Deephaven and Selected Stories

Deephaven and Selected Stories

Sarah Orne Jewett

MINT EDITIONS

Deephaven and Selected Stories was first published in 1896.

This edition published by Mint Editions 2020.

ISBN 9781513279848 | E-ISBN 9781513284866

Published by Mint Editions®

 MINT
EDITIONS

minteditionbooks.com

Publishing Director: Jennifer Newens
Design & Production: Rachel Lopez Metzger
Project Manager: Micaela Clark
Typesetting: Westchester Publishing Services

Contents

DEEPHAVEN

Preface

This book is not wholly new, several of the chapters having already been published in the "Atlantic Monthly." It has so often been asked if Deephaven may not be found on the map of New England under another name, that, to prevent any misunderstanding, I wish to say, while there is a likeness to be traced, few of the sketches are drawn from that town itself, and the characters will in almost every case be looked for there in vain.

I dedicate this story of out-of-door life and country people first to my father and mother, my two best friends, and also to all my other friends, whose names I say to myself lovingly, though I do not write them here.

S. O. J.

I

KATE LANCASTER'S PLAN

I had been spending the winter in Boston, and Kate Lancaster and I had been together a great deal, for we are the best of friends. It happened that the morning when this story begins I had waked up feeling sorry, and as if something dreadful were going to happen. There did not seem to be any good reason for it, so I undertook to discourage myself more by thinking that it would soon be time to leave town, and how much I should miss being with Kate and my other friends. My mind was still disquieted when I went down to breakfast; but beside my plate I found, with a hoped-for letter from my father, a note from Kate. To this day I have never known any explanation of that depression of my spirits, and I hope that the good luck which followed will help some reader to lose fear, and to smile at such shadows if any chance to come.

Kate had evidently written to me in an excited state of mind, for her note was not so trig-looking as usual; but this is what she said:—

> Dear Helen,
>
> I have a plan—I think it a most delightful plan—in which you and I are chief characters. Promise that you will say yes; if you do not you will have to remember all your life that you broke a girl's heart. Come round early, and lunch with me and dine with me. I'm to be all alone, and it's a long story and will need a great deal of talking over.
>
> K.

I showed this note to my aunt, and soon went round, very much interested. My latch-key opened the Lancasters' door, and I hurried to the parlor, where I heard my friend practising with great diligence. I went up to her, and she turned her head and kissed me solemnly. You need not smile; we are not sentimental girls, and are both much averse to indiscriminate kissing, though I have not the adroit habit of shying in which Kate is proficient. It would sometimes be impolite in any one else, but she shies so affectionately.

"Won't you sit down, dear?" she said, with great ceremony, and went on with her playing, which was abominable that morning; her fingers stepped on each other, and, whatever the tune might have been in reality, it certainly had a most remarkable incoherence as I heard it then. I took up the new Littell and made believe read it, and finally threw it at Kate; you would have thought we were two children.

"Have you heard that my grand-aunt, Miss Katharine Brandon of Deephaven, is dead?" I knew that she had died in November, at least six months before.

"Don't be nonsensical, Kate!" said I. "What is it you are going to tell me?"

"My grand-aunt died very old, and was the last of her generation. She had a sister and three brothers, one of whom had the honor of being my grandfather. Mamma is sole heir to the family estates in Deephaven, wharf-property and all, and it is a great inconvenience to her. The house is a charming old house, and some of my ancestors who followed the sea brought home the greater part of its furnishings. Miss Katharine was a person who ignored all frivolities, and her house was as sedate as herself. I have been there but little, for when I was a child my aunt found no pleasure in the society of noisy children who upset her treasures, and when I was older she did not care to see strangers, and after I left school she grew more and more feeble; I had not been there for two years when she died. Mamma went down very often. The town is a quaint old place which has seen better days. There are high rocks at the shore, and there is a beach, and there are woods inland, and hills, and there is the sea. It might be dull in Deephaven for two young ladies who were fond of gay society and dependent upon excitement, I suppose; but for two little girls who were fond of each other and could play in the boats, and dig and build houses in the sea-sand, and gather shells, and carry their dolls wherever they went, what could be pleasanter?"

"Nothing," said I, promptly.

Kate had told this a little at a time, with a few appropriate bars of music between, which suddenly reminded me of the story of a Chinese procession which I had read in one of Marryat's novels when I was a child: "A thousand white elephants richly caparisoned,—ti-tum tilly-lily," and so on, for a page or two. She seemed to have finished her story for that time, and while it was dawning upon me what she meant, she sang a bit from one of Jean Ingelow's verses:—

> *"Will ye step aboard, my dearest,*
> *For the high seas lie before us?"*

and then came over to sit beside me and tell the whole story in a more sensible fashion.

"You know that my father has been meaning to go to England in the autumn? Yesterday he told us that he is to leave in a month and will be away all summer, and mamma is going with him. Jack and Willy are to join a party of their classmates who are to spend nearly the whole of the long vacation at Lake Superior. I don't care to go abroad again now, and I did not like any plan that was proposed to me. Aunt Anna was here all the afternoon, and she is going to take the house at Newport, which is very pleasant and unexpected, for she hates housekeeping. Mamma thought of course that I would go with her, but I did not wish to do that, and it would only result in my keeping house for her visitors, whom I know very little; and she will be much more free and independent by herself. Beside, she can have my room if I am not there. I have promised to make her a long visit in Baltimore next winter instead. I told mamma that I should like to stay here and go away when I choose. There are ever so many visits which I have promised; I could stay with you and your Aunt Mary at Lenox if she goes there, for a while, and I have always wished to spend a summer in town; but mamma did not encourage that at all. In the evening papa gave her a letter which had come from Mr. Dockum, the man who takes care of Aunt Katharine's place, and the most charming idea came into my head, and I said I meant to spend my summer in Deephaven.

"At first they laughed at me, and then they said I might go if I chose, and at last they thought nothing could be pleasanter, and mamma wishes she were going herself. I asked if she did not think you would be the best person to keep me company, and she does, and papa announced that he was just going to suggest my asking you. I am to take Ann and Maggie, who will be overjoyed, for they came from that part of the country, and the other servants are to go with Aunt Anna, and old Nora will come to take care of this house, as she always does. Perhaps you and I will come up to town once in a while for a few days. We shall have such jolly housekeeping. Mamma and I sat up very late last night, and everything is planned. Mr. Dockum's house is very near Aunt Katharine's, so we shall not be lonely; though I know you're no more afraid of that than I. O Helen, won't you go?"

Do you think it took me long to decide?

Mr. and Mrs. Lancaster sailed the 10th of June, and my Aunt Mary went to spend her summer among the Berkshire Hills, so I was at the Lancasters' ready to welcome Kate when she came home, after having said good by to her father and mother. We meant to go to Deephaven in a week, but were obliged to stay in town longer. Boston was nearly deserted of our friends at the last, and we used to take quiet walks in the cool of the evening after dinner, up and down the street, or sit on the front steps in company with the servants left in charge of the other houses, who also sometimes walked up and down and looked at us wonderingly. We had much shopping to do in the daytime, for there was a probability of our spending many days in doors, and as we were not to be near any large town, and did not mean to come to Boston for weeks at least, there was a great deal to be remembered and arranged. We enjoyed making our plans, and deciding what we should want, and going to the shops together. I think we felt most important the day we conferred with Ann and made out a list of the provisions which must be ordered. This was being housekeepers in earnest. Mr. Dockum happened to come to town, and we sent Ann and Maggie, with most of our boxes, to Deephaven in his company a day or two before we were ready to go ourselves, and when we reached there the house was opened and in order for us.

On our journey to Deephaven we left the railway twelve miles from that place, and took passage in a stage-coach. There was only one passenger beside ourselves. She was a very large, thin, weather-beaten woman, and looked so tired and lonesome and good-natured, that I could not help saying it was very dusty; and she was apparently delighted to answer that she should think everybody was sweeping, and she always felt, after being in the cars a while, as if she had been taken all to pieces and left in the different places. And this was the beginning of our friendship with Mrs. Kew.

After this conversation we looked industriously out of the window into the pastures and pine-woods. I had given up my seat to her, for I do not mind riding backward in the least, and you would have thought I had done her the greatest favor of her life. I think she was the most grateful of women, and I was often reminded of a remark one of my friends once made about some one: "If you give Bessie a half-sheet of letter-paper, she behaves to you as if it were the most exquisite of presents!" Kate and I had some fruit left in our lunch-basket, and divided it with Mrs. Kew, but after the first mouthful we looked at each other in dismay. "Lemons with oranges' clothes on, aren't they?" said she, as Kate threw hers out of the window, and mine went after it for company; and after this we began to be very friendly indeed. We both liked the odd woman, there was something so straightforward and kindly about her.

"Are you going to Deephaven, dear?" she asked me, and then: "I wonder if you are going to stay long? All summer? Well, that's clever! I do hope you will come out to the Light to see me; young folks 'most always like my place. Most likely your friends will fetch you."

"Do you know the Brandon house?" asked Kate.

"Well as I do the meeting-house. There! I wonder I didn't know from the beginning, but I have been a trying all the way to settle it who you could be. I've been up country some weeks, stopping with my mother, and she seemed so set to have me stay till strawberry-time, and would hardly let me come now. You see she's getting to be old; why, every time I've come away for fifteen years she's said it was the last time I'd ever see her, but she's a dreadful smart woman of her age. 'He' wrote me some o' Mrs. Lancaster's folks were going to take the Brandon house this summer; and so you are the ones? It's a sightly old place; I used to go and see Miss Katharine. She must have left a power of china-ware. She set a great deal by the house, and she kept everything just as it used to be in her mother's day."

"Then you live in Deephaven too?" asked Kate.

"I've been here the better part of my life. I was raised up among the hills in Vermont, and I shall always be a real up-country woman if I live here a hundred years. The sea doesn't come natural to me, it kind of worries me, though you won't find a happier woman than I be, 'long shore. When I was first married 'he' had a schooner and went to the banks, and once he was off on a whaling voyage, and I hope I may never come to so long a three years as those were again, though I was up to mother's. Before I was married he had been 'most everywhere. When he came home that time from whaling, he found I'd taken it so to heart that he said he'd never go off again, and then he got the chance to keep Deephaven Light, and we've lived there seventeen years come January. There isn't great pay, but then nobody tries to get it away from us, and we've got so's to be contented, if it is lonesome in winter."

"Do you really live in the lighthouse? I remember how I used to beg to be taken out there when I was a child, and how I used to watch for the light at night," said Kate, enthusiastically.

So began a friendship which we both still treasure, for knowing

SARAH ORNE JEWETT

Mrs. Kew was one of the pleasantest things which happened to us in that delightful summer, and she used to do so much for our pleasure, and was so good to us. When we went out to the lighthouse for the last time to say good by, we were very sorry girls indeed. We had no idea until then how much she cared for us, and her affection touched us very much. She told us that she loved us as if we belonged to her, and begged us not to forget her,—as if we ever could!—and to remember that there was always a home and a warm heart for us if she were alive. Kate and I have often agreed that few of our acquaintances are half so entertaining. Her comparisons were most striking and amusing, and her comments upon the books she read—for she was a great reader—were very shrewd and clever, and always to the point. She was never out of temper, even when the barrels of oil were being rolled across her kitchen floor. And she was such a wise woman! This stage-ride, which we expected to find tiresome, we enjoyed very much, and we were glad to think, when the coach stopped, and "he" came to meet her with great satisfaction, that we had one friend in Deephaven at all events.

I liked the house from my very first sight of it. It stood behind a row of poplars which were as green and flourishing as the poplars which stand in stately processions in the fields around Quebec. It was an imposing great white house, and the lilacs were tall, and there were crowds of rose-bushes not yet out of bloom; and there were box borders, and there were great elms at the side of the house and down the road. The hall door stood wide open, and my hostess turned to me as we went in, with one of her sweet, sudden smiles. "Won't we have a good time, Nelly?" said she. And I thought we should.

So our summer's housekeeping began in most pleasant fashion. It was just at sunset, and Ann's and Maggie's presence made the house seem familiar at once. Maggie had been unpacking for us, and there was a delicious supper ready for the hungry girls. Later in the evening we went down to the shore, which was not very far away; the fresh sea-air was welcome after the dusty day, and it seemed so quiet and pleasant in Deephaven.

II

The Brandon House
and the Lighthouse

I do not know that the Brandon house is really very remarkable, but I never have been in one that interested me in the same way. Kate used to recount to select audiences at school some of her experiences with her Aunt Katharine, and it was popularly believed that she once carried down some indestructible picture-books when they were first in fashion, and the old lady basted them for her to hem round the edges at the rate of two a day. It may have been fabulous. It was impossible to imagine any children in the old place; everything was for grown people; even the stair-railing was too high to slide down on. The chairs looked as if they had been put, at the furnishing of the house, in their places, and there they meant to remain. The carpets were particularly interesting, and I remember Kate's pointing out to me one day a great square figure in one, and telling me she used to keep house there with her dolls for lack of a better play-house, and if one of them chanced to fall outside the boundary stripe, it was immediately put to bed with a cold. It is a house with great possibilities; it might easily be made charming. There are four very large rooms on the lower floor, and six above, a wide hall in each story, and a fascinating garret over the whole, where were many mysterious old chests and boxes, in one of which we found Kate's grandmother's love-letters; and you may be sure the vista of rummages which Mr. Lancaster had laughed about was explored to its very end. The rooms all have elaborate cornices, and the lower hall is very fine, with an archway dividing it, and panellings of all sorts, and a great door at each end, through which the lilacs in front and the old pensioner plum-trees in the garden are seen exchanging bows and gestures. Coming from the Lancasters' high city house, it did not seem as if we had to go up stairs at all there, for every step of the stairway is so broad and low, and you come half-way to a square landing with an old straight-backed chair in each farther corner; and between them a large, round-topped window, with a cushioned seat, looking out on the garden and the village, the hills far inland, and the sunset beyond all. Then you turn and go up a few more steps to the upper hall, where we used to stay a great deal. There were more old chairs and a pair of remarkable sofas, on which we used to deposit the treasures collected in our wanderings. The wide window which looks out on the lilacs and the sea was a favorite seat of ours. Facing each other on either side of it are two old secretaries, and one of them we ascertained to be the hiding-place of secret drawers, in which may be found valuable records deposited by ourselves one rainy day when we first explored it. We wrote, between us, a tragic "journal" on some yellow old letter-paper we found in the desk. We put it in the most hidden drawer by itself, and flatter ourselves that it will be regarded with great interest some time or other. Of one of the front rooms, "the best chamber," we stood rather in dread. It is very remarkable that there seem to be no ghost-stories connected with any part of the house, particularly this. We are neither of us nervous; but there is certainly something dismal about the room. The huge curtained bed and immense easy-chairs, windows, and everything were draped in some old-fashioned kind of white cloth which always seemed to be waving and moving about of itself. The carpet was most singularly colored with dark reds and indescribable grays and browns, and the pattern, after a whole summer's study, could never be followed with one's eye. The paper was captured in a French prize somewhere some time in the last century, and part of the figure was shaggy, and therein little spiders found habitation, and went visiting their acquaintances across the shiny places. The color was an unearthly pink and a forbidding maroon, with dim white spots, which gave it the appearance of having moulded. It made you low-spirited to look long in the mirror; and the great lounge one could not have cheerful associations with, after hearing that Miss Brandon herself did not like it, having seen so many of her relatives lie there dead. There were fantastic china ornaments from Bible subjects on the mantel, and the only picture was one of the Maid of Orleans tied with an unnecessarily strong rope to a very stout stake. The best parlor we also rarely used, because all the portraits which hung there had for some unaccountable reason taken a violent dislike to us, and followed us suspiciously with their eyes. The furniture was stately and very uncomfortable, and there was something about the room which suggested an invisible funeral.

There is not very much to say about the dining-room. It was not specially interesting, though the sea was in sight from one of the windows. There were some old Dutch pictures on the wall, so dark that one could scarcely make out what they were meant to represent, and one or two engravings. There was a huge sideboard, for which Kate had brought down from Boston Miss Brandon's own silver which had stood there for so many years, and looked so much more at home and in place than any other possibly could have looked, and Kate also found in the closet the three great decanters with silver labels chained round their necks, which had always been the companions of the tea-service in her aunt's lifetime. From the little closets in the sideboard there came a most significant odor of cake and wine whenever one opened the doors. We used Miss Brandon's beautiful old blue India china which she had given to Kate, and which had been carefully packed all winter. Kate sat at the head and I at the foot of the round table, and I must confess that we were apt to have either a feast or a famine, for at first we often forgot to provide our dinners. If this were the case Maggie was sure to serve us with most derisive elegance, and make us wait for as much ceremony as she thought necessary for one of Mrs. Lancaster's dinner-parties.

The west parlor was our favorite room down stairs. It had a great fireplace framed in blue and white Dutch tiles which ingeniously and instructively represented the careers of the good and the bad man; the starting-place of each being a very singular cradle in the centre at the top. The last two of the series are very high art: a great coffin stands in the foreground of each, and the virtuous man is being led off by two disagreeable-looking angels, while the wicked one is hastening from an indescribable but unpleasant assemblage of claws and horns and eyes which is rapidly advancing from the distance, open-mouthed, and bringing a chain with it.

There was a large cabinet holding all the small curiosities and knick-knacks there seemed to be no other place for,—odd china figures and cups and vases, unaccountable Chinese carvings and exquisite corals and sea-shells, minerals and Swiss wood-work, and articles of *vertu* from the South Seas. Underneath were stored boxes of letters and old magazines; for this was one of the houses where nothing seems to have been thrown away. In one parting we found a parcel of old manuscript sermons, the existence of which was a mystery, until Kate remembered there had been a gifted son of the house who entered the ministry and soon died. The windows had each a pane of stained glass, and on the wide sills we used to put our immense bouquets of field-flowers. There was one place which I liked and sat in more than any other. The chimney filled nearly the whole side of the room, all but this little corner, where there was just room for a very comfortable high-backed cushioned chair, and a narrow window where I always had a bunch of fresh green ferns in a tall champagne-glass. I used to write there often, and always sat there when Kate sang and played. She sent for a tuner, and used to successfully coax the long-imprisoned music from the antiquated piano, and sing for her visitors by the hour. She almost always sang her oldest songs, for they seemed most in keeping with everything about us. I used to fancy that the portraits liked our being there. There was one young girl who seemed solitary and forlorn among the rest in the room, who were all middle-aged. For their part they looked amiable, but rather unhappy, as if she had come in and interrupted their conversation. We both grew very fond of her, and it seemed, when we went in the last morning on purpose to take leave of her, as if she looked at us imploringly. She was soon afterward boxed up, and now enjoys society after her own heart in Kate's room in Boston.

There was the largest sofa I ever saw opposite the fireplace; it must have been brought in in pieces, and built in the room. It was broad enough for Kate and me to lie on together, and very high and square; but there was a pile of soft cushions at one end. We used to enjoy it greatly in September, when the evenings were long and cool, and we had many candles, and a fire—and crickets too—on the hearth, and the dear dog lying on the rug. I remember one rainy night, just before Miss Tennant and Kitty Bruce went away; we had a real drift-wood fire, and blew out the lights and told stories. Miss Margaret knows so many and tells them so well. Kate and I were unusually entertaining, for we became familiar with the family record of the town, and could recount marvellous adventures by land and sea, and ghost-stories by the dozen. We had never either of us been in a society consisting of so many travelled people! Hardly a man but had been the most of his life at sea. Speaking of ghost-stories, I must tell you that once in the summer two Cambridge girls who were spending a week with us unwisely enticed us into giving some thrilling recitals, which nearly frightened them out of their wits, and Kate and I were finally in terror ourselves. We had all been on the sofa in the dark, singing and talking, and were waiting in great suspense after I had finished one of such particular horror that I declared it should be the last, when we heard footsteps on the hall stairs. There were lights in the dining-room which shone faintly through the half-closed door, and we saw something white and shapeless come slowly down, and clutched each other's gowns in agony. It was only Kate's dog, who came in and laid his head in her lap and slept peacefully.

We thought we could not sleep a wink after this, and I bravely went alone out to the light to see my watch, and, finding it was past twelve, we concluded to sit up all night and to go down to the shore at sunrise, it would be so much easier than getting up early some morning. We had been out rowing and had taken a long walk the day before, and were obliged to dance and make other slight exertions to keep ourselves awake at one time. We lunched at two, and I never shall forget the sunrise that morning; but we were singularly quiet and abstracted that day, and indeed for several days after Deephaven was "a land in which it seemed always afternoon," we breakfasted so late.

As Mrs. Kew had said, there was "a power of china." Kate and I were convinced that the lives of her grandmothers must have been spent in giving tea-parties. We counted ten sets of cups, beside quantities of stray ones; and some member of the family had evidently devoted her time to making a collection of pitchers.

There was an escritoire in Miss Brandon's own room, which we looked over one day. There was a little package of letters; ship letters mostly, tied with a very pale and tired-looking blue ribbon. They were in a drawer with a locket holding a faded miniature on ivory and a lock of brown hair, and there were also some dry twigs and bits of leaf which had long ago been bright wild-roses, such as still bloom among the Deephaven rocks. Kate said that she had often heard her mother wonder why her aunt never had cared to marry, for she had chances enough doubtless, and had been rich and handsome and finely educated. So there was a sailor lover after all, and perhaps he had been lost at sea and she faithfully kept the secret, never mourning outwardly. "And I always thought her the most matter-of-fact old lady," said Kate; "yet here's her romance, after all." We put the letters outside on a chair to read, but afterwards carefully replaced them, without untying them. I'm glad we did. There were other letters which we did read, and which interested us very much,—letters from her girl friends written in the boarding-school vacations, and just after she finished school. Those in one of the smaller packages were charming; it must have been such a bright, nice girl who wrote them! They were very few, and were tied with black ribbon, and marked on the outside in girlish writing: "My dearest friend, Dolly McAllister, died September 3, 1809, aged eighteen." The ribbon had evidently been untied and the letters read many times. One began: "My dear, delightful Kitten: I am quite overjoyed to find my father has business which will force him to go to Deephaven next week, and he kindly says if there be no more rain I may ride with him to see you. I will surely come, for if there is danger of spattering my gown, and he bids me stay at home, I shall go galloping after him and overtake him when it is too late to send me back. I have so much to tell you." I wish I knew more about the visit. Poor Miss Katharine! it made us sad to look over these treasures of her girlhood. There were her compositions and exercise-books; some samplers and queer little keepsakes; withered flowers and some pebbles and other things of like value, with which there was probably some pleasant association. "Only think of her keeping them all her days," said I to Kate. "I am continually throwing some relic of the kind away, because I forget why I have it!"

There was a box in the lower part which Kate was glad to find, for she had heard her mother wonder if some such things were not in existence. It held a crucifix and a mass-book and some rosaries, and Kate told me Miss Katharine's youngest and favorite brother had become a Roman Catholic while studying in Europe. It was a dreadful blow to the family; for in those days there could have been few deeper disgraces to the Brandon family than to have one of its sons go over to popery. Only Miss Katharine treated him with kindness, and after a time he disappeared without telling even her where he was going, and was only heard from indirectly once or twice afterward. It was a great grief to her. "And mamma knows," said Kate, "that she always had a lingering hope of his return, for one of the last times she saw Aunt Katharine before she was ill she spoke of soon going to be with all the rest, and said, 'Though your Uncle Henry, dear,'—and stopped and smiled sadly; 'you'll think me a very foolish old woman, but I never quite gave up thinking he might come home.'"

Mrs. Kew did the honors of the lighthouse thoroughly on our first visit; but I think we rarely went to see her that we did not make some entertaining discovery. Mr. Kew's nephew, a guileless youth of forty, lived with them, and the two men were of a mechanical turn and had invented numerous aids to housekeeping,—appendages to the stove, and fixtures on the walls for everything that could be hung up; catches in the floor to hold the doors open, and ingenious apparatus to close them; but, above all, a system of barring and bolting for the wide "fore door," which would have disconcerted an energetic battering-ram. After all this work being expended, Mrs. Kew informed us that it was usually wide open all night in summer weather. On the back of this door I discovered one day a row of marks, and asked their significance.

It seemed that Mrs. Kew had attempted one summer to keep count of the number of people who inquired about the depredations of the neighbors' chickens. Mrs. Kew's bedroom was partly devoted to the fine arts. There was a large collection of likenesses of her relatives and friends on the wall, which was interesting in the extreme. Mrs. Kew was always much pleased to tell their names, and her remarks about any feature not exactly perfect were very searching and critical. "That's my oldest brother's wife, Clorinthy Adams that was. She's well featured, if it were not for her nose, and that looks as if it had been thrown at her, and she wasn't particular about having it on firm, in hopes of getting a better one. She sets by her looks, though."

There were often sailing-parties that came there from up and down the coast. One day Kate and I were spending the afternoon at the Light; we had been fishing, and were sitting in the doorway listening to a reminiscence of the winter Mrs. Kew kept school at the Four Corners; saw a boatful coming, and all lost our tempers. Mrs. Kew had a lame ankle, and Kate offered to go up with the visitors. There were some girls and young men who stood on the rocks awhile, and then asked us, with much better manners than the people who usually came, if they could see the lighthouse, and Kate led the way. She was dressed that day in a costume we both frequently wore, of gray skirts and blue sailor-jacket, and her boots were much the worse for wear. The celebrated Lancaster complexion was rather darkened by the sun. Mrs. Kew expressed a wish to know what questions they would ask her, and I followed after a few minutes. They seemed to have finished asking about the lantern, and to have become personal.

"Don't you get tired staying here?"

"No, indeed!" said Kate.

"Is that your sister down stairs?"

"No, I have no sister."

"I should think you would wish she was. Aren't you ever lonesome?"

"Everybody is, sometimes," said Kate.

"But it's such a lonesome place!" said one of the girls. "I should think you would get work away. I live in Boston. Why, it's so awful quiet! nothing but the water, and the wind, when it blows; and I think either of them is worse than nothing. And only this little bit of a rocky place! I should want to go to walk."

I heard Kate pleasantly refuse the offer of pay for her services, and then they began to come down the steep stairs laughing and chattering with each other. Kate stayed behind to close the doors and leave everything all right, and the girl who had talked the most waited too, and when they were on the stairs just above me, and the others out of hearing, she said, "You're real good to show us the things. I guess you'll think I'm silly, but I do like you ever so much! I wish you would come to Boston. I'm in a real nice store,—H——'s, on Winter Street; and they will want new saleswomen in October. Perhaps you could be at my counter. I'd teach you, and you could board with me. I've got a real comfortable room, and I suppose I might have more things, for I get good pay; but I like to send money home to mother. I'm at my aunt's now, but I am going back next Monday, and if you will tell me what your name is, I'll find out for certain about the place, and write you. My name's Mary Wendell."

I knew by Kate's voice that this had touched her. "You are very kind; thank you heartily," said she; "but I cannot go and work with you. I should like to know more about you. I live in Boston too; my friend and I are staying over in Deephaven for the summer only." And she held out her hand to the girl, whose face had changed from its first expression of earnest good-humor to a very startled one; and when she noticed Kate's hand, and a ring of hers, which had been turned round, she looked really frightened.

"O, will you please excuse me?" said she, blushing. "I ought to have known better; but you showed us round so willing, and I never thought of your not living here. I didn't mean to be rude."

"Of course you did not, and you were not. I am very glad you said it, and glad you like me," said Kate; and just then the party called the girl, and she hurried away, and I joined Kate. "Then you heard it all. That was worth having!" said she. "She was such an honest little soul, and I mean to look for her when I get home."

Sometimes we used to go out to the Light early in the morning with the fishermen who went that way to the fishing-grounds, but we usually made the voyage early in the afternoon if it were not too hot, and we went fishing off the rocks or sat in the house with Mrs. Kew, who often related some of her Vermont experiences, or Mr. Kew would tell us surprising sea-stories and ghost-stories like a story-book sailor. Then we would have an unreasonably good supper and afterward climb the ladder to the lantern to see the lamps lighted, and sit there for a while watching the ships and the sunset. Almost all the coasters came in sight of Deephaven, and the sea outside the light was their grand highway.

Twice from the lighthouse we saw a yacht squadron like a flock of great white birds. As for the sunsets, it used to seem often as if we were near the heart of them, for the sea all around us caught the color of the clouds, and though the glory was wonderful, I remember best one still evening when there was a bank of heavy gray clouds in the west shutting down like a curtain, and the sea was silver-colored. You could look under and beyond the curtain of clouds into the palest, clearest yellow sky. There was a little black boat in the distance drifting slowly, climbing one white wave after another, as if it were bound out into that other world beyond. But presently the sun came from behind the clouds, and the dazzling golden light changed the look of everything, and it was the time then to say one thought it a beautiful sunset; while before one could only keep very still, and watch the boat, and wonder if heaven would not be somehow like that far, faint color, which was neither sea nor sky.

When we came down from the lighthouse and it grew late, we would beg for an hour or two longer on the water, and row away in the twilight far out from land, where, with our faces turned from the Light, it seemed as if we were alone, and the sea shoreless; and as the darkness closed round us softly, we watched the stars come out, and were always glad to see Kate's star and my star, which we had chosen when we were children. I used long ago to be sure of one thing,—that, however far away heaven might be, it could not be out of sight of the stars. Sometimes in the evening we waited out at sea for the moonrise, and then we would take the oars again and go slowly in, once in a while singing or talking, but oftenest silent.

III

My Lady Brandon and the Widow Jim

When it was known that we had arrived in Deephaven, the people who had known Miss Brandon so well, and Mrs. Lancaster also, seemed to consider themselves Kate's friends by inheritance, and were exceedingly polite to us, in either calling upon us or sending pleasant messages. Before the first week had ended we had no lack of society. They were not strangers to Kate, to begin with, and as for me, I think it is easy for me to be contented, and to feel at home anywhere. I have the good fortune and the misfortune to belong to the navy,—that is, my father does,—and my life has been consequently an unsettled one, except during the years of my school life, when my friendship with Kate began.

I think I should be happy in any town if I were living there with Kate Lancaster. I will not praise my friend as I can praise her, or say half the things I might say honestly. She is so fresh and good and true, and enjoys life so heartily. She is so child-like, without being childish; and I do not tell you that she is faultless, but when she makes mistakes she is sorrier and more ready to hopefully try again than any girl I know. Perhaps you would like to know something about us, but I am not writing Kate's biography and my own, only telling you of one summer which we spent together. Sometimes in Deephaven we were between six and seven years old, but at other times we have felt irreparably grown-up, and as if we carried a crushing weight of care and duty. In reality we are both twenty-four, and it is a pleasant age, though I think next year is sure to be pleasanter, for we do not mind growing older, since we have lost nothing that we mourn about, and are gaining so much. I shall be glad if you learn to know Kate a little in my stories. It is not that I am fond of her and endow her with imagined virtues and graces; no one can fail to see how unaffected she is, or not notice her thoughtfulness and generosity and her delightful fun, which never has a trace of coarseness or silliness. It was very pleasant having her for one's companion, for she has an unusual power of winning people's confidence, and of knowing with surest instinct how to meet them on their own ground. It is the girl's being so genuinely sympathetic and interested which makes every one ready to talk to her and be friends with her; just as the sunshine makes it easy for flowers to grow which the chilly winds hinder. She is not polite for the sake of seeming polite, but polite for the sake of being kind, and there is not a particle of what Hugh Miller justly calls the insolence of condescension about her; she is not brilliantly talented, yet she does everything in a charming fashion of her own; she is not profoundly learned, yet she knows much of which many wise people are ignorant, and while she is a patient scholar in both little things and great, she is no less a teacher to all her friends,— dear Kate Lancaster!

We knew that we were considered Miss Brandon's representatives in Deephaven society, and this was no slight responsibility, as she had received much honor and respect. We heard again and again what a loss she had been to the town, and we tried that summer to do nothing to lessen the family reputation, and to give pleasure as well as take it, though we were singularly persistent in our pursuit of a good time. I grew much interested in what I heard of Miss Brandon, and it seems to me that it is a great privilege to have an elderly person in one's neighborhood, in town or country, who is proud, and conservative, and who lives in stately fashion; who is intolerant of sham and of useless novelties, and clings to the old ways of living and behaving as if it were part of her religion. There is something immensely respectable about the gentlewomen of the old school. They ignore all bustle and flashiness, and the conceit of the younger people, who act as if at last it had been time for them to appear and manage this world as it ought to have been managed before. Their position in modern society is much like that of the King's Chapel in its busy street in Boston. It perhaps might not have been easy to approach Miss Brandon, but I am sure that if I had visited in Deephaven during her lifetime I should have been very proud if I had been asked to take tea at her house, and should have liked to speak afterward of my acquaintance with her. It would have been impossible not to pay her great deference; it is a pleasure to think that she must have found this world a most polite world, and have had the highest opinion of its good manners. *Noblesse oblige*: that is true in more ways than one!

I cannot help wondering if those of us who will be left by and by to represent our own generation will seem to have such superior elegance of behavior; if we shall receive so much respect and be so much valued. It is hard to imagine it. We know that the world gains new refinements and a better culture; but to us there never will be such imposing ladies and gentlemen as these who belong to the old school.

The morning after we reached Deephaven we were busy up stairs, and there was a determined blow at the knocker of the front door. I went down to see who was there, and had the pleasure of receiving our first caller. She was a prim little old woman who looked pleased and expectant, who wore a neat cap and front, and whose eyes were as bright as black beads. She wore no bonnet, and had thrown a little three-cornered shawl, with palm-leaf figures, over her shoulders; and it was evident that she was a near neighbor. She was very short and straight and thin, and so quick that she darted like a pickerel when she moved about. It occurred to me at once that she was a very capable person, and had "faculty," and, dear me, how fast she talked! She hesitated a moment when she saw me, and dropped a fragment of a courtesy. "Miss Lan'k'ster?" said she, doubtfully.

"No," said I, "I'm Miss Denis: Miss Lancaster is at home, though: come in, won't you?"

"O Mrs. Patton!" said Kate, who came down just then. "How very kind of you to come over so soon! I should have gone to see you to-day. I was asking Mrs. Kew last night if you were here."

"Land o' compassion!" said Mrs. Patton, as she shook Kate's hand delightedly. "Where'd ye s'pose I'd be, dear? I ain't like to move away from Deephaven now, after I've held by the place so long, I've got as many roots as the big ellum. Well, I should know you were a Brandon, no matter where I see you. You've got a real Brandon look; tall and straight, ain't you? It's four or five years since I saw you, except once at church, and once you went by, down to the shore, I suppose. It was a windy day in the spring of the year."

"I remember it very well," said Kate. "Those were both visits of only a day or two, and I was here at Aunt Katharine's funeral, and went away that same evening. Do you remember once I was here in the summer for a longer visit, five or six years ago, and I helped you pick currants in the garden? You had a very old mug."

"Now, whoever would ha' thought o' your rec'lecting that?" said Mrs. Patton. "Yes. I had that mug because it was handy to carry about among the bushes, and then I'd empt' it into the basket as fast as I got it full. Your aunt always told me to pick all I wanted; she couldn't use 'em, but they used to make sights o' currant wine in old times. I s'pose that mug would be considerable of a curiosity to anybody that wasn't used to seeing it round. My grand'ther Joseph Toggerson—my mother was a Toggerson—picked it up on the long sands in a wad of sea-weed: strange it wasn't broke, but it's tough; I've dropped it on the floor, many's the time, and it ain't even chipped. There's some Dutch reading on it and it's marked 1732. Now I shouldn't ha' thought you'd remembered that old mug, I declare. Your aunt she had a monstrous sight of chiny. She's told me where 'most all of it come from, but I expect I've forgot. My memory fails me a good deal by spells. If you hadn't come down I suppose your mother would have had the chiny packed up this spring,—what she didn't take with her after your aunt died. S'pose she hasn't made up her mind what to do with the house?"

"No," said Kate; "she wishes she could: it is a great puzzle to us."

"I hope you will find it in middling order," said Mrs. Patton, humbly. "Me and Mis' Dockum have done the best we knew,—opened the windows and let in the air and tried to keep it from getting damp. I fixed all the woollens with fresh camphire and tobacco the last o' the winter; you have to be dreadful careful in one o' these old houses, 'less everything gets creaking with moths in no time. Miss Katharine, how she did hate the sight of a moth-miller! There's something I'll speak about before I forget it: the mice have eat the backs of a pile o' old books that's stored away in the west chamber closet next to Miss Katharine's room, and I set a trap there, but it was older 'n the ten commandments, that trap was, and the spring's rusty. I guess you'd better get some new ones and set round in different places, 'less the mice'll pester you. There ain't been no chance for 'em to get much of a living 'long through the winter, but they'll be sure to come back quick as they find there's likely to be good board. I see your aunt's cat setting out on the front steps. She never was no great of a mouser, but it went to my heart to see how pleased she looks! Come right back, didn't she? How they do hold to their old haunts!"

"Was that Miss Brandon's cat?" I asked, with great interest. "She has been up stairs with us, but I supposed she belonged to some neighbor, and had strayed in. She behaved as if she felt at home, poor old pussy!"

"We must keep her here," said Kate.

"Mis' Dockum took her after your mother went off, and Miss Katharine's maids," said Mrs. Patton; "but she told me that it was a long spell before she seemed to feel contented. She used to set on the steps and cry by the hour together, and try to get in, to first one door and then another. I used to think how bad Miss Katharine would feel; she set a great deal by a cat, and she took notice of this as long as she did of anything. Her mind failed her, you know. Great loss to Deephaven, she was. Proud woman, and some folks were scared of her; but I always got along with her, and I wouldn't ask for no kinder friend nor neighbor. I've had my troubles, and I've seen the day I was suffering poor, and I couldn't have brought myself to ask town help nohow, but I wish ye'd ha' heared her scold me when she found it out; and she come marching into my kitchen one morning, like a grenadier, and says she, 'Why didn't you send and tell me how sick and poor you are?' says she. And she said she'd ha' been so glad to help me all along, but she thought I had means,—everybody did; and I see the tears in her eyes, but she was scolding me and speaking as if she was dreadful mad. She made me comfortable, and she sent over one o' her maids to see to me, and got the doctor, and a load o' stuff come up from the store, so I didn't have to buy anything for a good many weeks. I got better and so's to work, but she never'd let me say nothing about it. I had a good deal o' trouble, and I thought I'd lost my health, but I hadn't, and that was thirty or forty years ago. There never was nothing going on at the great house that she didn't have me over, sewing or cleaning or company; and I got so that I knew how she liked to have things done. I felt as if it was my own sister, though I never had one, when I was going over to help lay her out. She used to talk as free to me as she would to Miss Lorimer or Miss Carew. I s'pose ye ain't seen nothing o' them yet? She was a good Christian woman, Miss Katharine was. 'The memory of the just is blessed'; that's what Mr. Lorimer said in his sermon the Sunday after she died, and there wasn't a blood-relation there to hear it. I declare it looked pitiful to see that pew empty that ought to ha' been the mourners' pew. Your mother, Mis' Lancaster, had to go home Saturday, your father was going away sudden to Washington, I've understood, and she come back again the first of the week. There! it didn't make no sort o' difference, p'r'aps nobody thought of it but me. There hadn't been anybody in the pew more than a couple o' times since she used to sit there herself, regular as Sunday come." And Mrs. Patton looked for a minute as if she were going to cry, but she changed her mind upon second thought.

"Your mother gave me most of Miss Katharine's clothes; this cap belonged to her, that I've got on now; it's 'most wore out, but it does for mornings."

"O," said Kate, "I have two new ones for you in one of my trunks! Mamma meant to choose them herself, but she had not time, and so she told me, and I think I found the kind she thought you would like."

"Now I'm sure!" said Mrs. Patton, "if that ain't kind; you don't tell me that Mis' Lancaster thought of me just as she was going off? I shall set everything by them caps, and I'm much obliged to you too, Miss Kate. I was just going to speak of that time you were here and saw the mug; you trimmed a cap for Miss Katharine to give me, real Boston style. I guess that box of cap-fixings is up on the top shelf of Miss Katharine's closet now, to the left hand," said Mrs. Patton, with wistful certainty. "She used to make her every-day caps herself, and she had some beautiful materials laid away that she never used. Some folks has laughed at me for being so particular 'bout wearing caps except for best, but I don't know's it's presuming beyond my station, and somehow I feel more respect for myself when I have a good cap on. I can't get over your mother's rec'lecting about me; and she sent me a handsome present o' money this spring for looking after the house. I never should have asked for a cent; it's a pleasure to me to keep an eye on it, out o' respect to your aunt. I was so pleased when I heard you were coming long o' your friend. I like to see the old place open; it was about as bad as having no meeting. I miss seeing the lights, and your aunt was a great hand for lighting up bright; the big hall lantern was lit every night, and she put it out when she went up stairs. She liked to go round same's if it was day. You see I forget all the time she was sick, and go back to the days when she was well and about the house. When her mind was failing her, and she was up stairs in her room, her eyesight seemed to be lost part of the time, and sometimes she'd tell us to get the lamp and a couple o' candles in the middle o' the day, and then she'd be as satisfied! But she used to take a notion to set in the dark, some nights, and think, I s'pose. I should have forty fits, if I undertook it. That was a good while ago; and do you rec'lect how she used to play the piano? She used to be a great hand to play when she was young."

"Indeed I remember it," said Kate, who told me afterward how her aunt used to sit at the piano in the twilight and play to herself. "She was formerly a skilful musician," said my friend, "though one would not have imagined she cared for music. When I was a child she used to play in company of an evening, and once when I was here one of her old friends asked for a tune, and she laughingly said that her day was over and her fingers were stiff; though I believe she might have played as well as ever then, if she had cared to try. But once in a while when she had been quiet all day and rather sad—I am ashamed that I used to think she was cross—she would open the piano and sit there until late, while I used to be enchanted by her memories of dancing-tunes, and old psalms, and marches and songs. There was one tune which I am sure had a history: there was a sweet wild cadence in it, and she would come back to it again and again, always going through with it in the same measured way. I have remembered so many things about my aunt since I have been here," said Kate, "which I hardly noticed and did not understand when they happened. I was afraid of her when I was a little girl, but I think if I had grown up sooner, I should have enjoyed her heartily. It never used to occur to me that she had a spark of tenderness or of sentiment, until just before she was ill, but I have been growing more fond of her ever since. I might have given her a great deal more pleasure. It was not long after I was through school that she became so feeble, and of course she liked best having mamma come to see her; one of us had to be at home. I have thought lately how careful one ought to be, to be kind and thoughtful to one's old friends. It is so soon too late to be good to them, and then one is always so sorry."

I must tell you more of Mrs. Patton; of course it was not long before we returned her call, and we were much entertained; we always liked to see our friends in their own houses. Her house was a little way down the road, unpainted and gambrel-roofed, but so low that the old lilac-bushes which clustered round it were as tall as the eaves. The Widow Jim (as nearly every one called her in distinction to the widow Jack Patton, who was a tailoress and lived at the other end of the town) was a very useful person. I suppose there must be her counterpart in all old New England villages. She sewed, and she made elaborate rugs, and she had a decided talent for making carpets,—if there were one to be made, which must have happened seldom. But there were a great many to be turned and made over in Deephaven, and she went to the Carews' and Lorimers' at house-cleaning time or in seasons of great festivity. She had no equal in sickness, and knew how to brew every old-fashioned dose and to make every variety of herb-tea, and when her nursing was put to an end by her patient's death, she was commander-in-chief at the funeral, and stood near the doorway to direct the mourning friends to their seats; and I have no reason to doubt that she sometimes even had the immense responsibility of making out the order of the procession, since she had all genealogy and relationship at her tongue's end. It was an awful thing in Deephaven, we found, if the precedence was wrongly assigned, and once we chanced to hear some bitter remarks because the cousins of the departed wife had been placed after the husband's relatives,—"the blood-relations ridin' behind them that was only kin by marriage! I don't wonder they felt hurt!" said the person who spoke; a most unselfish and unassuming soul, ordinarily.

Mrs. Patton knew everybody's secrets, but she told them judiciously if at all. She chattered all day to you as a sparrow twitters, and you did not tire of her; and Kate and I were never more agreeably entertained than when she told us of old times and of Kate's ancestors and their contemporaries; for her memory was wonderful, and she had either seen everything that had happened in Deephaven for a long time, or had received the particulars from reliable witnesses. She had known much trouble; her husband had been but small satisfaction to her, and it was not to be wondered at if she looked upon all proposed marriages with compassion. She was always early at church, and she wore the same bonnet that she had when Kate was a child; it was such a well-preserved, proper black straw bonnet, with discreet bows of ribbon, and a useful lace veil to protect it from the weather.

She showed us into the best room the first time we went to see her. It was the plainest little room, and very dull, and there was an exact sufficiency about its furnishings. Yet there was a certain dignity about it; it was unmistakably a best room, and not a place where one might make a litter or carry one's every-day work. You felt at once that somebody valued the prim old-fashioned chairs, and the two half-moon tables, and the thin carpet, which must have needed anxious stretching every spring to make it come to the edge of the floor. There were some mourning-pieces by way of decoration, inscribed with the names of Mrs. Patton's departed friends,—two worked in crewel to the memory of her father and mother, and two paper memorials, with the woman weeping under the willow at the side of a monument. They were all brown with age; and there was a sampler beside, worked by "Judith Beckett, aged ten," and all five were framed in slender black frames and hung very high on the walls. There was a rocking-chair which looked as if it felt too grand for use, and considered itself imposing. It tilted far back on its rockers, and was bent forward at the top to make one's head uncomfortable. It need not have troubled itself; nobody would ever wish to sit there. It was such a big rocking-chair, and Mrs. Patton was proud of it; always generously urging her guests to enjoy its comfort, which was imaginary with her, as she was so short that she could hardly have climbed into it without assistance.

Mrs. Patton was a little ceremonious at first, but soon recovered herself and told us a great deal which we were glad to hear. I asked her once if she had not always lived at Deephaven. "Here and beyond East Parish," said she. "Mr. Patton,—that was my husband,—he owned a good farm there when I married him, but I come back here again after he died; place was all mortgaged. I never got a cent, and I was poorer than when I started. I worked harder 'n ever I did before or since to keep things together, but 't wasn't any kind o' use. Your mother knows all about it, Miss Kate,"—as if we might not be willing to believe it on her authority. "I come back here a widow and destitute, and I tell you the world looked fair to me when I left this house first to go over there. Don't you run no risks, you're better off as you be, dears. But land sakes alive, 'he' didn't mean no hurt! and he set everything by me when he was himself. I don't make no scruples of speaking about it, everybody knows how it was, but I did go through with everything. I never knew what the day would bring forth," said the widow, as if this were the first time she had had a chance to tell her sorrows to a sympathizing audience. She did not seem to mind talking about the troubles of her married life any more than a soldier minds telling the story of his campaigns, and dwells with pride on the worst battle of all.

Her favorite subject always was Miss Brandon, and after a pause she said that she hoped we were finding everything right in the house; she had meant to take up the carpet in the best spare room, but it didn't seem to need it; it was taken up the year before, and the room had not been used since, there was not a mite of dust under it last time. And Kate assured her, with an appearance of great wisdom, that she did not think it could be necessary at all.

"I come home and had a good cry yesterday after I was over to see you," said Mrs. Patton, and I could not help wondering if she really could cry, for she looked so perfectly dried up, so dry that she might rustle in the wind. "Your aunt had been failin' so long that just after she died it was a relief, but I've got so's to forget all about that, and I miss her as she used to be; it seemed as if you had stepped into her place, and you look some as she used to when she was young."

"You must miss her," said Kate, "and I know how much she used to depend upon you. You were very kind to her."

"I sat up with her the night she died," said the widow, with mournful satisfaction. "I have lived neighbor to her all my life except the thirteen years I was married, and there wasn't a week I wasn't over to the great house except I was off to a distance taking care of the sick. When she got to be feeble she always wanted me to 'tend to the cleaning and to see to putting the canopies and curtains on the bedsteads, and she wouldn't trust nobody but me to handle some of the best china. I used to say, 'Miss Katharine, why don't you have some young folks come and stop with you? There's Mis' Lancaster's daughter a growing up'; but she didn't seem to care for nobody but your mother. You wouldn't believe what a hand she used to be for company in her younger days. Surprisin' how folks alters. When I first rec'lect her much she was as straight as an arrow, and she used to go to Boston visiting and come home with the top of the fashion. She always did dress elegant. It used to be gay here, and she was always going down to the Lorimers' or the Carews' to tea, and they coming here. Her sister was married; she was a good deal older; but some of her brothers were at home. There was your grandfather and Mr. Henry. I don't think she ever got it over,—his disappearing so. There were lots of folks then that's dead and gone, and they used to have their card-parties, and old Cap'n Manning—he's dead and gone— used to have 'em all to play whist every fortnight, sometimes three or four tables, and they always had cake and wine handed round, or the cap'n made some punch, like's not, with oranges in it, and lemons; *he* knew how! He was a bachelor to the end of his days, the old cap'n was, but he used to entertain real handsome. I rec'lect one night they was a playin' after the wine was brought in, and he upset his glass all over Miss Martha Lorimer's invisible-green watered silk, and spoilt the better part of two breadths. She sent right over for me early the next morning to see if I knew of anything to take out the spots, but I didn't, though I can take grease out o' most any material. We tried clear alcohol, and saleratus-water, and hartshorn, and pouring water through, and heating of it, and when we got through it was worse than when we started. She felt dreadful bad about it, and at last she says, 'Judith, we won't work over it any more, but if you 'll give me a day some time or 'nother, we'll rip it up and make a quilt of it.' I see that quilt last time I was in Miss Rebecca's north chamber. Miss Martha was her aunt; you never saw her; she was dead and gone before your day. It was a silk old Cap'n Peter Lorimer, her brother, who left 'em his money, brought home from sea, and she had worn it for best and second best eleven year. It looked as good as new, and she never would have ripped it up if she could have matched it. I said it seemed to be a shame, but it was a curi's figure. Cap'n Manning fetched her one to pay for it the next time he went to Boston. She didn't want to take it, but he wouldn't take no for an answer; he was free-handed, the cap'n was. I helped 'em make it 'long of Mary Ann Simms the dressmaker,—she's dead and gone too,—the time it was made. It was brown, and a beautiful-looking piece, but it wore shiny, and she made a double-gown of it before she died."

Mrs. Patton brought Kate and me some delicious old-fashioned cake with much spice in it, and told us it was made by old Mrs. Chantrey Brandon's receipt which she got in England, that it would keep a year, and she always kept a loaf by her, now that she could afford it; she supposed we knew Miss Katharine had named her in her will long before she was sick. "It has put me beyond fear of want," said Mrs. Patton. "I won't deny that I used to think it would go hard with me when I got so old I couldn't earn my living. You see I never laid up but a little, and it's hard for a woman who comes of respectable folks to be a pauper in her last days; but your aunt, Miss Kate, she thought of it too, and I'm sure I'm thankful to be so comfortable, and to stay in my house, which I couldn't have done, like's not. Miss Rebecca Lorimer said to me after I got news of the will, 'Why, Mis' Patton, you don't suppose your friends would ever have let you want!' And I says, 'My friends are kind,—the Lord bless 'em!—but I feel better to be able to do for myself than to be beholden.'"

After this long call we went down to the post-office, and coming home stopped for a while in the old burying-ground, which we had noticed the day before; and we sat for the first time on the great stone in the wall, in the shade of a maple-tree, where we so often waited afterward for the stage to come with the mail, or rested on our way home from a walk. It was a comfortable perch; we used to read our letters there, I remember.

I must tell you a little about the Deephaven burying-ground, for its interest was inexhaustible, and I do not know how much time we may have spent in reading the long epitaphs on the grave-stones and trying to puzzle out the inscriptions, which were often so old and worn that we could only trace a letter here and there. It was a neglected corner of the world, and there were straggling sumachs and acacias scattered about the enclosure, while a row of fine old elms marked the boundary of two sides. The grass was long and tangled, and most of the stones leaned one way or the other, and some had fallen flat. There were a few handsome old family monuments clustered in one corner, among which the one that marked Miss Brandon's grave looked so new and fresh that it seemed inappropriate. "It should have been dingy to begin with, like the rest," said Kate one day; "but I think it will make itself look like its neighbors as soon as possible."

There were many stones which were sacred to the memory of men who had been lost at sea, almost always giving the name of the departed ship, which was so kept in remembrance; and one felt as much interest in the ship Starlight, supposed to have foundered off the Cape of Good Hope, as in the poor fellow who had the ill luck to be one of her crew. There were dozens of such inscriptions, and there were other stones perpetuating the fame of Honourable gentlemen who had been members of His Majesty's Council, or surveyors of His Majesty's Woods, or King's Officers of Customs for the town of Deephaven. Some of the epitaphs were beautiful, showing that tenderness for the friends who had died, that longing to do them justice, to fully acknowledge their virtues and dearness, which is so touching, and so unmistakable even under the stiff, quaint expressions and formal words which were thought suitable to be chiselled on the stones, so soon to be looked at carelessly by the tearless eyes of strangers. We often used to notice names, and learn their history from the old people whom we knew, and in this way we heard many stories which we never shall forget. It is wonderful, the romance and tragedy and adventure which one may find in a quiet old-fashioned country town, though to heartily enjoy the every-day life one must care to study life and character, and must find pleasure in thought and observation of simple things, and have an instinctive, delicious interest in what to other eyes is unflavored dulness.

To go back to Mrs. Patton; on our way home, after our first call upon her, we stopped to speak to Mrs. Dockum, who mentioned that she had seen us going in to the "Widow Jim's."

"Willin' woman," said Mrs. Dockum, "always been respected; got an uncommon facility o' speech. I never saw such a hand to talk, but then she has something to say, which ain't the case with everybody. Good neighbor, does according to her means always. Dreadful tough time of it with her husband, shif'less and drunk all his time. Noticed that dent in the side of her forehead, I s'pose? That's where he liked to have killed her; slung a stone bottle at her."

"*What!*" said Kate and I, very much shocked.

"She don't like to have it inquired about; but she and I were sitting up with 'Manda Damer one night, and she gave me the particulars. I knew he did it, for she had a fit o' sickness afterward. Had sliced

SARAH ORNE JEWETT

cucumbers for breakfast that morning; he was very partial to them, and he wanted some vinegar. Happened to be two bottles in the cellar-way; were just alike, and one of 'em was vinegar and the other had sperrit in it at haying-time. He takes up the wrong one and pours on quick, and out come the hayseed and flies, and he give the bottle a sling, and it hit her there where you see the scar; might put the end of your finger into the dent. He said he meant to break the bottle ag'in the door, but it went slant-wise, sort of. I don' know, I'm sure" (meditatively). "She said he was good-natured; it was early in the mornin', and he hadn't had time to get upset; but he had a high temper naturally, and so much drink hadn't made it much better. She had good prospects when she married him. Six-foot-two and red cheeks and straight as a Noroway pine; had a good property from his father, and his mother come of a good family, but he died in debt; drank like a fish. Yes, 'twas a shame, nice woman; good consistent church-member; always been respected; useful among the sick."

IV

Deephaven Society

I t was curious to notice, in this quaint little fishing-village by the sea, how clearly the gradations of society were defined. The place prided itself most upon having been long ago the residence of one Governor Chantrey, who was a rich shipowner and East India merchant, and whose fame and magnificence were almost fabulous. It was a never-ceasing regret that his house should have burned down after he died, and there is no doubt that if it were still standing it would rival any ruin of the Old World.

The elderly people, though laying claim to no slight degree of present consequence, modestly ignored it, and spoke with pride of the grand way in which life was carried on by their ancestors, the Deephaven families of old times. I think Kate and I were assured at least a hundred times that Governor Chantrey kept a valet, and his wife, Lady Chantrey, kept a maid, and that the governor had an uncle in England who was a baronet; and I believe this must have been why our friends felt so deep an interest in the affairs of the English nobility: they no doubt felt themselves entitled to seats near the throne itself. There were formerly five families who kept their coaches in Deephaven; there were balls at the governor's, and regal entertainments at other of the grand mansions; there is not a really distinguished person in the country who will not prove to have been directly or indirectly connected with Deephaven. We were shown the cellar of the Chantrey house, and the terraces, and a few clumps of lilacs, and the grand rows of elms. There are still two of the governor's warehouses left, but his ruined wharves are fast disappearing, and are almost deserted, except by small barefooted boys who sit on the edges to fish for sea-perch when the tide comes in. There is an imposing monument in the burying-ground to the great man and his amiable consort. I am sure that if there were any surviving relatives of the governor they would receive in Deephaven far more deference than is consistent with the principles of a republican government; but the family became extinct long since, and I have heard, though it is not a subject that one may speak of lightly, that the sons were unworthy their noble descent and came to inglorious ends.

SARAH ORNE JEWETT

There were still remaining a few representatives of the old families, who were treated with much reverence by the rest of the townspeople, although they were, like the conies of Scripture, a feeble folk.

Deephaven is utterly out of fashion. It never recovered from the effects of the embargo of 1807, and a sand-bar has been steadily filling in the mouth of the harbor. Though the fishing gives what occupation there is for the inhabitants of the place, it is by no means sufficient to draw recruits from abroad. But nobody in Deephaven cares for excitement, and if some one once in a while has the low taste to prefer a more active life, he is obliged to go elsewhere in search of it, and is spoken of afterward with kind pity. I well remember the Widow Moses said to me, in speaking of a certain misguided nephew of hers, "I never could see what could 'a' sot him out to leave so many privileges and go way off to Lynn, with all them children too. Why, they lived here no more than a cable's length from the meetin'-house!"

There were two schooners owned in town, and 'Bijah Mauley and Jo Sands owned a trawl. There were some schooners and a small brig slowly going to pieces by the wharves, and indeed all Deephaven looked more or less out of repair. All along shore one might see dories and wherries and whale-boats, which had been left to die a lingering death. There is something piteous to me in the sight of an old boat. If one I had used much and cared for were past its usefulness, I should say good by to it, and have it towed out to sea and sunk; it never should be left to fall to pieces above high-water mark.

Even the commonest fishermen felt a satisfaction, and seemed to realize their privilege, in being residents of Deephaven; but among the nobility and gentry there lingered a fierce pride in their family and town records, and a hardly concealed contempt and pity for people who were obliged to live in other parts of the world. There were acknowledged to be a few disadvantages,—such as living nearly a dozen miles from the railway,—but, as Miss Honora Carew said, the tone of Deephaven society had always been very high, and it was very nice that there had never been any manufacturing element introduced. She could not feel too grateful, herself, that there was no disagreeable foreign population.

"But," said Kate one day, "wouldn't you like to have some pleasant new people brought into town?"

"Certainly, my dear," said Miss Honora, rather doubtfully; "I have always been public-spirited; but then, we always have guests in summer, and I am growing old. I should not care to enlarge my acquaintance to any great extent." Miss Honora and Mrs. Dent had lived gay lives in their younger days, and were interested and connected with the outside world more than any of our Deephaven friends; but they were quite contented to stay in their own house, with their books and letters and knitting, and they carefully read Littell and "the new magazine," as they called the Atlantic.

The Carews were very intimate with the minister and his sister, and there were one or two others who belonged to this set. There was Mr. Joshua Dorsey, who wore his hair in a queue, was very deaf, and carried a ponderous cane which had belonged to his venerated father,—a much taller man than he. He was polite to Kate and me, but we never knew him much. He went to play whist with the Carews every Monday evening, and commonly went out fishing once a week. He had begun the practice of law, but he had lost his hearing, and at the same time his lady-love had inconsiderately fallen in love with somebody else; after which he retired from active business life. He had a fine library, which he invited us to examine. He had many new books, but they looked shockingly overdressed, in their fresher bindings, beside the old brown volumes of essays and sermons, and lighter works in many-volume editions.

A prominent link in society was Widow Tully, who had been the much-respected housekeeper of old Captain Manning for forty years. When he died he left her the use of his house and family pew, besides an annuity. The existence of Mr. Tully seemed to be a myth. During the first of his widow's residence in town she had been much affected when obliged to speak of him, and always represented herself as having seen better days and as being highly connected. But she was apt to be ungrammatical when excited, and there was a whispered tradition that she used to keep a toll-bridge in a town in Connecticut; though the mystery of her previous state of existence will probably never be solved. She wore mourning for the captain which would have befitted his widow, and patronized the townspeople conspicuously, while she herself was treated with much condescension by the Carews and Lorimers. She occupied, on the whole, much the same position that Mrs. Betty Barker did in Cranford. And, indeed, Kate and I were often reminded of that estimable town. We heard that Kate's aunt, Miss Brandon, had never been appreciative of Mrs. Tully's merits, and that since her death the others had received Mrs. Tully into their society rather more.

It seemed as if all the clocks in Deephaven, and all the people with them, had stopped years ago, and the people had been doing over and over what they had been busy about during the last week of their unambitious progress. Their clothes had lasted wonderfully well, and they had no need to earn money when there was so little chance to spend it; indeed, there were several families who seemed to have no more visible means of support than a balloon. There were no young people whom we knew, though a number used to come to church on Sunday from the inland farms, or "the country," as we learned to say. There were children among the fishermen's families at the shore, but a few years will see Deephaven possessed by two classes instead of the time-honored three.

As for our first Sunday at church, it must be in vain to ask you to imagine our delight when we heard the tuning of a bass-viol in the gallery just before service. We pressed each other's hands most tenderly, looked up at the singers' seats, and then trusted ourselves to look at each other. It was more than we had hoped for. There were also a violin and sometimes a flute, and a choir of men and women singers, though the congregation were expected to join in the psalm-singing. The first hymn was

> *"The Lord our God is full of might,*
> *The winds obey his will,"*

to the tune of St. Ann's. It was all so delightfully old-fashioned; our pew was a square pew, and was by an open window looking seaward. We also had a view of the entire congregation, and as we were somewhat early, we watched the people come in, with great interest. The Deephaven aristocracy came with stately step up the aisle; this was all the chance there was for displaying their unquestioned dignity in public.

Many of the people drove to church in wagons that were low and old and creaky, with worn buffalo-robes over the seat, and some hay tucked underneath for the sleepy, undecided old horse. Some of the younger farmers and their wives had high, shiny wagons, with tall horsewhips,— which they sometimes brought into church,—and they drove up to the steps with a consciousness of being conspicuous and enviable. They had a bashful look when they came in, and for a few minutes after they took their seats they evidently felt that all eyes were fixed upon them; but after a little while they were quite at their ease, and looked critically at the new arrivals.

The old folks interested us most. "Do you notice how many more old women there are than old men?" whispered Kate to me. And we wondered if the husbands and brothers had been drowned, and if it must not be sad to look at the blue, sunshiny sea beyond the marshes, if the far-away white sails reminded them of some ships that had never sailed home into Deephaven harbor, or of fishing-boats that had never come back to land.

The girls and young men adorned themselves in what they believed to be the latest fashion, but the elderly women were usually relics of old times in manner and dress. They wore to church thin, soft silk gowns that must have been brought from over the seas years upon years before, and wide collars fastened with mourning-pins holding a lock of hair. They had big black bonnets, some of them with stiff capes, such as Kate and I had not seen before since our childhood. They treasured large rusty lace veils of scraggly pattern, and wore sometimes, on pleasant Sundays, white China-crape shawls with attenuated fringes; and there were two or three of these shawls in the congregation which had been dyed black, and gave an aspect of meekness and general unworthiness to the aged wearer, they clung and drooped about the figure in such a hopeless way. We used to notice often the most interesting scarfs, without which no Deephaven woman considered herself in full dress. Sometimes there were red India scarfs in spite of its being hot weather; but our favorite ones were long strips of silk, embroidered along the edges and at the ends with dismal-colored floss in odd patterns. I think there must have been a fashion once, in Deephaven, of working these scarfs, and I should not be surprised to find that it was many years before the fashion of working samplers came about. Our friends always wore black mitts on warm Sundays, and many of them carried neat little bags of various designs on their arms, containing a precisely folded pocket-handkerchief, and a frugal lunch of caraway seeds or red and white peppermints. I should like you to see, with your own eyes, Widow Ware and Miss Exper'ence Hull, two old sisters whose personal appearance we delighted in, and whom we saw feebly approaching down the street this first Sunday morning under the shadow of the two last members of an otherwise extinct race of parasols.

There were two or three old men who sat near us. They were sailors,—there is something unmistakable about a sailor,—and they had a curiously ancient, uncanny look, as if they might have belonged to the crew of the Mayflower, or even have cruised about with the

Northmen in the times of Harold Harfager and his comrades. They had been blown about by so many winter winds, so browned by summer suns, and wet by salt spray, that their hands and faces looked like leather, with a few deep folds instead of wrinkles. They had pale blue eyes, very keen and quick; their hair looked like the fine sea-weed which clings to the kelp-roots and mussel-shells in little locks. These friends of ours sat solemnly at the heads of their pews and looked unflinchingly at the minister, when they were not dozing, and they sang with voices like the howl of the wind, with an occasional deep note or two.

Have you never seen faces that seemed old-fashioned? Many of the people in Deephaven church looked as if they must be—if not supernaturally old—exact copies of their remote ancestors. I wonder if it is not possible that the features and expression may be almost perfectly reproduced. These faces were not modern American faces, but belonged rather to the days of the early settlement of the country, the old colonial times. We often heard quaint words and expressions which we never had known anywhere else but in old books. There was a great deal of sea-lingo in use; indeed, we learned a great deal ourselves, unconsciously, and used it afterward to the great amusement of our friends; but there were also many peculiar provincialisms, and among the people who lived on the lonely farms inland we often noticed words we had seen in Chaucer, and studied out at school in our English literature class. Everything in Deephaven was more or less influenced by the sea; the minister spoke oftenest of Peter and his fishermen companions, and prayed most earnestly every Sunday morning for those who go down to the sea in ships. He made frequent allusions and drew numberless illustrations of a similar kind for his sermons, and indeed I am in doubt whether, if the Bible had been written wholly in inland countries, it would have been much valued in Deephaven.

The singing was very droll, for there was a majority of old voices, which had seen their best days long before, and the bass-viol was excessively noticeable, and apt to be a little ahead of the time the singers kept, while the violin lingered after. Somewhere on the other side of the church we heard an acute voice which rose high above all the rest of the congregation, sharp as a needle, and slightly cracked, with a limitless supply of breath. It rose and fell gallantly, and clung long to the high notes of Dundee. It was like the wail of the banshee, which sounds clear to the fated hearer above all other noises. We afterward became acquainted with the owner of this voice, and were surprised to find her a meek widow, who was like a thin black beetle in her pathetic cypress veil and big black bonnet. She looked as if she had forgotten who she was, and spoke with an apologetic whine; but we heard she had a temper as high as her voice, and as much to be dreaded as the equinoctial gale.

Near the church was the parsonage, where Mr. Lorimer lived, and the old Lorimer house not far beyond was occupied by Miss Rebecca Lorimer. Some stranger might ask the question why the minister and his sister did not live together, but you would have understood it at once after you had lived for a little while in town. They were very fond of each other, and the minister dined with Miss Rebecca on Sundays, and she passed the day with him on Wednesdays, and they ruled their separate households with decision and dignity. I think Mr. Lorimer's house showed no signs of being without a mistress, any more than his sister's betrayed the want of a master's care and authority.

The Carews were very kind friends of ours, and had been Miss Brandon's best friends. We heard that there had always been a coolness between Miss Brandon and Miss Lorimer, and that, though they exchanged visits and were always polite, there was a chill in the politeness, and one would never have suspected them of admiring each other at all. We had the whole history of the trouble, which dated back scores of years, from Miss Honora Carew, but we always took pains to appear ignorant of the feud, and I think Miss Lorimer was satisfied that it was best not to refer to it, and to let bygones be bygones. It would not have been true Deephaven courtesy to prejudice Kate against her grand-aunt, and Miss Rebecca cherished her dislike in silence, which gave us a most grand respect for her, since we knew she thought herself in the right; though I think it never had come to an open quarrel between these majestic aristocrats.

Miss Honora Carew and Mr. Dick and their elder sister, Mrs. Dent, had a charmingly sedate and quiet home in the old Carew house. Mrs. Dent was ill a great deal while we were there, but she must have been a very brilliant woman, and was not at all dull when we knew her. She had outlived her husband and her children, and she had, several years before our summer there, given up her own home, which was in the city, and had come back to Deephaven. Miss Honora—dear Miss Honora!—had been one of the brightest, happiest girls, and had lost none of her brightness and happiness by growing old. She had lost none of her fondness for society, though she was so contented in quiet Deephaven, and I think she enjoyed Kate's and my stories of our pleasures as much as we did hers of old times. We used to go to see her almost every day. "Mr. Dick," as they called their brother, had once been a merchant in the East Indies, and there were quantities of curiosities and most beautiful china which he had brought and sent home, which gave the house a character of its own. He had been very rich and had lost some of his money, and then he came home and was still considered to possess princely wealth by his neighbors. He had a great fondness for reading and study, which had not been lost sight of during his business life, and he spent most of his time in his library. He and Mr. Lorimer had their differences of opinion about certain points of theology, and this made them much fonder of each other's society, and gave them a great deal of pleasure; for after every series of arguments, each was sure that he had vanquished the other, or there were alternate victories and defeats which made life vastly interesting and important.

Miss Carew and Mrs. Dent had a great treasury of old brocades and laces and ornaments, which they showed us one day, and told us stories of the wearers, or, if they were their own, there were always some reminiscences which they liked to talk over with each other and with us. I never shall forget the first evening we took tea with them; it impressed us very much, and yet nothing wonderful happened. Tea was handed round by an old-fashioned maid, and afterward we sat talking in the twilight, looking out at the garden. It was such a delight to have tea served in this way. I wonder that the fashion has been almost forgotten. Kate and I took much pleasure in choosing our tea-poys; hers had a mandarin parading on the top, and mine a flight of birds and a pagoda; and we often used them afterward, for Miss Honora asked us to come to tea whenever we liked. "A stupid, common country town" some one dared to call Deephaven in a letter once, and how bitterly we resented it! That was a house where one might find the best society, and the most charming manners and good-breeding, and if I were asked to tell you what I mean by the word "lady," I should ask you to go, if it were possible, to call upon Miss Honora Carew.

After a while the elder sister said, "My dears, we always have prayers at nine, for I have to go up stairs early nowadays." And then the servants came in, and she read solemnly the King of glory Psalm, which I have always liked best, and then Mr. Dick read the church prayers, the form of prayer to be used in families. We stayed later to talk with Miss Honora after we had said good night to Mrs. Dent. And we told each other, as we went home in the moonlight down the quiet street, how much we had enjoyed the evening, for somehow the house and the people had nothing to do with the present, or the hurry of modern life. I have never heard that psalm since without its bringing back that summer night in Deephaven, the beautiful quaint old room, and Kate and I feeling so young and worldly, by contrast, the flickering, shaded light of the candles, the old book, and the voices that said Amen.

There were several other fine old houses in Deephaven beside this and the Brandon house, though that was rather the most imposing. There were two or three which had not been kept in repair, and were deserted, and of course they were said to be haunted, and we were told of their ghosts, and why they walked, and when. From some of the local superstitions Kate and I have vainly endeavored ever since to shake ourselves free. There was a most heathenish fear of doing certain things on Friday, and there were countless signs in which we still have confidence. When the moon is very bright and other people grow sentimental, we only remember that it is a fine night to catch hake.

SARAH ORNE JEWETT

V

THE CAPTAINS

I should consider my account of Deephaven society incomplete if I did not tell you something of the ancient mariners, who may be found every pleasant morning sunning themselves like turtles on one of the wharves. Sometimes there was a considerable group of them, but the less constant members of the club were older than the rest, and the epidemics of rheumatism in town were sadly frequent. We found that it was etiquette to call them each captain, but I think some of the Deephaven men took the title by brevet upon arriving at a proper age.

They sat close together because so many of them were deaf, and when we were lucky enough to overhear the conversation, it seemed to concern their adventures at sea, or the freight carried out by the Sea Duck, the Ocean Rover, or some other Deephaven ship,—the particulars of the voyage and its disasters and successes being as familiar as the wanderings of the children of Israel to an old parson. There were sometimes violent altercations when the captains differed as to the tonnage of some craft that had been a prey to the winds and waves, dry-rot, or barnacles fifty years before. The old fellows puffed away at little black pipes with short stems, and otherwise consumed tobacco in fabulous quantities. It is needless to say that they gave an immense deal of attention to the weather. We used to wish we could join this agreeable company, but we found that the appearance of an outsider caused a disapproving silence, and that the meeting was evidently not to be interfered with. Once we were impertinent enough to hide ourselves for a while just round the corner of the warehouse, but we were afraid or ashamed to try it again, though the conversation was inconceivably edifying. Captain Isaac Horn, the eldest and wisest of all, was discoursing upon some cloth he had purchased once in Bristol, which the shopkeeper delayed sending until just as they were ready to weigh anchor.

"I happened to take a look at that cloth," said the captain, in a loud droning voice, "and as quick as I got sight of it, I spoke onpleasant of that swindling English fellow, and the crew, they stood back. I was dreadful high-tempered in them days, mind ye; and I had the gig manned. We was out in the stream, just ready to sail. 'T was no use waiting any longer for the wind to change, and we was going north-about. I went ashore, and when I walks into his shop ye never see a creatur' so wilted. Ye see the miser'ble sculpin thought I'd never stop to open the goods, an' it was a chance I did, mind ye! 'Lor,' says he, grinning and turning the color of a biled lobster, 'I s'posed ye were a standing out to sea by this time.' 'No,' says I, 'and I've got my men out here on the quay a landing that cloth o' yourn, and if you don't send just what I bought and paid for down there to go back in the gig within fifteen minutes, I'll take ye by the collar and drop ye into the dock.' I was twice the size of him, mind ye, and master strong. 'Don't ye like it?' says he, edging round; 'I'll change it for ye, then.' Ter'ble perlite he was. 'Like it?' says I, 'it looks as if it were built of dog's hair and divil's wool, kicked together by spiders; and it's coarser than Irish frieze; three threads to an *armful*,' says I."

This was evidently one of the captain's favorite stories, for we heard an approving grumble from the audience.

In the course of a walk inland we made a new acquaintance, Captain Lant, whom we had noticed at church, and who sometimes joined the company on the wharf. We had been walking through the woods, and coming out to his fields we went on to the house for some water. There was no one at home but the captain, who told us cheerfully that he should be pleased to serve us, though his women-folks had gone off to a funeral, the other side of the P'int. He brought out a pitcherful of milk, and after we had drunk some, we all sat down together in the shade. The captain brought an old flag-bottomed chair from the woodhouse, and sat down facing Kate and me, with an air of certainty that he was going to hear something new and make some desirable new acquaintances, and also that he could tell something it would be worth our while to hear. He looked more and more like a well-to-do old English sparrow, and chippered faster and faster.

"Queer ye should know I'm a sailor so quick; why, I've been a-farming it this twenty years; have to go down to the shore and take a day's fishing every hand's turn, though, to keep the old hulk clear of barnacles. There! I do wish I lived nigher the shore, where I could see the folks I know, and talk about what's been a-goin' on. You don't know anything about it, you don't; but it's tryin' to a man to be called 'old Cap'n Lant,' and, so to speak, be forgot when there's anything stirring, and be called gran'ther by clumsy creatur's goin' on fifty and sixty, who

SARAH ORNE JEWETT

can't do no more work to-day than I can; an' then the women-folks keeps a-tellin' me to be keerful and not fall, and as how I'm too old to go out fishing; and when they want to be soft-spoken, they say as how they don't see as I fail, and how wonderful I keep my hearin'. I never did want to farm it, but 'she' always took it to heart when I was off on a v'y'ge, and this farm and some consider'ble means beside come to her from her brother, and they all sot to and give me no peace of mind till I sold out my share of the Ann Eliza and come ashore for good. I did keep an eighth of the Pactolus, and I was ship's husband for a long spell, but she never was heard from on her last voyage to Singapore. I was the lonesomest man, when I first come ashore, that ever you see. Well, you are master hands to walk, if you come way up from the Brandon house. I wish the women was at home. Know Miss Brandon? Why, yes; and I remember all her brothers and sisters, and her father and mother. I can see 'em now coming into meeting, proud as Lucifer and straight as a mast, every one of 'em. Miss Katharine, she always had her butter from this very farm. Some of the folks used to go down every Saturday, and my wife, she's been in the house a hundred times, I s'pose. So you are Hathaway Brandon's grand-daughter?" (to Kate); "why, he and I have been out fishing together many's the time,—he and Chantrey, his next younger brother. Henry, he was a disapp'intment; he went to furrin parts and turned out a Catholic priest, I s'pose you've heard? I never was so set ag'in Mr. Henry as some folks was. He was the pleasantest spoken of the whole on 'em. You do look like the Brandons; you really favor 'em consider'ble. Well, I'm pleased to see ye, I'm sure."

We asked him many questions about the old people, and found he knew all the family histories and told them with great satisfaction. We found he had his pet stories, and it must have been gratifying to have an entirely new and fresh audience. He was adroit in leading the conversation around to a point where the stories would come in appropriately, and we helped him as much as possible. In a small neighborhood all the people know each other's stories and experiences by heart, and I have no doubt the old captain had been snubbed many times on beginning a favorite anecdote. There was a story which he told us that first day, which he assured us was strictly true, and it is certainly a remarkable instance of the influence of one mind upon another at a distance. It seems to me worth preserving, at any rate; and as we heard it from the old man, with his solemn voice and serious expression and quaint gestures, it was singularly impressive.

"When I was a youngster," said Captain Lant, "I was an orphan, and I was bound out to old Mr. Peletiah Daw's folks, over on the Ridge Road. It was in the time of the last war, and he had a nephew, Ben Dighton, a dreadful high-strung, wild fellow, who had gone off on a privateer. The old man, he set everything by Ben; he would disoblige his own boys any day to please him. This was in his latter days, and he used to have spells of wandering and being out of his head; and he used to call for Ben and talk sort of foolish about him, till they would tell him to stop. Ben never did a stroke of work for him, either, but he was a handsome fellow, and had a way with him when he was good-natured. One night old Peletiah had been very bad all day and was getting quieted down, and it was after supper; we sat round in the kitchen, and he lay in the bedroom opening out. There were some pitch-knots blazing, and the light shone in on the bed, and all of a sudden something made me look up and look in; and there was the old man setting up straight, with his eyes shining at me like a cat's. 'Stop 'em!' says he; *'stop 'em!'* and his two sons run in then to catch hold of him, for they thought he was beginning with one of his wild spells; but he fell back on the bed and began to cry like a baby. 'O, dear me,' says he, 'they've hung him,—hung him right up to the yard-arm! O, they oughtn't to have done it; cut him down quick! he didn't think; he means well, Ben does; he was hasty. O my God, I can't bear to see him swing round by the neck! It's poor Ben hung up to the yard-arm. Let me alone, I say!' Andrew and Moses, they were holding him with all their might, and they were both hearty men, but he 'most got away from them once or twice, and he screeched and howled like a mad creatur', and then he would cry again like a child. He was worn out after a while and lay back quiet, and said over and over, 'Poor Ben!' and 'hung at the yard-arm'; and he told the neighbors next day, but nobody noticed him much, and he seemed to forget it as his mind come back. All that summer he was miser'ble, and towards cold weather he failed right along, though he had been a master strong man in his day, and his timbers held together well. Along late in the fall he had taken to his bed, and one day there came to the house a fellow named Sim Decker, a reckless fellow he was too, who had gone out in the same ship with Ben. He pulled a long face when he came in, and said he had brought bad news. They had been taken prisoner and carried into port and put in jail, and Ben Dighton had got a fever there and died.

"'You lie!' says the old man from the bedroom, speaking as loud and f'erce as ever you heard. 'They hung him to the yard-arm!'

"'Don't mind him,' says Andrew; 'he's wandering-like, and he had a bad dream along back in the spring; I s'posed he'd forgotten it.' But the Decker fellow he turned pale, and kept talking crooked while he listened to old Peletiah a-scolding to himself. He answered the questions the women-folks asked him,—they took on a good deal,—but pretty soon he got up and winked to me and Andrew, and we went out in the yard. He began to swear, and then says he, 'When did the old man have his dream?' Andrew couldn't remember, but I knew it was the night before he sold the gray colt, and that was the 24th of April.

"'Well,' says Sim Decker, 'on the twenty-third day of April Ben Dighton was hung to the yard-arm, and I see 'em do it, Lord help him! I didn't mean to tell the women, and I s'posed you'd never know, for I'm all the one of the ship's company you're ever likely to see. We were taken prisoner, and Ben was mad as fire, and they were scared of him and chained him to the deck; and while he was sulking there, a little parrot of a midshipman come up and grinned at him, and snapped his fingers in his face; and Ben lifted his hands with the heavy irons and sprung at him like a tiger, and the boy dropped dead as a stone; and they put the bight of a rope round Ben's neck and slung him right up to the yard-arm, and there he swung back and forth until as soon as we dared one of us clim' up and cut the rope and let him go over the ship's side; and they put us in irons for that, curse 'em! How did that old man in there know, and he bedridden here, nigh upon three thousand miles off?' says he. But I guess there wasn't any of us could tell him," said Captain Lant in conclusion. "It's something I never could account for, but it's true as truth. I've known more such cases; some folks laughs at me for believing 'em,—'the cap'n's yarns,' they calls 'em,—but if you'll notice, everybody's got some yarn of that kind they do believe, if they won't believe yours. And there's a good deal happens in the world that's myster'ous. Now there was Widder Oliver Pinkham, over to the P'int, told me with her own lips that she—" But just here we saw the captain's expression alter suddenly, and looked around to see a wagon coming up the lane. We immediately said we must go home, for it was growing late, but asked permission to come again and hear the Widow Oliver Pinkham story. We stopped, however, to see "the women-folks," and afterward became so intimate with them that we were invited to spend the afternoon and take tea, which invitation we accepted with great pride. We went out fishing, also, with the captain and "Danny," of whom I will tell you presently. I often think of Captain Lant in the

VI

DANNY

D eephaven seemed more like one of the lazy little English seaside towns than any other. It was not in the least American. There was no excitement about anything; there were no manufactories; nobody seemed in the least hurry. The only foreigners were a few stranded sailors. I do not know when a house or a new building of any kind had been built; the men were farmers, or went outward in boats, or inward in fish-wagons, or sometimes mackerel and halibut fishing in schooners for the city markets. Sometimes a schooner came to one of the wharves to load with hay or firewood; but Deephaven used to be a town of note, rich and busy, as its forsaken warehouses show.

We knew almost all the fisher-people at the shore, even old Dinnett, who lived an apparently desolate life by himself in a hut and was reputed to have been a bloodthirsty pirate in his youth. He was consequently feared by all the children, and for misdemeanors in his latter days avoided generally. Kate talked with him awhile one day on the shore, and made him come up with her for a bandage for his hand which she saw he had hurt badly; and the next morning he brought us a "new" lobster apiece,—fishermen mean that a thing is only not salted when they say it is "fresh." We happened to be in the hall, and received him ourselves, and gave him a great piece of tobacco and (unintentionally) the means of drinking our health. "Bless your pretty hearts!" said he; "may ye be happy, and live long, and get good husbands, and if they ain't good to you may they die from you!"

None of our friends were more interesting than the fishermen. The fish-houses, which might be called the business centre of the town, were at a little distance from the old warehouses, farther down the harbor shore, and were ready to fall down in despair. There were some fishermen who lived near by, but most of them were also farmers in a small way, and lived in the village or farther inland. From our eastern windows we could see the moorings, and we always liked to watch the boats go out or come straying in, one after the other, ripping and skimming under the square little sails; and we often went down to the fish-houses to see what kind of a catch there had been.

I should have imagined that the sea would become very commonplace to men whose business was carried on in boats, and who had spent night after night and day after day from their boyhood on the water; but that is a mistake. They have an awe of the sea and of its mysteries, and of what it hides away from us. They are childish in their wonder at any strange creature which they find. If they have not seen the sea-serpent, they believe, I am sure, that other people have, and when a great shark or black-fish or sword-fish was taken and brought in shore, everybody went to see it, and we talked about it, and how brave its conqueror was, and what a fight there had been, for a long time afterward.

I said that we liked to see the boats go out, but I must not give you the impression that we saw them often, for they weighed anchor at an early hour in the morning. I remember once there was a light fog over the sea, lifting fast, as the sun was coming up, and the brownish sails disappeared in the mist, while voices could still be heard for some minutes after the men were hidden from sight. This gave one a curious feeling, but afterward, when the sun had risen, everything looked much the same as usual; the fog had gone, and the dories and even the larger boats were distant specks on the sparkling sea.

One afternoon we made a new acquaintance in this wise. We went down to the shore to see if we could hire a conveyance to the lighthouse the next morning. We often went out early in one of the fishing-boats, and after we had stayed as long as we pleased, Mr. Kew would bring us home. It was quiet enough that day, for not a single boat had come in, and there were no men to be seen along-shore. There was a solemn company of lobster-coops or cages which had been brought in to be mended. They always amused Kate. She said they seemed to her like droll old women telling each other secrets. These were scattered about in different attitudes, and looked more confidential than usual.

Just as we were going away we happened to see a man at work in one of the sheds. He was the fisherman whom we knew least of all; an odd-looking, silent sort of man, more sunburnt and weather-beaten than any of the others. We had learned to know him by the bright red flannel shirt he always wore, and besides, he was lame; some one told us he had had a bad fall once, on board ship. Kate and I had always wished we could find a chance to talk with him. He looked up at us pleasantly, and when we nodded and smiled, he said "Good day" in a gruff, hearty voice, and went on with his work, cleaning mackerel.

"Do you mind our watching you?" asked Kate.

"No, *ma'am*!" said the fisherman emphatically. So there we stood.

Those fish-houses were curious places, so different from any other kind of workshop. In this there was a seine, or part of one, festooned among the cross-beams overhead, and there were snarled fishing-lines, and barrows to carry fish in, like wheelbarrows without wheels; there were the queer round lobster-nets, and "kits" of salt mackerel, tubs of bait, and piles of clams; and some queer bones, and parts of remarkable fish, and lobster-claws of surprising size fastened on the walls for ornament. There was a pile of rubbish down at the end; I dare say it was all useful, however,—there is such mystery about the business.

Kate and I were never tired of hearing of the fish that come at different times of the year, and go away again, like the birds; or of the actions of the dog-fish, which the 'longshore-men hate so bitterly; and then there are such curious legends and traditions, of which almost all fishermen have a store.

"I think mackerel are the prettiest fish that swim," said I presently.

"So do I, miss," said the man, "not to say but I've seen more fancy-looking fish down in southern waters, bright as any flower you ever see; but a mackerel," holding up one admiringly, "why, they're so clean-built and trig-looking! Put a cod alongside, and he looks as lumbering as an old-fashioned Dutch brig aside a yacht.

"Those are good-looking fish, but they an't made much account of," continued our friend, as he pushed aside the mackerel and took another tub. "They're hake, I s'pose you know. But I forgot,—I can't stop to bother with them now." And he pulled forward a barrow full of small fish, flat and hard, with pointed, bony heads.

"Those are porgies, aren't they?" asked Kate.

"Yes," said the man, "an' I'm going to sliver them for the trawls."

We knew what the trawls were, and supposed that the porgies were to be used for bait; and we soon found out what "slivering" meant, by seeing him take them by the head and cut a slice from first one side and then the other in such a way that the pieces looked not unlike smaller fish.

"It seems to me," said I, "that fishermen always have sharper knives than other people."

"Yes, we do like a sharp knife in our trade; and then we are mostly strong-handed."

He was throwing the porgies' heads and backbones—all that was left of them after slivering—in a heap, and now several cats walked in as if they felt at home, and began a hearty lunch. "What a troop of pussies there is round here," said I; "I wonder what will become of them in the winter,—though, to be sure, the fishing goes on just the same."

"The better part of them don't get through the cold weather," said Danny. "Two or three of the old ones have been here for years, and are as much belonging to Deephaven as the meetin'-house; but the rest of them an't to be depended on. You'll miss the young ones by the dozen, come spring. I don't know myself but they move inland in the fall of the year; they're knowing enough, if that's all!"

Kate and I stood in the wide doorway, arm in arm, looking sometimes at the queer fisherman and the porgies, and sometimes out to sea. It was low tide; the wind had risen a little, and the heavy salt air blew toward us from the wet brown ledges in the rocky harbor. The sea was bright blue, and the sun was shining. Two gulls were swinging lazily to and fro; there was a flock of sand-pipers down by the water's edge, in a great hurry, as usual.

Presently the fisherman spoke again, beginning with an odd laugh: "I *was* scared last winter! Jack Scudder and me, we were up in the Cap'n Manning storehouse hunting for a half-bar'l of salt the skipper said was there. It was an awful blustering kind of day, with a thin icy rain blowing from all points at once; sea roaring as if it wished it could come ashore and put a stop to everything. Bad days at sea, them are; rigging all froze up. As I was saying, we were hunting for a half-bar'l of salt, and I laid hold of a bar'l that had something heavy in the bottom, and tilted it up, and my eye! there was a stir and a scratch and a squeal, and out went some kind of a creatur', and I jumped back, not looking for anything live, but I see in a minute it was a cat; and perhaps you think it is a big story, but there were eight more in there, hived in together to keep warm. I car'd 'em up some new fish that night; they seemed short of provisions. We hadn't been out fishing as much as common, and they hadn't dared to be round the fish-houses much, for a fellow who came in on a coaster had a dog, and he used to chase 'em. Hard chance they had, and lots of 'em died, I guess; but there seem to be some survivin' relatives, an' al'ays just so hungry! I used to feed them some when I was ashore. I think likely you've heard that a cat will fetch you bad luck; but I don't know's that made much difference to me. I kind of like to keep on the right side of 'em, too; if ever I have a bad dream there's sure to be a cat in it; but I was brought up to be clever to dumb beasts, an' I guess it's my natur'. Except fish," said Danny after a minute's thought; "but then it never seems like they had feelin's like creatur's that live ashore." And we all laughed heartily and felt well acquainted.

"I s'pose you misses will laugh if I tell ye I kept a kitty once myself." This was said rather shyly, and there was evidently a story, so we were much interested, and Kate said, "Please tell us about it; was it at sea?"

"Yes, it was at sea; leastways, on a coaster. I got her in a sing'lar kind of way: it was one afternoon we were lying alongside Charlestown Bridge, and I heard a young cat screeching real pitiful; and after I looked all round, I see her in the water clutching on to the pier of the bridge, and some little divils of boys were heaving rocks down at her. I got into the schooner's tag-boat quick, I tell ye, and pushed off for her, 'n' she let go just as I got there, 'n' I guess you never saw a more miser'ble-looking creatur' than I fished out of the water. Cold weather it was. Her leg was hurt, and her eye, and I thought first I'd drop her overboard again, and then I didn't, and I took her aboard the schooner and put her by the stove. I thought she might as well die where it was warm. She eat a little mite of chowder before night, but she was very slim; but next morning, when I went to see if she was dead, she fell to licking my finger, and she did purr away like a dolphin. One of her eyes was out, where a stone had took her, and she never got any use of it, but she used to look at you so clever with the other, and she got well of her lame foot after a while. I got to be ter'ble fond of her. She was just the knowingest thing you ever saw, and she used to sleep alongside of me in my bunk, and like as not she would go on deck with me when it was my watch. I was coasting then for a year and eight months, and I kept her all the time. We used to be in harbor consider'ble, and about eight o'clock in the forenoon I used to drop a line and catch her a couple of cunners. Now, it is cur'us that she used to know when I was fishing for her. She would pounce on them fish and carry them off and growl, and she knew when I got a bite,—she'd watch the line; but when we were mackereling she never give us any trouble. She would never lift a paw to touch any of our fish. She didn't have the thieving ways common to most cats. She used to set round on deck in fair weather, and when the wind blew she al'ays kept herself below. Sometimes when we were in port she would go ashore awhile, and fetch back a bird or a mouse, but she wouldn't eat it till she come and showed it to me. She never wanted to stop long ashore, though I never shut her up; I always give her her liberty. I got a good deal of joking about her from the fellows, but she was a sight of company. I don' know as I ever had anything like me as much as she did. Not to say as I ever had much of any trouble with anybody, ashore or afloat. I'm a still kind of fellow, for all I look so rough.

"But then, I han't had a home, what I call a home, since I was going on nine year old."

"How has that happened?" asked Kate.

"Well, mother, she died, and I was bound out to a man in the tanning trade, and I hated him, and I hated the trade; and when I was a little bigger I ran away, and I've followed the sea ever since. I wasn't much use to him, I guess; leastways, he never took the trouble to hunt me up.

"About the best place I ever was in was a hospital. It was in foreign parts. Ye see I'm crippled some? I fell from the topsail yard to the deck, and I struck my shoulder, and broke my leg, and banged myself all up. It was to a nuns' hospital where they took me. All of the nuns were Catholics, and they wore big white things on their heads. I don't suppose you ever saw any. Have you? Well, now, that's queer! When I was first there I was scared of them; they were real ladies, and I wasn't used to being in a house, any way. One of them, that took care of me most of the time, why, she would even set up half the night with me, and I couldn't begin to tell you how good-natured she was, an' she'd look real sorry too. I used to be ugly, I ached so, along in the first of my being there, but I spoke of it when I was coming away, and she said it was all right. She used to feed me, that lady did; and there were some days I couldn't lift my head, and she would rise it on her arm. She give me a little mite of a book, when I come away. I'm not much of a hand at reading, but I always kept it on account of her. She was so pleased when I got so's to set up in a chair and look out of the window. She wasn't much of a hand to talk English. I did feel bad to come away from there; I 'most wished I could be sick a while longer. I never said much of anything either, and I don't know but she thought it was queer, but I am a dreadful clumsy man to say anything, and I got flustered. I don't know's I mind telling you; I was 'most a-crying. I used to think I'd lay by some money and ship for there and carry her something real pretty. But I don't rank able-bodied seaman like I used, and it's as much as I can do to get a berth on a coaster; I suppose I might go as cook. I liked to have died with my hurt at that hospital, but when I was getting well it made me think of when I was a mite of a chap to home before mother died, to be laying there in a clean bed with somebody to do for me. Guess you think I'm a good hand to spin long yarns; somehow it comes easy to talk to-day."

"What became of your cat?" asked Kate, after a pause, during which our friend sliced away at the porgies.

"I never rightfully knew; it was in Salem harbor, and a windy night. I was on deck consider'ble, for the schooner pitched lively, and once or twice she dragged her anchor. I never saw the kitty after she eat her supper. I remember I gave her some milk,—I used to buy her a pint once in a while for a treat; I don't know but she might have gone off on a cake of ice, but it did seem as if she had too much sense for that. Most likely she missed her footing, and fell overboard in the dark. She was marked real pretty, black and white, and kep' herself just as clean! She knew as well as could be when foul weather was coming; she would bother round and act queer; but when the sun was out she would sit round on deck as pleased as a queen. There! I feel bad sometimes when I think of her, and I never went into Salem since without hoping that I should see her. I don't know but if I was a-going to begin my life over again, I'd settle down ashore and have a snug little house and farm it. But I guess I shall do better at fishing. Give me a trig-built topsail schooner painted up nice, with a stripe on her, and clean sails, and a fresh wind with the sun a-shining, and I feel first-rate."

"Do you believe that codfish swallow stones before a storm?" asked Kate. I had been thinking about the lonely fisherman in a sentimental way, and so irrelevant a question shocked me. "I saw he felt slightly embarrassed at having talked about his affairs so much," Kate told me afterward, "and I thought we should leave him feeling more at his ease if we talked about fish for a while." And sure enough he did seem relieved, and gave us his opinion about the codfish at once, adding that he never cared much for cod any way; folks up country bought 'em a good deal, he heard. Give him a haddock right out of the water for his dinner!

"I never can remember," said Kate, "whether it is cod or haddock that have a black stripe along their sides—"

"O, those are haddock," said I; "they say that the Devil caught a haddock once, and it slipped through his fingers and got scorched; so all the haddock had the same mark afterward."

"Well, now, how did you know that old story?" said Danny, laughing heartily; "ye mustn't believe all the old stories ye hear, mind ye!"

"O, no," said we.

"Hullo! There's Jim Toggerson's boat close in shore. She sets low in the water, so he's done well. He and Skipper Scudder have been out deep-sea fishing since yesterday."

Our friend pushed the porgies back into a corner, stuck his knife into a beam, and we hurried down to the shore. Kate and I sat on the pebbles, and he went out to the moorings in a dirty dory to help unload the fish.

We afterward saw a great deal of Danny, as all the men called him. But though Kate and I tried our best and used our utmost skill and tact to make him tell us more about himself, he never did. But perhaps there was nothing more to be told.

The day we left Deephaven we went down to the shore to say good by to him and to some other friends, and he said, "Goin', are ye? Well, I'm sorry; ye've treated me first-rate; the Lord bless ye!" and then was so much mortified at the way he had said farewell that he turned and fled round the corner of the fish-house.

VII

CAPTAIN SANDS

Old Captain Sands was one of the most prominent citizens of Deephaven, and a very good friend of Kate's and mine. We often met him, and grew much interested in him before we knew him well. He had a reputation in town for being peculiar and somewhat visionary; but every one seemed to like him, and at last one morning, when we happened to be on our way to the wharves, we stopped at the door of an old warehouse which we had never seen opened before. Captain Sands sat just inside, smoking his pipe, and we said good morning, and asked him if he did not think there was a fog coming in by and by. We had thought a little of going out to the lighthouse. The cap'n rose slowly, and came out so that he could see farther round to the east. "There's some scud coming in a'ready," said he. "None to speak of yet, I don't know's you can see it,—yes, you're right; there's a heavy bank of fog lyin' off, but it won't be in under two or three hours yet, unless the wind backs round more and freshens up. Weren't thinking of going out, were ye?"

"A little," said Kate, "but we had nearly given it up. We are getting to be very weather-wise, and we pride ourselves on being quick at seeing fogs." At which the cap'n smiled and said we were consider'ble young to know much about weather, but it looked well that we took some interest in it; most young people were fools about weather, and would just as soon set off to go anywhere right under the edge of a thunder-shower. "Come in and set down, won't ye?" he added; "it ain't much of a place; I've got a lot of old stuff stowed away here that the women-folks don't want up to the house. I'm a great hand for keeping things." And he looked round fondly at the contents of the wide low room. "I come down here once in a while and let in the sun, and sometimes I want to hunt up something or 'nother; kind of stow-away place, ye see." And then he laughed apologetically, rubbing his hands together, and looking out to sea again as if he wished to appear unconcerned; yet we saw that he wondered if we thought it ridiculous for a man of his age to have treasured up so much trumpery in that cobwebby place. There were some whole oars and the sail of his boat and two or three killicks and painters, not to forget a heap of worn-out oars and sails in one corner and a sailor's hammock slung across the beam overhead, and there were some sailor's chests and the capstan of a ship and innumerable boxes which all seemed to be stuffed full, besides no end of things lying on the floor and packed away on shelves and hanging to rusty big-headed nails in the wall. I saw some great lumps of coral, and large, rough shells, a great hornet's nest, and a monstrous lobster-shell. The cap'n had cobbled and tied up some remarkable old chairs for the accommodation of himself and his friends.

"What a nice place!" said Kate in a frank, delighted way which could not have failed to be gratifying.

"Well, no," said the cap'n, with his slow smile, "it ain't what you'd rightly call 'nice,' as I know of: it ain't never been cleared out all at once since I began putting in. There's nothing that's worth anything, either, to anybody but me. Wife, she's said to me a hundred times, 'Why don't you overhaul them old things and burn 'em?' She's al'ays at me about letting the property, as if it were a corner-lot in Broadway. That's all women-folks know about business!" And here the captain caught himself tripping, and looked uneasy for a minute. "I suppose I might have let it for a fish-house, but it's most too far from the shore to be handy—and—well—there are some things here that I set a good deal by."

"Isn't that a sword-fish's sword in that piece of wood?" Kate asked presently; and was answered that it was found broken off as we saw it, in the hull of a wreck that went ashore on Blue P'int when the captain was a young man, and he had sawed it out and kept it ever since,— fifty-nine years. Of course we went closer to look at it, and we both felt a great sympathy for this friend of ours, because we have the same fashion of keeping worthless treasures, and we understood perfectly how dear such things may be.

"Do you mind if we look round a little?" I asked doubtfully, for I knew how I should hate having strangers look over my own treasury. But Captain Sands looked pleased at our interest, and said cheerfully that we might overhaul as much as we chose. Kate discovered first an old battered wooden figure-head of a ship,—a woman's head with long curly hair falling over the shoulders. The paint was almost gone, and the dust covered most of what was left: still there was a wonderful spirit and grace, and a wild, weird beauty which attracted us exceedingly; but the captain could only tell us that it had belonged to the wreck of a Danish brig which had been driven on the reef where the lighthouse stands now, and his father had found this on the long sands a day or two afterward. "That was a dreadful storm," said the captain. "I've heard the old folks tell about it; it was when I was only a year or two old. There were three merchantmen wrecked within five miles of Deephaven. This one was all stove to splinters, and they used to say she had treasure aboard. When I was small I used to have a great idea of going out there to the rocks at low water and trying to find some gold, but I never made out no great." And he smiled indulgently at the thought of his youthful dream.

"Kate," said I, "do you see what beauties these Turk's-head knots are?" We had been taking a course of first lessons in knots from Danny, and had followed by learning some charmingly intricate ones from Captain Lant, the stranded mariner who lived on a farm two miles or so inland. Kate came over to look at the Turk's-heads, which were at either end of the rope handles of a little dark-blue chest.

Captain Sands turned in his chair and nodded approval. "That's a neat piece of work, and it was a first-rate seaman who did it; he's dead and gone years ago, poor young fellow; an I-talian he was, who sailed on the Ranger three or four long voyages. He fell from the mast-head on the voyage home from Callao. Cap'n Manning and old Mr. Lorimer, they owned the Ranger, and when she come into port and they got the news they took it as much to heart as if he'd been some relation. He was smart as a whip, and had a way with him, and the pleasantest kind of a voice; you couldn't help liking him. They found out that he had a mother alive in Port Mahon, and they sent his pay and some money he had in the bank at Riverport out to her by a ship that was going to the Mediterranean. He had some clothes in his chest, and they sold those and sent her the money,—all but some trinkets they supposed he was keeping for her; I rec'lect he used to speak consider'ble about his mother. I shipped one v'y'ge with him before the mast, before I went out mate of the Daylight. I happened to be in port the time the Ranger got in, an' I see this chist lying round in Cap'n Manning's storehouse, and I offered to give him what it was worth; but we was good friends, and he told me take it if I wanted it, it was no use to him, and I've kept it ever since.

"There are some of his traps in it now, I believe; ye can look." And we took off some tangled cod-lines and opened the chest. There was only a round wooden box in the till, and in some idle hour at sea the young sailor had carved his initials and an anchor and the date on the cover.

We found some sail-needles and a palm in this "kit," as the sailors call it, and a little string of buttons with some needles and yarn and thread in a neat little bag, which perhaps his mother had made for him when he started off on his first voyage. Besides these things there was only a fanciful little broken buckle, green and gilt, which he might have picked up in some foreign street, and his protection-paper carefully folded, wherein he was certified as being a citizen of the United States, with dark complexion and dark hair.

"He was one of the pleasantest fellows that ever I shipped with," said the captain, with a gruff tenderness in his voice. "Always willin' to do his work himself, and like's not when the other fellows up the rigging were cold, or ugly about something or 'nother, he'd say something that would set them all laughing, and somehow it made you good-natured to see him round. He was brought up a Catholic, I s'pose; anyway, he had some beads, and sometimes they would joke him about 'em on board ship, but he would blaze up in a minute, ugly as a tiger. I never saw him mad about anything else, though he wouldn't stand it if anybody tried to crowd him. He fell from the main-to'-gallant yard to the deck, and was dead when they picked him up. They were off the Bermudas. I suppose he lost his balance, but I never could see how; he was sure-footed, and as quick as a cat. They said they saw him try to catch at the stay, but there was a heavy sea running, and the ship rolled just so's to let him through between the rigging, and he struck the deck like a stone. I don't know's that chest has been opened these ten years,—I declare it carries me back to look at those poor little traps of his. Well, it's the way of the world; we think we're somebody, and we have our day, but it isn't long afore we're forgotten."

The captain reached over for the paper, and taking out a clumsy pair of steel-bowed spectacles, read it through carefully. "I'll warrant he took good care of this," said he. "He was an I-talian, and no more of an American citizen than a Chinese; I wonder he hadn't called himself John Jones, that's the name most of the foreigners used to take when they got their papers. I remember once I was sick with a fever in Chelsea Hospital, and one morning they came bringing in the mate of a Portugee brig on a stretcher, and the surgeon asked what his name was. 'John Jones,' says he. 'O, say something else,' says the surgeon; 'we've got five John Joneses here a'ready, and it's getting to be no name at all.' Sailors are great hands for false names; they have a trick of using them when they have any money to leave ashore, for fear their shipmates will go and draw it out. I suppose there are thousands of dollars unclaimed in New York banks, where men have left it charged to their false names; then they get lost at sea or something, and never go to get it, and nobody knows whose it is. They're curious folks, take 'em altogether, sailors is; specially these foreign fellows that wander about from ship to ship. They're getting to be a dreadful low set, too, of late years. It's the last thing I'd want a boy of mine to do,—ship before the mast with one of these mixed crews. It's a dog's life, anyway, and the risks and the chances against you are awful. It's a good while before you can lay up anything, unless you are part owner. I saw all the p'ints a good deal plainer after I quit followin' the sea myself, though I've always been more or less into navigation until this last war come on. I know when I was ship's husband of the Polly and Susan there was a young man went out cap'n of her,—her last voyage, and she never was heard from. He had a wife and two or three little children, and for all he was so smart, they would have been about the same as beggars, if I hadn't happened to have his life insured the day I was having the papers made out for the ship. I happened to think of it. Five thousand dollars there was, and I sent it to the widow along with his primage. She hadn't expected nothing, or next to nothing, and she was pleased, I tell ye."

"I think it was very kind in you to think of that, Captain Sands," said Kate. And the old man said, flushing a little, "Well, I'm not so smart as some of the men who started when I did, and some of 'em went ahead of me, but some of 'em didn't, after all. I've tried to be honest, and to do just about as nigh right as I could, and you know there's an old sayin' that a cripple in the right road will beat a racer in the wrong."

VIII

The Circus at Denby

K ate and I looked forward to a certain Saturday with as much eagerness as if we had been little school-boys, for on that day we were to go to a circus at Denby, a town perhaps eight miles inland. There had not been a circus so near Deephaven for a long time, and nobody had dared to believe the first rumor of it, until two dashing young men had deigned to come themselves to put up the big posters on the end of 'Bijah Mauley's barn. All the boys in town came as soon as possible to see these amazing pictures, and some were wretched in their secret hearts at the thought that they might not see the show itself. Tommy Dockum was more interested than any one else, and mentioned the subject so frequently one day when he went blackberrying with us, that we grew enthusiastic, and told each other what fun it would be to go, for everybody would be there, and it would be the greatest loss to us if we were absent. I thought I had lost my childish fondness for circuses, but it came back redoubled; and Kate may contradict me if she chooses, but I am sure she never looked forward to the Easter Oratorio with half the pleasure she did to this "caravan," as most of the people called it.

We felt that it was a great pity that any of the boys and girls should be left lamenting at home, and finding that there were some of our acquaintances and Tommy's who saw no chance of going, we engaged Jo Sands and Leander Dockum to carry them to Denby in two fish-wagons, with boards laid across for the extra seats. We saw them join the straggling train of carriages which had begun to go through the village from all along shore, soon after daylight, and they started on their journey shouting and carousing, with their pockets crammed with early apples and other provisions. We thought it would have been fun enough to see the people go by, for we had had no idea until then how many inhabitants that country held.

We had asked Mrs. Kew to go with us; but she was half an hour later than she had promised, for, since there was no wind, she could not come ashore in the sail-boat, and Mr. Kew had had to row her in in the dory. We saw the boat at last nearly in shore, and drove down to meet it: even the horse seemed to realize what a great day it was, and showed a disposition to friskiness, evidently as surprising to himself as to us.

Mrs. Kew was funnier that day than we had ever known her, which is saying a great deal, and we should not have had half so good a time if she had not been with us; although she lived in the lighthouse, and had no chance to "see passing," which a woman prizes so highly in the country, she had a wonderful memory for faces, and could tell us the names of all Deephaveners and of most of the people we met outside its limits. She looked impressed and solemn as she hurried up from the water's edge, giving Mr. Kew some parting charges over her shoulder as he pushed off the boat to go back; but after we had convinced her that the delay had not troubled us, she seemed more cheerful. It was evident that she felt the importance of the occasion, and that she was pleased at our having chosen her for company. She threw back her veil entirely, sat very straight, and took immense pains to bow to every acquaintance whom she met. She wore her best Sunday clothes, and her manner was formal for the first few minutes; it was evident that she felt we were meeting under unusual circumstances, and that, although we had often met before on the friendliest terms, our having asked her to make this excursion in public required a different sort of behavior at her hands, and a due amount of ceremony and propriety. But this state of things did not last long, as she soon made a remark at which Kate and I laughed so heartily in lighthouse-acquaintance fashion, that she unbent, and gave her whole mind to enjoying herself.

When we came by the store where the post-office was kept we saw a small knot of people gathered round the door, and stopped to see what had happened. There was a forlorn horse standing near, with his harness tied up with fuzzy ends of rope, and the wagon was cobbled together with pieces of board; the whole craft looked as if it might be wrecked with the least jar. In the wagon were four or five stupid-looking boys and girls, one of whom was crying softly. Their father was sick, some one told us. "He was took faint, but he is coming to all right; they have give him something to take: their name is Craper, and they live way over beyond the Ridge, on Stone Hill. They were goin' over to Denby to the circus, and the man was calc'lating to get doctored, but I d' know's he can get so fur; he's powerful slim-looking to me." Kate and I went to see if we could be of any use, and when we went into the store we saw the man leaning back in his chair, looking ghastly pale, and as if he were far gone in consumption. Kate spoke to him, and he said he was better;

he had felt bad all the way along, but he hadn't given up. He was pitiful, poor fellow, with his evident attempt at dressing up. He had the bushiest, dustiest red hair and whiskers, which made the pallor of his face still more striking, and his illness had thinned and paled his rough, clumsy hands. I thought what a hard piece of work it must have been for him to start for the circus that morning, and how kind-hearted he must be to have made such an effort for his children's pleasure. As we went out they stared at us gloomily. The shadow of their disappointment touched and chilled our pleasure.

Somebody had turned the horse so that he was heading toward home, and by his actions he showed that he was the only one of the party who was glad. We were so sorry for the children; perhaps it had promised to be the happiest day of their lives, and now they must go back to their uninteresting home without having seen the great show.

"I am so sorry you are disappointed," said Kate, as we were wondering how the man who had followed us could ever climb into the wagon.

"Heh?" said he, blankly, as if he did not know what her words meant. "What fool has been a turning o' this horse?" he asked a man who was looking on.

"Why, which way be ye goin'?"

"To the circus," said Mr. Craper, with decision, "where d'ye s'pose? That's where I started for, anyways." And he climbed in and glanced round to count the children, struck the horse with the willow switch, and they started off briskly, while everybody laughed. Kate and I joined Mrs. Kew, who had enjoyed the scene.

"Well, there!" said she, "I wonder the folks in the old North burying-ground ain't a-rising up to go to Denby to that caravan!"

We reached Denby at noon; it was an uninteresting town which had grown up around some mills. There was a great commotion in the streets, and it was evident that we had lost much in not having seen the procession. There was a great deal of business going on in the shops, and there were two or three hand-organs at large, near one of which we stopped awhile to listen, just after we had met Leander and given the horse into his charge. Mrs. Kew finished her shopping as soon as possible, and we hurried toward the great tents, where all the flags were flying. I think I have not told you that we were to have the benefit of seeing a menagerie in addition to the circus, and you may be sure we went faithfully round to see everything that the cages held.

I cannot truthfully say that it was a good show; it was somewhat dreary, now that I think of it quietly and without excitement. The creatures looked tired, and as if they had been on the road for a great many years. The animals were all old, and there was a shabby great elephant whose look of general discouragement went to my heart, for it seemed as if he were miserably conscious of a misspent life. He stood dejected and motionless at one side of the tent, and it was hard to believe that there was a spark of vitality left in him. A great number of the people had never seen an elephant before, and we heard a thin little old man, who stood near us, say delightedly, "There's the old creatur', and no mistake, Ann 'Liza. I wanted to see him most of anything. My sakes alive, ain't he big!"

And Ann 'Liza, who was stout and sleepy-looking, droned out, "Ye-es, there's consider'ble of him; but he looks as if he ain't got no animation."

Kate and I turned away and laughed, while Mrs. Kew said confidentially, as the couple moved away, "*She* needn't be a reflectin' on the poor beast. That's Mis Seth Tanner, and there isn't a woman in Deephaven nor East Parish to be named the same day with her for laziness. I'm glad she didn't catch sight of me; she'd have talked about nothing for a fortnight."

There was a picture of a huge snake in Deephaven, and I was just wondering where he could be, or if there ever had been one, when we heard a boy ask the same question of the man whose thankless task it was to stir up the lions with a stick to make them roar. "The snake's dead," he answered good-naturedly. "Didn't you have to dig an awful long grave for him?" asked the boy; but the man said he reckoned they curled him up some, and smiled as he turned to his lions, who looked as if they needed a tonic. Everybody lingered longest before the monkeys, who seemed to be the only lively creatures in the whole collection; and finally we made our way into the other tent, and perched ourselves on a high seat, from whence we had a capital view of the audience and the ring, and could see the people come in. Mrs. Kew was on the lookout for acquaintances, and her spirits as well as our own seemed to rise higher and higher. She was on the alert, moving her head this way and that to catch sight of people, giving us a running commentary in the mean time. It was very pleasant to see a person so happy as Mrs. Kew was that day, and I dare say in speaking of the occasion she would say the same thing of Kate and me,—for it was such a good time! We bought some peanuts, without which no circus seems complete, and we listened to the conversations which were being carried on around us while we were waiting for the performance to begin. There were two old farmers whom we had noticed occasionally in Deephaven; one was telling the other, with great confusion of pronouns, about a big pig which had lately been killed. "John did feel dreadful disappointed at having to kill now," we heard him say, "bein' as he had calc'lated to kill along near Thanksgivin' time; there was goin' to be a new moon then, and he expected to get seventy-five or a hundred pound more on to him. But he didn't seem to gain, and me and 'Bijah both told him he'd be better to kill now, while everything was favor'ble, and if he set out to wait something might happen to him, and then I've always held that you can't get no hog only just so fur, and for my part I don't like these great overgrown creatur's. I like well enough to see a hog that'll weigh six hunderd, just for the beauty on't, but for my eatin' give me one that'll just rise three. 'Bijah's accurate, and he says he is goin' to weigh risin' five hundred and fifty. I shall stop, as I go home, to John's wife's brother's and see if they've got the particulars yet; John was goin' to get the scales this morning. I guess likely consider'ble many'll gather there to-morrow after meeting. John didn't calc'late to cut up till Monday."

"I guess likely I 'll stop in to-morrow," said the other man; "I like to see a han'some hog. Chester White, you said? Consider them best, don't ye?" But this question never was answered, for the greater part of the circus company in gorgeous trappings came parading in.

The circus was like all other circuses, except that it was shabbier than most, and the performers seemed to have less heart in it than usual. They did their best, and went through with their parts conscientiously, but they looked as if they never had had a good time in their lives. The audience was hilarious, and cheered and laughed at the tired clown until he looked as if he thought his speeches might possibly be funny, after all. We were so glad we had pleased the poor thing; and when he sang a song our satisfaction was still greater, and so he sang it all over again. Perhaps he had been associating with people who were used to circuses. The afternoon was hot, and the boys with Japanese fans and trays of lemonade did a remarkable business for so late in the season; the brass band on the other side of the tent shrieked its very best, and all the young men of the region had brought their girls, and some of these countless pairs of country lovers we watched a great deal, as they "kept company" with more or less depth of satisfaction in each other. We had a grand chance to see the fashions, and there were many old people and a great number of little children, and some families had evidently locked their house door behind them, since they had brought both the dog and the baby.

"Doesn't it seem as if you were a child again?" Kate asked me. "I am sure this is just the same as the first circus I ever saw. It grows more and more familiar, and it puzzles me to think they should not have altered in the least while I have changed so much, and have even had time to grow up. You don't know how it is making me remember other things of which I have not thought for years. I was seven years old when I went that first time. Uncle Jack invited me. I had a new parasol, and he laughed because I would hold it over my shoulder when the sun was in my face. He took me into the side-shows and bought me everything I asked for, on the way home, and we did not get home until twilight. The rest of the family had dined at four o'clock and gone out for a long drive, and it was such fun to have our dinner by ourselves. I sat at the head of the table in mamma's place, and when Bridget came down and insisted that I must go to bed, Uncle Jack came softly up stairs and sat by the window, smoking and telling me stories. He ran and hid in the closet when we heard mamma coming up, and when she found him out by the cigar-smoke, and made believe scold him, I thought she was in earnest, and begged him off. Yes; and I remember that Bridget sat in the next room, making her new dress so she could wear it to church next day. I thought it a beautiful dress, and besought mamma to have one like it. It was bright green with yellow spots all over it," said Kate. "Ah, poor Uncle Jack! he was so good to me! We were always telling stories of what we would do when I was grown up. He died in Canton the next year, and I cried myself ill; but for a long time I thought he might not be dead, after all, and might come home any day. He used to seem so old to me, and he really was just out of college and not so old as I am now. That day at the circus he had a pink rosebud in his buttonhole, and—ah! when have I ever thought of this before!—a woman sat before us who had a stiff little cape on her bonnet like a shelf, and I carefully put peanuts round the edge of it, and when she moved her head they would fall. I thought it was the best fun in the world, and I wished Uncle Jack to ride the donkey; I was sure he could keep on, because his horse had capered about with him one day on Beacon Street, and I thought him a perfect rider, since nothing had happened to him then."

"I remember," said Mrs. Kew, presently, "that just before I was married 'he' took me over to Wareham Corners to a caravan. My sister

Hannah and the young man who was keeping company with her went too. I haven't been to one since till to-day, and it does carry me back same's it does you, Miss Kate. It doesn't seem more than five years ago, and what would I have thought if I had known 'he' and I were going to keep a lighthouse and be contented there, what's more, and sometimes not get ashore for a fortnight; settled, gray-headed old folks! We were gay enough in those days. I know old Miss Sabrina Smith warned me that I'd better think twice before I took up with Tom Kew, for he was a light-minded young man. I speak o' that to him in the winter-time, when he sets reading the almanac half asleep and I'm knitting, and the wind's a' howling and the waves coming ashore on those rocks as if they wished they could put out the light and blow down the lighthouse. We were reflected on a good deal for going to that caravan; some of the old folks didn't think it was improvin'—Well, I should think that man was a trying to break his neck!"

Coming out of the great tent was disagreeable enough, and we seemed to have chosen the worst time, for the crowd pushed fiercely, though I suppose nobody was in the least hurry, and we were all severely jammed, while from somewhere underneath came the wails of a deserted dog. We had not meant to see the side-shows, and went carelessly past two or three tents; but when we came in sight of the picture of the Kentucky giantess, we noticed that Mrs. Kew looked at it wistfully, and we immediately asked if she cared anything about going to see the wonder, whereupon she confessed that she never heard of such a thing as a woman's weighing six hundred and fifty pounds, so we all three went in. There were only two or three persons inside the tent, beside a little boy who played the hand-organ.

The Kentucky giantess sat in two chairs on a platform, and there was a large cage of monkeys just beyond, toward which Kate and I went at once. "Why, she isn't more than two thirds as big as the picture," said Mrs. Kew, in a regretful whisper; "but I guess she's big enough; doesn't she look discouraged, poor creatur'?" Kate and I felt ashamed of ourselves for being there. No matter if she had consented to be carried round for a show, it must have been horrible to be stared at and joked about day after day; and we gravely looked at the monkeys, and in a few minutes turned to see if Mrs. Kew were not ready to come away, when to our surprise we saw that she was talking to the giantess with great interest, and we went nearer.

"I thought your face looked natural the minute I set foot inside the door," said Mrs. Kew; "but you've—altered some since I saw you, and I couldn't place you till I heard you speak. Why, you used to be spare; I am amazed, Marilly! Where are your folks?"

"I don't wonder you are surprised," said the giantess. "I was a good ways from this when you knew me, wasn't I? But father he run through with every cent he had before he died, and 'he' took to drink and it killed him after a while, and then I begun to grow worse and worse, till I couldn't do nothing to earn a dollar, and everybody was a coming to see me, till at last I used to ask 'em ten cents apiece, and I scratched along somehow till this man came round and heard of me, and he offered me my keep and good pay to go along with him. He had another giantess before me, but she had begun to fall away consider'ble, so he paid her off and let her go. This other giantess was an awful expense to him, she was such an eater; now I don't have no great of an appetite,"—this was said plaintively,—"and he's raised my pay since I've been with him because we did so well. I took up with his offer because I was nothing but a drag and never will be. I'm as comfortable as I can be, but it's a pretty hard business. My oldest boy is able to do for himself, but he's married this last year, and his wife don't want me. I don't know's I blame her either. It would be something like if I had a daughter now; but there, I'm getting to like travelling first-rate; it gives anybody a good deal to think of."

"I was asking the folks about you when I was up home the early part of the summer," said Mrs. Kew, "but all they knew was that you were living out in New York State. Have you been living in Kentucky long? I saw it on the picture outside."

"No," said the giantess, "that was a picture the man bought cheap from another show that broke up last year. It says six hundred and fifty pounds, but I don't weigh more than four hundred. I haven't been weighed for some time past. Between you and me I don't weigh so much as that, but you mustn't mention it, for it would spoil my reputation, and might hender my getting another engagement." And then the poor giantess lost her professional look and tone as she said, "I believe I'd rather die than grow any bigger. I do lose heart sometimes, and wish I was a smart woman and could keep house. I'd be smarter than ever I was when I had the chance; I tell you that! Is Tom along with you?"

"No. I came with these young ladies, Miss Lancaster and Miss Denis, who are stopping over to Deephaven for the summer." Kate and I turned as we heard this introduction; we were standing close by, and

I am proud to say that I never saw Kate treat any one more politely than she did that absurd, pitiful creature with the gilt crown and many bracelets. It was not that she said much, but there was such an exquisite courtesy in her manner, and an apparent unconsciousness of there being anything in the least surprising or uncommon about the giantess.

Just then a party of people came in, and Mrs. Kew said good by reluctantly. "It has done me sights of good to see you," said our new acquaintance; "I was feeling down-hearted just before you came in. I'm pleased to see somebody that remembers me as I used to be." And they shook hands in a way that meant a great deal, and when Kate and I said good afternoon the giantess looked at us gratefully, and said, "I'm very much obliged to you for coming in, young ladies."

"Walk in! walk in!" the man was shouting as we came away. "Walk in and see the wonder of the world, ladies and gentlemen,—the largest woman ever seen in America,—the great Kentucky giantess!"

"Wouldn't you have liked to stay longer?" Kate asked Mrs. Kew as we came down the street. But she answered that it would be no satisfaction; the people were coming in, and she would have no chance to talk. "I never knew her very well; she is younger than I, and she used to go to meeting where I did, but she lived five or six miles from our house. She's had a hard time of it, according to her account," said Mrs. Kew. "She used to be a dreadful flighty, high-tempered girl, but she's lost that now, I can see by her eyes. I was running over in my mind to see if there was anything I could do for her, but I don't know as there is. She said the man who hired her was kind. I guess your treating her so polite did her as much good as anything. She used to be real ambitious. I had it on my tongue's end to ask her if she couldn't get a few days' leave and come out to stop with me, but I thought just in time that she'd sink the dory in a minute. There! seeing her has took away all the fun," said Mrs. Kew ruefully; and we were all dismal for a while, but at last, after we were fairly started for home, we began to be merry again.

We passed the Craper family whom we had seen at the store in the morning; the children looked as stupid as ever, but the father, I am sorry to say, had been tempted to drink more whiskey than was good for him. He had a bright flush on his cheeks, and he was flourishing his whip, and hoarsely singing some meaningless tune. "Poor creature!" said I, "I should think this day's pleasuring would kill him." "Now, wouldn't you think so?" said Mrs. Kew, sympathizingly; "but the truth is, you couldn't kill one of those Crapers if you pounded him in a mortar."

SARAH ORNE JEWETT

We had a pleasant drive home, and we kept Mrs. Kew to supper, and afterward went down to the shore to see her set sail for home. Mr. Kew had come in some time before, and had been waiting for the moon to rise. Mrs. Kew told us that she should have enough to think of for a year, she had enjoyed the day so much; and we stood on the pebbles watching the boat out of the harbor, and wishing ourselves on board, it was such a beautiful evening.

WE WENT TO ANOTHER SHOW that summer, the memory of which will never fade. It is somewhat impertinent to call it a show, and "public entertainment" is equally inappropriate, though we certainly were entertained. It had been raining for two or three days; the Deephavenites spoke of it as "a spell of weather." Just after tea, one Thursday evening, Kate and I went down to the post-office. When we opened the great hall door, the salt air was delicious, but we found the town apparently wet through and discouraged; and though it had almost stopped raining just then, there was a Scotch mist, like a snow-storm with the chill taken off, and the Chantrey elms dripped hurriedly, and creaked occasionally in the east-wind.

"There will not be a cap'n on the wharves for a week after this," said I to Kate; "only think of the cases of rheumatism!"

We stopped for a few minutes at the Carews', who were as much surprised to see us as if we had been mermaids out of the sea, and begged us to give ourselves something warm to drink, and to change our boots the moment we got home. Then we went on to the post-office. Kate went in, but stopped, as she came out with our letters, to read a written notice securely fastened to the grocery door by four large carpet-tacks with wide leathers round their necks.

"Dear," said she, exultantly, "there's going to be a lecture to-night in the church,—a free lecture on the Elements of True Manhood. Wouldn't you like to go?" And we went.

We were fifteen minutes later than the time appointed, and were sorry to find that the audience was almost imperceptible. The dampness had affected the antiquated lamps so that those on the walls and on the front of the gallery were the dimmest lights I ever saw, and sent their feeble rays through a small space the edges of which were clearly defined. There were two rather more energetic lights on the table near the pulpit, where the lecturer sat, and as we were in the rear of the church, we could see the yellow fog between ourselves and him.

There were fourteen persons in the audience, and we were all huddled together in a cowardly way in the pews nearest the door: three old men, four women, and four children, besides ourselves and the sexton, a deaf little old man with a wooden leg.

The children whispered noisily, and soon, to our surprise, the lecturer rose and began. He bowed, and treated us with beautiful deference, and read his dreary lecture with enthusiasm. I wish I could say, for his sake, that it was interesting; but I cannot tell a lie, and it was so long! He went on and on, until it seemed as if I had been there ever since I was a little girl. Kate and I did not dare to look at each other, and in my desperation at feeling her quiver with laughter, I moved to the other end of the pew, knocking over a big hymn-book on the way, which attracted so much attention that I have seldom felt more embarrassed in my life. Kate's great dog rose several times to shake himself and yawn loudly, and then lie down again despairingly.

You would have thought the man was addressing an enthusiastic Young Men's Christian Association. He exhorted with fervor upon our duties as citizens and as voters, and told us a great deal about George Washington and Benjamin Franklin, whom he urged us to choose as our examples. He waited for applause after each of his outbursts of eloquence, and presently went on again, in no wise disconcerted at the silence, and as if he were sure that he would fetch us next time. The rain began to fall again heavily, and the wind wailed around the meeting-house. If the lecture had been upon any other subject it would not have been so hard for Kate and me to keep sober faces; but it was directed entirely toward young men, and there was not a young man there.

The children in front of us mildly scuffled with each other at one time, until the one at the end of the pew dropped a marble, which struck the floor and rolled with a frightful noise down the edge of the aisle where there was no carpet. The congregation instinctively started up to look after it, but we recollected ourselves and leaned back again in our places, while the awed children, after keeping unnaturally quiet, fell asleep, and tumbled against each other helplessly. After a time the man sat down and wiped his forehead, looking well satisfied; and when we were wondering whether we might with propriety come away, he rose again, and said it was a free lecture, and he thanked us for our kind patronage on that inclement night; but in other places which he had visited there had been a contribution taken up for the cause. It would, perhaps, do no harm,—would the sexton—But the sexton could not

SARAH ORNE JEWETT

have heard the sound of a cannon at that distance, and slumbered on. Neither Kate nor I had any money, except a twenty-dollar bill in my purse, and some coppers in the pocket of her water-proof cloak which she assured me she was prepared to give; but we saw no signs of the sexton's waking, and as one of the women kindly went forward to wake the children, we all rose and came away.

After we had made as much fun and laughed as long as we pleased that night, we became suddenly conscious of the pitiful side of it all; and being anxious that every one should have the highest opinion of Deephaven, we sent Tom Dockum early in the morning with an anonymous note to the lecturer, whom he found without much trouble; but afterward we were disturbed at hearing that he was going to repeat his lecture that evening,—the wind having gone round to the northwest,—and I have no doubt there were a good many women able to be out, and that he harvested enough ten-cent pieces to pay his expenses without our help; though he had particularly told us it was for "the cause," the evening before, and that ought to have been a consolation.

IX

CUNNER-FISHING

O ne of the chief pleasures in Deephaven was our housekeeping. Going to market was apt to use up a whole morning, especially if we went to the fish-houses. We depended somewhat upon supplies from Boston, but sometimes we used to chase a butcher who took a drive in his old canvas-topped cart when he felt like it, and as for fish, there were always enough to be caught, even if we could not buy any. Our acquaintances would often ask if we had anything for dinner that day, and would kindly suggest that somebody had been boiling lobsters, or that a boat had just come in with some nice mackerel, or that somebody over on the Ridge was calculating to kill a lamb, and we had better speak for a quarter in good season. I am afraid we were looked upon as being in danger of becoming epicures, which we certainly are not, and we undoubtedly roused a great deal of interest because we used to eat mushrooms, which grew in the suburbs of the town in wild luxuriance.

One morning Maggie told us that there was nothing in the house for dinner, and, taking an early start, we went at once down to the store to ask if the butcher had been seen, but finding that he had gone out deep-sea fishing for two days, and that when he came back he had planned to kill a veal, we left word for a sufficient piece of the doomed animal to be set apart for our family, and strolled down to the shore to see if we could find some mackerel; but there was not a fisherman in sight, and after going to all the fish-houses we concluded that we had better provide for ourselves. We had not brought our own lines, but we knew where Danny kept his, and after finding a basket of suitable size, and taking some clams from Danny's bait-tub, we went over to the hull of an old schooner which was going to pieces alongside one of the ruined wharves. We looked down the hatchway into the hold, and could see the flounders and sculpin swimming about lazily, and once in a while a little pollock scooted down among them impertinently and then disappeared. "There is that same big flounder that we saw day before yesterday," said I. "I know him because one of his fins is half gone. I don't believe he can get out, for the hole in the side of the schooner isn't very wide, and it is higher up than flounders ever swim.

Perhaps he came in when he was young, and was too lazy to go out until he was so large he couldn't. Flounders always look so lazy, and as if they thought a great deal of themselves."

"I hope they will think enough of themselves to keep away from my hook this morning," said Kate, philosophically, "and the sculpin too. I am going to fish for cunners alone, and keep my line short." And she perched herself on the quarter, baited her hook carefully, and threw it over, with a clam-shell to call attention. I went to the rail at the side, and we were presently much encouraged by pulling up two small cunners, and felt that our prospects for dinner were excellent. Then I unhappily caught so large a sculpin that it was like pulling up an open umbrella, and after I had thrown him into the hold to keep company with the flounder, our usual good luck seemed to desert us. It was one of the days when, in spite of twitching the line and using all the tricks we could think of, the cunners would either eat our bait or keep away altogether. Kate at last said we must starve unless we could catch the big flounder, and asked me to drop my hook down the hatchway; but it seemed almost too bad to destroy his innocent happiness. Just then we heard the noise of oars, and to our delight saw Cap'n Sands in his dory just beyond the next wharf. "Any luck?" said he. "S'pose ye don't care anything about going out this morning?"

"We are not amusing ourselves; we are trying to catch some fish for dinner," said Kate. "Could you wait out by the red buoy while we get a few more, and then should you be back by noon, or are you going for a longer voyage, Captain Sands?"

"I was going out to Black Rock for cunners myself," said the cap'n. "I should be pleased to take ye, if ye'd like to go." So we wound up our lines, and took our basket and clams and went round to meet the boat. I felt like rowing, and took the oars while Kate was mending her sinker and the cap'n was busy with a snarled line.

"It's pretty hot," said he, presently, "but I see a breeze coming in, and the clouds seem to be thickening; I guess we shall have it cooler 'long towards noon. It looked last night as if we were going to have foul weather, but the scud seemed to blow off, and it was as pretty a morning as ever I see. 'A growing moon chaws up the clouds,' my gran'ther used to say. He was as knowing about the weather as anybody I ever come across; 'most always hit it just about right. Some folks lay all the weather to the moon, accordin' to where she quarters, and when she's in perigee we're going to have this kind of weather, and when she's in apogee she's got to do so and so for sartain; but gran'ther he used to laugh at all them things. He said it never made no kind of difference, and he went by the looks of the clouds and the feel of the air, and he thought folks couldn't make no kind of rules that held good, that had to do with the moon. Well, he did use to depend on the moon some; everybody knows we aren't so likely to have foul weather in a growing moon as we be when she's waning. But some folks I could name, they can't do nothing without having the moon's opinion on it. When I went my second voyage afore the mast we was in port ten days at Cadiz, and the ship she needed salting dreadful. The mate kept telling the captain how low the salt was in her, and we was going a long voyage from there, but no, he wouldn't have her salted nohow, because it was the wane of the moon. He was an amazing set kind of man, the cap'n was, and would have his own way on sea or shore. The mate was his own brother, and they used to fight like a cat and dog; they owned most of the ship between 'em. I was slushing the mizzen-mast, and heard 'em a disputin' about the salt. The cap'n was a first-rate seaman and died rich, but he was dreadful notional. I know one time we were a lyin' out in the stream all ready to weigh anchor, and everything was in trim, the men were up in the rigging and a fresh breeze going out, just what we'd been waiting for, and the word was passed to take in sail and make everything fast. The men swore, and everybody said the cap'n had had some kind of a warning. But that night it began to blow, and I tell you afore morning we were glad enough we were in harbor. The old Victor she dragged her anchor, and the fore-to'gallant sail and r'yal got loose somehow and was blown out of the bolt-ropes. Most of the canvas and rigging was old, but we had first-rate weather after that, and didn't bend near all the new sail we had aboard, though the cap'n was most afraid we'd come short when we left Boston. That was 'most sixty year ago," said the captain, reflectively. "How time does slip away! You young folks haven't any idea. She was a first-rate ship, the old Victor was, though I suppose she wouldn't cut much of a dash now 'longside of some of the new clippers.

"There used to be some strange-looking crafts in those days; there was the old brig Hannah. They used to say she would sail backwards as fast as forwards, and she was so square in the bows, they used to call her the sugar-box. She was master old, the Hannah was, and there wasn't a port from here to New Orleans where she wasn't known; she used to carry a master cargo for her size, more than some ships that ranked two hundred and fifty ton, and she was put down for two hundred. She used to make good voyages, the Hannah did, and then there was the Pactolus; she was just about such another,—you would have laughed to see her. She sailed out of this port for a good many years. Cap'n Wall he told me that if he had her before the wind with a cargo of cotton, she would make a middling good run, but load her deep with salt, and you might as well try to sail a stick of oak timber with a handkerchief. She was a stout-built ship: I shouldn't wonder if her timbers were afloat somewhere yet; she was sold to some parties out in San Francisco. There! everything's changed from what it was when I used to follow the sea. I wonder sometimes if the sailors have as queer works aboard ship as they used. Bless ye! Deephaven used to be a different place to what it is now; there was hardly a day in the year that you didn't hear the shipwrights' hammers, and there was always something going on at the wharves. You would see the folks from up country comin' in with their loads of oak knees and plank, and logs o' rock-maple for keels when there was snow on the ground in winter-time, and the big sticks of timber-pine for masts would come crawling along the road with their three and four yoke of oxen all frosted up, the sleds creaking and the snow growling and the men flapping their arms to keep warm, and hallooing as if there wan't nothin' else goin' on in the world except to get them masts to the ship-yard. Bless ye! two o' them teams together would stretch from here 'most up to the Widow Jim's place,—no such timber-pines nowadays."

"I suppose the sailors are very jolly together sometimes," said Kate, meditatively, with the least flicker of a smile at me. The captain did not answer for a minute, as he was battling with an obstinate snarl in his line; but when he had found the right loop he said, "I've had the best times and the hardest times of my life at sea, that's certain! I was just thinking it over when you spoke. I'll tell you some stories one day or 'nother that'll please you. Land! you've no idea what tricks some of those wild fellows will be up to. Now, saying they fetch home a cargo of wines and they want a drink; they've got a trick so they can get it. Saying it's champagne, they'll fetch up a basket, and how do you suppose they'll get into it?"

Of course we didn't know.

"Well, every basket will be counted, and they're fastened up particular, so they can tell in a minute if they've been tampered with; and neither must you draw the corks if you could get the basket open. I suppose ye may have seen champagne, how it's all wired and waxed. Now, they take a clean tub, them fellows do, and just shake the basket and jounce it up and down till they break the bottles and let the wine drain out; then they take it down in the hold and put it back with the rest, and when the cargo is delivered there's only one or two whole bottles in that basket, and there's a dreadful fuss about its being stowed so foolish." The captain told this with an air of great satisfaction, but we did not show the least suspicion that he might have assisted at some such festivity.

"Then they have a way of breaking into a cask. It won't do to start the bung, and it won't do to bore a hole where it can be seen, but they're up to that: they slip back one of the end hoops and bore two holes underneath it, one for the air to go in and one for the liquor to come out, and after they get all out they want they put in some spigots and cut them down close to the stave, knock back the hoop again, and there ye are, all trig."

"I never should have thought of it," said Kate, admiringly.

"There isn't nothing," Cap'n Sands went on, "that'll hender some masters from cheating the owners a little. Get them off in a foreign port, and there's nobody to watch, and they most of them have a feeling that they ain't getting full pay, and they'll charge things to the ship that she never seen nor heard of. There were two shipmasters that sailed out of Salem. I heard one of 'em tell the story. They had both come into port from Liverpool nigh the same time, and one of 'em, he was dressed up in a handsome suit of clothes, and the other looked kind of poverty-struck. 'Where did you get them clothes?' says he. 'Why, to Liverpool,' says the other; 'you don't mean to say you come away without none, cheap as cloth was there?' 'Why, yes,' says the other cap'n,—'I can't afford to wear such clothes as those be, and I don't see how you can, either.' 'Charge 'em to the ship, bless ye; the owners expect it.'

"So the next v'y'ge the poor cap'n he had a nice rig for himself made to the best tailor's in Bristol, and charged it, say ten pounds, in the ship's account; and when he came home the ship's husband he was looking over the papers, and 'What's this?' says he, 'how come the ship to run up a tailor's bill?' 'Why, them's mine,' says the cap'n, very meaching. 'I understood that there wouldn't be no objection made.' 'Well, you made a mistake,' says the other, laughing; 'guess I'd better scratch this out.' And it wasn't long before the cap'n met the one who had put him up to doing it, and he give him a blowing up for getting him into such a fix. 'Land sakes alive!' says he, 'were you fool enough to set it down in the account? Why, I put mine in, so many bolts of Russia duck.'"

Captain Sands seemed to enjoy this reminiscence, and to our satisfaction, in a few minutes, after he had offered to take the oars, he went on to tell us another story.

"Why, as for cheating, there's plenty of that all over the world. The first v'y'ge I went into Havana as master of the Deerhound, she had never been in the port before and had to be measured and recorded, and then pay her tonnage duties every time she went into port there afterward, according to what she was registered on the custom-house books. The inspector he come aboard, and he went below and looked round, and he measured her between decks; but he never offered to set down any figgers, and when we came back into the cabin, says he, 'Yes—yes—good ship! you put one bloon front of this eye, *so!*' says he, 'an' I not see with him; and you put one more doubloon front of other eye, and how you think I see at all what figger you write?' So I took his book and I set down her measurements and made her out twenty ton short, and he took his doubloons and shoved 'em into his pocket. There, it isn't what you call straight dealing, but everybody done it that dared, and you'd eat up all the profits of a v'y'ge and the owners would just as soon you'd try a little up-country air, if you paid all those dues according to law. Tonnage was dreadful high and wharfage too, in some ports, and they'd get your last cent some way or 'nother if ye weren't sharp.

"Old Cap'n Carew, uncle to them ye see to meeting, did a smart thing in the time of the embargo. Folks got tired of it, and it was dreadful hard times; ships rotting at the wharves, and Deephaven never was quite the same afterward, though the old place held out for a good while before she let go as ye see her now. You'd 'a' had a hard grip on't when I was a young man to make me believe it would ever be so dull here. Well, Cap'n Carew he bought an old brig that was lying over by East Parish, and he began fitting her up and loading her for the West Indies, and the farmers they'd come in there by night from all round the country, to sell salt-fish and lumber and potatoes, and glad enough they were, I tell ye. The rigging was put in order, and it wasn't long before she was ready to sail, and it was all kept mighty quiet. She lay up to an old wharf in a cove where she wouldn't be much noticed, and they took care not to paint her any or to attract any attention.

"One day Cap'n Carew was over in Riverport dining out with some gentlemen, and the revenue officer sat next to him, and by and by says he, 'Why won't ye take a ride with me this afternoon? I've had warning that there's a brig loading for the West Indies over beyond Deephaven somewheres, and I'm going over to seize her.' And he laughed to himself as if he expected fun, and something in his pocket beside. Well, the first minute that Cap'n Carew dared, after dinner, he slipped out, and he hired the swiftest horse in Riverport and rode for dear life, and told the folks who were in the secret, and some who weren't, what was the matter, and every soul turned to and helped finish loading her and getting the rigging ready and the water aboard; but just as they were leaving the cove—the wind was blowing just right—along came the revenue officer with two or three men, and they come off in a boat and boarded her as important as could be.

"'Won't ye step into the cabin, gentlemen, and take a glass o' wine?' says Cap'n Carew, very polite; and the wind came in fresher,—something like a squall for a few minutes,—and the men had the sails spread before you could say Jack Robi'son, and before those fellows knew what they were about the old brig was a standing out to sea, and the folks on the wharves cheered and yelled. The Cap'n gave the officers a good scare and offered 'em a free passage to the West Indies, and finally they said they wouldn't report at headquarters if he'd let 'em go ashore; so he told the sailors to lower their boat about two miles off Deephaven, and they pulled ashore meek enough. Cap'n Carew had a first-rate run, and made a lot of money, so I have heard it said. Bless ye! every shipmaster would have done just the same if he had dared, and everybody was glad when they heard about it. Dreadful foolish piece of business that embargo was!

"Now I declare," said Captain Sands, after he had finished this narrative, "here I'm a telling stories and you're doin' all the work. You'll pull a boat ahead of anybody, if you keep on. Tom Kew was a-praisin' up both of you to me the other day: says he, 'They don't put on no airs, but I tell ye they can pull a boat well, and swim like fish,' says he. There now, if you'll give me the oars I'll put the dory just where I want her, and you can be getting your lines ready. I know a place here where it's always toler'ble fishing, and I guess we'll get something."

Kate and I cracked our clams on the gunwale of the boat, and cut them into nice little bits for bait with a piece of the shell, and by the time the captain had thrown out the killick we were ready to begin, and found the fishing much more exciting than it had been at the wharf.

"I don't know as I ever see 'em bite faster," said the old sailor, presently; "guess it's because they like the folks that's fishing. Well, I'm pleased. I thought I'd let 'Bijah take some along to Denby in the cart to-morrow if I got more than I could use at home. I didn't calc'late on having such a lively crew aboard. I s'pose ye wouldn't care about going out a little further by and by to see if we can't get two or three haddock?" And we answered that we should like nothing better.

It was growing cloudy, and was much cooler,—the perfection of a day for fishing,—and we sat there diligently pulling in cunners, and talking a little once in a while. The tide was nearly out, and Black Rock looked almost large enough to be called an island. The sea was smooth and the low waves broke lazily among the seaweed-covered ledges, while our boat swayed about on the water, lifting and falling gently as the waves went in shore. We were not a very long way from the lighthouse, and once we could see Mrs. Kew's big white apron as she stood in the doorway for a few minutes. There was no noise except the plash of the low-tide waves and the occasional flutter of a fish in the bottom of the dory. Kate and I always killed our fish at once by a rap on the head, for it certainly saved the poor creatures much discomfort, and ourselves as well, and it made it easier to take them off the hook than if they were flopping about and making us aware of our cruelty.

Suddenly the captain wound up his line and said he thought we'd better be going in, and Kate and I looked at him with surprise. "It is only half past ten," said I, looking at my watch. "Don't hurry in on our account," added Kate, persuasively, for we were having a very good time.

"I guess we won't mind about the haddock. I've got a feelin' we'd better go ashore." And he looked up into the sky and turned to see the west. "I knew there was something the matter; there's going to be a shower." And we looked behind us to see a bank of heavy clouds coming over fast. "I wish we had two pair of oars," said Captain Sands. "I'm afraid we shall get caught."

"You needn't mind us," said Kate. "We aren't in the least afraid of our clothes, and we don't get cold when we're wet; we have made sure of that."

"Well, I'm glad to hear that," said the cap'n. "Women-folks are apt to be dreadful scared of a wetting; but I'd just as lief not get wet myself. I had a twinge of rheumatism yesterday. I guess we'll get ashore fast enough. No. I feel well enough to-day, but you can row if you want to, and I'll take the oars the last part of the way."

When we reached the moorings the clouds were black, and the thunder rattled and boomed over the sea, while heavy spatters of rain were already falling. We did not go to the wharves, but stopped down the shore at the fish-houses, the nearer place of shelter. "You just select some of those cunners," said the captain, who was beginning to be a little out of breath, "and then you can run right up and get under cover, and I'll put a bit of old sail over the rest of the fish to keep the fresh water off." By the time the boat touched the shore and we had pulled it up on the pebbles, the rain had begun in good earnest. Luckily there was a barrow lying near, and we loaded that in a hurry, and just then the captain caught sight of a well-known red shirt in an open door, and shouted, "Halloa, Danny! lend us a hand with these fish, for we're nigh on to being shipwrecked." And then we ran up to the fish-house and waited awhile, though we stood in the doorway watching the lightning, and there were so many leaks in the roof that we might almost as well have been out of doors. It was one of Danny's quietest days, and he silently beheaded hake, only winking at us once very gravely at something our other companion said.

"There!" said Captain Sands, "folks may say what they have a mind to; I didn't see that shower coming up, and I know as well as I want to that my wife did, and impressed it on my mind. Our house sets high, and she watches the sky and is al'ays a worrying when I go out fishing for fear something's going to happen to me,' specially sence I've got to be along in years."

This was just what Kate and I wished to hear, for we had been told that Captain Sands had most decided opinions on dreams and other mysteries, and could tell some stories which were considered incredible by even a Deephaven audience, to whom the marvellous was of every-day occurrence.

"Then it has happened before?" asked Kate. "I wondered why you started so suddenly to come in."

"Happened!" said the captain. "Bless ye, yes! I'll tell you my views about these p'ints one o' those days. I've thought a good deal about 'em by spells. Not that I can explain 'em, nor anybody else, but it's no use to laugh at 'em as some folks do. Cap'n Lant—you know Cap'n Lant?—he and I have talked it over consider'ble, and he says to me, 'Everybody's got some story of the kind they will believe in spite of everything, and yet they won't believe yourn.'"

The shower seemed to be over now, and we felt compelled to go home, as the captain did not go on with his remarks. I hope he did not see Danny's wink. Skipper Scudder, who was Danny's friend and partner, came up just then and asked us if we knew what the sign was when the sun came out through the rain. I said that I had always heard it would rain again next day. "O no," said Skipper Scudder, "the Devil is whipping his wife."

After dinner Kate and I went for a walk through some pine woods which were beautiful after the rain; the mosses and lichens which had been dried up were all freshened and blooming out in the dampness. The smell of the wet pitch-pines was unusually sweet, and we wandered about for an hour or two there, to find some ferns we wanted, and then walked over toward East Parish, and home by the long beach late in the afternoon. We came as far as the boat-landing, meaning to go home through the lane, but to our delight we saw Captain Sands sitting alone on an old overturned whaleboat, whittling busily at a piece of dried kelp. "Good evenin'," said our friend, cheerfully. And we explained that we had taken a long walk and thought we would rest awhile before we went home to supper. Kate perched herself on the boat, and I sat down on a ship's knee which lay on the pebbles.

"Didn't get any hurt from being out in the shower, I hope?"

"No, indeed," laughed Kate, "and we had such a good time. I hope you won't mind taking us out again some time."

"Bless ye! no," said the captain. "My girl Lo'isa, she that's Mis Winslow over to Riverport, used to go out with me a good deal, and it seemed natural to have you aboard. I missed Lo'isa after she got married, for she was al'ays ready to go anywhere 'long of father. She's had slim health of late years. I tell 'em she's been too much shut up out of the fresh air and sun. When she was young her mother never could pr'vail on her to set in the house stiddy and sew, and she used to have great misgivin's that Lo'isa never was going to be capable. How about those fish you caught this morning? good, were they? Mis Sands had dinner on the stocks when I got home, and she said she wouldn't fry any 'til supper-time; but I calc'lated to have 'em this noon. I like 'em best right out o' the water. Little more and we should have got them wet. That's one of my whims; I can't bear to let fish get rained on."

"O Captain Sands!" said I, there being a convenient pause, "you were speaking of your wife just now; did you ask her if she saw the shower?"

"First thing she spoke of when I got into the house. 'There,' says she, 'I was afraid you wouldn't see the rain coming in time, and I had my heart in my mouth when it began to thunder. I thought you'd get soaked through, and be laid up for a fortnight,' says she. 'I guess a summer shower won't hurt an old sailor like me,' says I." And the captain reached for another piece of his kelp-stalk, and whittled away more busily than ever. Kate took out her knife and also began to cut kelp, and I threw pebbles in the hope of hitting a spider which sat complacently on a stone not far away, and when he suddenly vanished there was nothing for me to do but to whittle kelp also.

"Do you suppose," said Kate, "that Mrs. Sands really made you know about that shower?"

The captain put on his most serious look, coughed slowly, and moved himself a few inches nearer us, along the boat. I think he fully understood the importance and solemnity of the subject. "It ain't for us to say what we do know or don't, for there's nothing sartain, but I made up my mind long ago that there's something about these p'ints that's myster'ous. My wife and me will be sitting there to home and there won't be no word between us for an hour, and then of a sudden we'll speak up about the same thing. Now the way I view it, she either puts it into my head or I into hers. I've spoke up lots of times about something, when I didn't know what I was going to say when I began, and she'll say she was just thinking of that. Like as not you have noticed it sometimes? There was something my mind was dwellin' on yesterday, and she come right out with it, and I'd a good deal rather she hadn't," said the captain, ruefully. "I didn't want to rake it all over ag'in, I'm sure." And then he recollected himself, and was silent, which his audience must confess to have regretted for a moment.

"I used to think a good deal about such things when I was younger, and I'm free to say I took more stock in dreams and such like than I do now. I rec'lect old Parson Lorimer—this Parson Lorimer's father who was settled here first—spoke to me once about it, and said it was a tempting of Providence, and that we hadn't no right to pry into secrets. I know I had a dream-book then that I picked up in a shop in Bristol once when I was there on the Ranger, and all the young folks were beset to get sight of it. I see what fools it made of folks, bothering their heads about such things, and I pretty much let them go: all this stuff about spirit-rappings is enough to make a man crazy. You don't get no good by it. I come across a paper once with a lot of letters in it from sperits, and I cast my eye over 'em, and I says to myself, 'Well, I always was given to understand that when we come to a futur' state we was goin' to have more wisdom than we can get afore'; but them letters hadn't any more sense to 'em, nor so much, as a man could write here without schooling, and I should think that if the letters be all straight, if the folks who wrote 'em had any kind of ambition they'd want to be movin' back here again. But as for one person's having something to do with another any distance off, why, that's another thing; there ain't any nonsense about that. I know it's true jest as well as I want to," said the cap'n, warming up. "I'll tell ye how I was led to make up my mind about it. One time I waked a man up out of a sound sleep looking at him, and it set me to thinking. First, there wasn't any noise, and then ag'in there wasn't any touch so he could feel it, and I says to myself, 'Why couldn't I ha' done it the width of two rooms as well as one, and why couldn't I ha' done it with my back turned?' It couldn't have been the looking so much as the thinking. And then I car'd it further, and I says, 'Why ain't a mile as good as a yard? and it's the thinking that does it,' says I, 'and we've got some faculty or other that we don't know much about. We've got some way of sending our thought like a bullet goes out of a gun and it hits. We don't know nothing except what we see. And some folks is scared, and some more thinks it is all nonsense and laughs. But there's something we haven't got the hang of.' It makes me think o' them little black polliwogs that turns into frogs in the fresh-water puddles in the ma'sh. There's a time before their tails drop off and their legs have sprouted out, when they don't get any use o' their legs, and I dare say they're in their way consider'ble; but after they get to be frogs they find out what they're for without no kind of trouble. I guess we shall turn these fac'lties to account some time or 'nother. Seems to me, though, that we might depend on 'em now more than we do."

The captain was under full sail on what we had heard was his pet subject, and it was a great satisfaction to listen to what he had to say. It loses a great deal in being written, for the old sailor's voice and gestures and thorough earnestness all carried no little persuasion. And it was impossible not to be sure that he knew more than people usually do about these mysteries in which he delighted.

"Now, how can you account for this?" said he. "I remember not more than ten years ago my son's wife was stopping at our house, and she had left her child at home while she come away for a rest. And after she had been there two or three days, one morning she was sitting in the kitchen 'long o' the folks, and all of a sudden she jumped out of her chair and ran into the bedroom, and next minute she come out laughing, and looking kind of scared. 'I could ha' taken my oath,' says she, 'that I heard Katy cryin' out mother,' says she, 'just as if she was hurt. I heard it so plain that before I stopped to think it seemed as if she were right in the next room. I'm afeard something has happened.' But the folks laughed, and said she must ha' heard one of the lambs. 'No, it wasn't,' says she, 'it was Katy.' And sure enough, just after dinner a young man who lived neighbor to her come riding into the yard post-haste to get her to go home, for the baby had pulled some hot water over on to herself and was nigh scalded to death and cryin' for her mother every minute. Now, who's going to explain that? It wasn't any common hearing that heard that child's cryin' fifteen miles. And I can tell you another thing that happened among my own folks. There was an own cousin of mine married to a man by the name of John Hathorn. He was trading up to Parsonsfield, and business run down, so he wound up there, and thought he'd make a new start. He moved down to Denby, and while he was getting under way, he left his family up to the old place, and at the time I speak of, was going to move 'em down in about a fortnight.

"One morning his wife was fidgeting round, and finally she came down stairs with her bonnet and shawl on, and said somebody must put the horse right into the wagon and take her down to Denby. 'Why, what for, mother?' they says. 'Don't stop to talk,' says she; 'your father is sick, and wants me. It's been a worrying me since before day, and I can't stand it no longer.' And the short of the story is that she kept hurrying 'em faster and faster, and then she got hold of the reins herself, and when they got within five miles of the place the horse fell dead, and she was nigh about crazy, and they took another horse at a farm-house on the road. It was the spring of the year, and the going was dreadful, and when they got to the house John Hathorn had just died, and he had been calling for his wife up to 'most the last breath he drew. He had been taken sick sudden the day before, but the folks knew it was bad travelling, and that she was a feeble woman to come near thirty miles, and they had no idee he was so bad off. I'm telling you the living truth," said Captain Sands, with an emphatic shake of his head. "There's more folks than me can tell about it, and if you were goin' to keel-haul me next minute, and hang me to the yard-arm afterward, I couldn't say it different. I was up to Parsonsfield to the funeral; it was just after I quit following the sea. I never saw a woman so broke down as she was. John was a nice man; stiddy and pleasant-spoken and straightforrard and kind to his folks. He belonged to the Odd Fellows, and they all marched to the funeral. There was a good deal of respect shown him, I tell ye.

"There is another story I'd like to have ye hear, if it's so that you ain't beat out hearing me talk. When I get going I slip along as easy as a schooner wing-and-wing afore the wind.

"This happened to my own father, but I never heard him say much about it; never could get him to talk it over to any length, best I could do. But gran'ther, his father, told me about it nigh upon fifty times, first and last, and always the same way. Gran'ther lived to be old, and there was ten or a dozen years after his wife died that he lived year and year about with Uncle Tobias's folks and our folks. Uncle Tobias lived over on the Ridge. I got home from my first v'y'ge as mate of the Daylight just in time for his funeral. I was disapp'inted to find the old man was gone. I'd fetched him some first-rate tobacco, for he was a great hand to smoke, and I was calc'latin' on his being pleased: old folks like to be thought of, and then he set more by me than by the other boys. I know I used to be sorry for him when I was a little fellow. My father's second wife she was a well-meaning woman, but an awful driver with her work, and she was always making of him feel he wasn't no use. I do' know as she meant to, either. He never said nothing, and he was always just so pleasant, and he was fond of his book, and used to set round reading, and tried to keep himself out of the way just as much as he could. There was one winter when I was small that I had the scarlet-fever, and was very slim for a long time afterward, and I used to keep along o' gran'ther, and he would tell me stories. He'd been a sailor,—it runs in our blood to foller the sea,—and he'd been wrecked two or three times and been taken by the Algerine pirates. You remind me to tell you some time about that; and I wonder if you ever heard about old Citizen Leigh, that used to be about here when I was a boy. He was taken by the Algerines once, same's gran'ther, and they was dreadful f'erce just then, and they sent him home to get the ransom money for the crew; but it was a monstrous price they asked, and the owners wouldn't give it to him, and they s'posed likely the men was dead by that time, any way. Old Citizen Leigh he went crazy, and used to go about the streets with a bundle of papers in his hands year in and year out. I've seen him a good many times. Gran'ther used to tell me how he escaped. I'll remember it for ye some day if you'll put me in mind.

"I got to be mate when I was twenty, and I was as strong a fellow as you could scare up, and darin'!—why, it makes my blood run cold when I think of the reckless things I used to do. I was off at sea after I was fifteen year old, and there wasn't anybody so glad to see me as gran'ther when I came home. I expect he used to be lonesome after I went off, but then his mind failed him quite a while before he died. Father was clever to him, and he'd get him anything he spoke about; but he wasn't a man to set round and talk, and he never took notice himself when gran'ther was out of tobacco, so sometimes it would be a day or two. I know better how he used to feel now that I'm getting to be along in years myself, and likely to be some care to the folks before long. I never could bear to see old folks neglected; nice old men and women who have worked hard in their day and been useful and willin'. I've seen 'em many a time when they couldn't help knowing that the folks would a little rather they'd be in heaven, and a good respectable headstone put up for 'em in the burying-ground.

"Well, now, I'm sure I've forgot what I was going to tell you. O, yes; about grandmother dreaming about father when he come home from sea. Well, to go back to the first of it, gran'ther never was rugged; he had ship-fever when he was a young man, and though he lived to be so old, he never could work hard and never got forehanded; and Aunt Hannah Starbird over at East Parish took my sister to fetch up, because she was named for her, and Melinda and Tobias stayed at home with the old folks, and my father went to live with an uncle over in Riverport, whom he was named for. He was in the West India trade and was well-off, and he had no children, so they expected he would do well by father. He was dreadful high-tempered. I've heard say he had the worst temper that was ever raised in Deephaven.

"One day he set father to putting some cherries into a bar'l of rum, and went off down to his wharf to see to the loading of a vessel, and afore he come back father found he'd got hold of the wrong bar'l, and had sp'ilt a bar'l of the best Holland gin; he tried to get the cherries out, but that wasn't any use, and he was dreadful afraid of Uncle Matthew, and he run away, and never was heard of from that time out. They supposed he'd run away to sea, as he had a leaning that way, but nobody ever knew for certain; and his mother she 'most mourned herself to death. Gran'ther told me that it got so at last that if they could only know for sure that he was dead it was all they would ask. But it went on four years, and gran'ther got used to it some; though grandmother never would give up. And one morning early, before day, she waked him up, and says she, 'We're going to hear from Matthew. Get up quick and go down to the store!' 'Nonsense,' says he. 'I've seen him,' says grandmother, 'and he's coming home. He looks older, but just the same other ways, and he's got long hair, like a horse's mane, all down over his shoulders.' 'Well, let the dead rest,' says gran'ther; 'you've thought about the boy till your head is turned.' 'I tell you I saw Matthew himself,' says she, 'and I want you to go right down to see if there isn't a letter.' And she kept at him till he saddled the horse, and he got down to the store before it was opened in the morning, and he had to wait round, and when the man came over to unlock it he was 'most ashamed to tell what his errand was, for he had been so many times, and everybody supposed the boy was dead. When he asked for a letter, the man said there was none there, and asked if he was expecting any particular one. He didn't get many letters, I s'pose; all his folks lived about here, and people didn't write any to speak of in those days. Gran'ther said he thought he wouldn't make such a fool of himself again, but he didn't say anything, and he waited round awhile, talking to one and another who came up, and by and by says the store-keeper, who was reading a newspaper that had just come, 'Here's some news for you, Sands, I do believe! There are three vessels come into Boston harbor that have been out whaling and sealing in the South Seas for three or four years, and your son Matthew's name is down on the list of the crew.' 'I tell ye,' says gran'ther, 'I took that paper, and I got on my horse and put for home, and your grandmother she hailed me, and she said, "You've heard, haven't you?" before I told her a word.'

"Gran'ther he got his breakfast and started right off for Boston, and got there early the second day, and went right down on the wharves. Somebody lent him a boat, and he went out to where there were two sealers laying off riding at anchor, and he asked a sailor if Matthew was aboard. 'Ay, ay,' says the sailor, 'he's down below.' And he sung out for him, and when he come up out of the hold his hair was long, down over his shoulders like a horse's mane, just as his mother saw it in the dream. Gran'ther he didn't know what to say,—it scared him,—and he asked how it happened; and father told how they'd been off sealing in the South Seas, and he and another man had lived alone on an island for months, and the whole crew had grown wild in their ways of living, being off so long, and for one thing had gone without caps and let their hair grow. The rest of the men had been ashore and got fixed up smart, but he had been busy, and had put it off till that morning; he was just going ashore then. Father was all struck up when he heard about the dream, and said his mind had been dwellin' on his mother and going home, and he come down to let her see him just as he was and she said it was the same way he looked in the dream. He never would have his hair cut—father wouldn't—and wore it in a queue. I remember seeing him with it when I was a boy; but his second wife didn't like the looks of it, and she come up behind him one day and cut it off with the scissors. He was terrible worked up about it. I never see father so mad as he was that day. Now this is just as true as the Bible," said Captain Sands. "I haven't put a word to it, and gran'ther al'ays told a story just as it was. That woman saw her son; but if you ask me what kind of eyesight it was, I can't tell you, nor nobody else."

Later that evening Kate and I drifted into a long talk about the captain's stories and these mysterious powers of which we know so little. It was somewhat chilly in the house, and we had kindled a fire in the fireplace, which at first made a blaze which lighted the old room royally, and then quieted down into red coals and lazy puffs of smoke. We had carried the lights away, and sat with our feet on the fender, and Kate's great dog was lying between us on the rug. I remember that evening so well; could see the stars through the window plainer and plainer as the fire went down, and we could hear the noise of the sea.

"Do you remember in the old myth of Demeter and Persephone," Kate asked me, "where Demeter takes care of the child and gives it ambrosia and hides it in fire, because she loves it and wishes to make it immortal, and to give it eternal youth; and then the mother finds it out and cries in terror to hinder her, and the goddess angrily throws the child down and rushes away? And he had to share the common destiny of mankind, though he always had some wonderful inscrutable grace and wisdom, because a goddess had loved him and held him in her arms. I always thought that part of the story beautiful where Demeter throws off her disguise and is no longer an old woman, and the great house is filled with brightness like lightning, and she rushes out through the halls with her yellow hair waving over her shoulders, and the people would give anything to bring her back again, and to undo their mistake. I knew it almost all by heart once," said Kate, "and I am always finding a new meaning in it. I was just thinking that it may be that we all have given to us more or less of another nature, as the child had whom Demeter wished to make like the gods. I believe old Captain Sands is right, and we have these instincts which defy all our wisdom and for which we never can frame any laws. We may laugh at them, but we are always meeting them, and one cannot help knowing that it has been the same through all history. They are powers which are imperfectly developed in this life, but one cannot help the thought that the mystery of this world may be the commonplace of the next."

"I wonder," said I, "why it is that one hears so much more of such things from simple country people. They believe in dreams, and they have a kind of fetichism, and believe so heartily in supernatural causes. I suppose nothing could shake Mrs. Patton's faith in warnings. There is no end of absurdity in it, and yet there is one side of such lives for which one cannot help having reverence; they live so much nearer to nature than people who are in cities, and there is a soberness about country people oftentimes that one cannot help noticing. I wonder if they are unconsciously awed by the strength and purpose in the world about them, and the mysterious creative power which is at work with them on their familiar farms. In their simple life they take their instincts for truths, and perhaps they are not always so far wrong as we imagine. Because they are so instinctive and unreasoning they may have a more complete sympathy with Nature, and may hear her voices when wiser ears are deaf. They have much in common, after all, with the plants which grow up out of the ground and the wild creatures which depend upon their instincts wholly."

"I think," said Kate, "that the more one lives out of doors the more personality there seems to be in what we call inanimate things. The strength of the hills and the voice of the waves are no longer only grand poetical sentences, but an expression of something real, and more and more one finds God himself in the world, and believes that we may read the thoughts that He writes for us in the book of Nature." And after this we were silent for a while, and in the mean time it grew very late, and we watched the fire until there were only a few sparks left in the ashes. The stars faded away and the moon came up out of the sea, and we barred the great hall door and went up stairs to bed. The lighthouse lamp burned steadily, and it was the only light that had not been blown out in all Deephaven.

X

Mrs. Bonny

I am sure that Kate Lancaster and I must have spent by far the greater part of the summer out of doors. We often made long expeditions out into the suburbs of Deephaven, sometimes being gone all day, and sometimes taking a long afternoon stroll and coming home early in the evening hungry as hunters and laden with treasure, whether we had been through the pine woods inland or alongshore, whether we had met old friends or made some desirable new acquaintances. We had a fashion of calling at the farm-houses, and by the end of the season we knew as many people as if we had lived in Deephaven all our days. We used to ask for a drink of water; this was our unfailing introduction, and afterward there were many interesting subjects which one could introduce, and we could always give the latest news at the shore. It was amusing to see the curiosity which we aroused. Many of the people came into Deephaven only on special occasions, and I must confess that at first we were often naughty enough to wait until we had been severely cross-questioned before we gave a definite account of ourselves. Kate was very clever at making unsatisfactory answers when she cared to do so. We did not understand, for some time, with what a keen sense of enjoyment many of those people made the acquaintance of an entirely new person who cordially gave the full particulars about herself; but we soon learned to call this by another name than impertinence.

I think there were no points of interest in that region which we did not visit with conscientious faithfulness. There were cliffs and pebble-beaches, the long sands and the short sands; there were Black Rock and Roaring Rock, High Point and East Point, and Spouting Rock; we went to see where a ship had been driven ashore in the night, all hands being lost and not a piece of her left larger than an axe-handle; we visited the spot where a ship had come ashore in the fog, and had been left high and dry on the edge of the marsh when the tide went out; we saw where the brig Methuselah had been wrecked, and the shore had been golden with her cargo of lemons and oranges, which one might carry away by the wherryful.

Inland there were not many noted localities, but we used to enjoy the woods, and our explorations among the farms, immensely. To the westward the land was better and the people well-to-do; but we went oftenest toward the hills and among the poorer people. The land was uneven and full of ledges, and the people worked hard for their living, at most laying aside only a few dollars each year. Some of the more enterprising young people went away to work in shops and factories; but the custom was by no means universal, and the people had a hungry, discouraged look. It is all very well to say that they knew nothing better, that it was the only life of which they knew anything; there was too often a look of disappointment in their faces, and sooner or later we heard or guessed many stories: that this young man had wished for an education, but there had been no money to spare for books or schooling; and that one had meant to learn a trade, but there must be some one to help his father with the farm-work, and there was no money to hire a man to work in his place if he went away. The older people had a hard look, as if they had always to be on the alert and must fight for their place in the world. One could only forgive and pity their petty sharpness, which showed itself in trifling bargains, when one understood how much a single dollar seemed where dollars came so rarely. We used to pity the young girls so much. It was plain that those who knew how much easier and pleasanter our lives were could not help envying us.

There was a high hill half a dozen miles from Deephaven which was known in its region as "the mountain." It was the highest land anywhere near us, and having been told that there was a fine view from the top, one day we went there, with Tommy Dockum for escort. We overtook Mr. Lorimer, the minister, on his way to make parochial calls upon some members of his parish who lived far from church, and to our delight he proposed to go with us instead. It was a great satisfaction to have him for a guide, for he knew both the country and the people more intimately than any one else. It was a long climb to the top of the hill, but not a hard one. The sky was clear, and there was a fresh wind, though we had left none at all at the sea-level. After lunch, Kate and I spread our shawls over a fine cushion of mountain-cranberry, and had a long talk with Mr. Lorimer about ancient and modern Deephaven. He always seemed as much pleased with our enthusiasm for the town as if it had been a personal favor and compliment to himself. I remember how far we could see, that day, and how we looked toward the far-away blue mountains, and then out over the ocean. Deephaven looked insignificant from that height and distance, and indeed the country seemed to be mostly covered with the pointed tops of pines and spruces, and there were long tracts of maple and beech woods with their coloring of lighter, fresher green.

"Suppose we go down, now," said Mr. Lorimer, long before Kate and I had meant to propose such a thing; and our feeling was that of dismay. "I should like to take you to make a call with me. Did you ever hear of old Mrs. Bonny?"

"No," said we, and cheerfully gathered our wraps and baskets; and when Tommy finally came panting up the hill after we had begun to think that our shoutings and whistling were useless, we sent him down to the horses, and went down ourselves by another path. It led us a long distance through a grove of young beeches; the last year's whitish leaves lay thick on the ground, and the new leaves made so close a roof overhead that the light was strangely purple, as if it had come through a great church window of stained glass. After this we went through some hemlock growth, where, on the lower branches, the pale green of the new shoots and the dark green of the old made an exquisite contrast each to the other. Finally we came out at Mrs. Bonny's. Mr. Lorimer had told us something about her on the way down, saying in the first place that she was one of the queerest characters he knew. Her husband used to be a charcoal-burner and basket-maker, and she used to sell butter and berries and eggs, and choke-pears preserved in molasses. She always came down to Deephaven on a little black horse, with her goods in baskets and bags which were fastened to the saddle in a mysterious way. She had the reputation of not being a neat housekeeper, and none of the wise women of the town would touch her butter especially, so it was always a joke when she coaxed a new resident or a strange shipmaster into buying her wares; but the old woman always managed to jog home without the freight she had brought. "She must be very old, now," said Mr. Lorimer; "I have not seen her in a long time. It cannot be possible that her horse is still alive!" And we all laughed when we saw Mrs. Bonny's steed at a little distance, for the shaggy old creature was covered with mud, pine-needles, and dead leaves, with half the last year's burdock-burs in all Deephaven snarled into his mane and tail and sprinkled over his fur, which looked nearly as long as a buffalo's. He had hurt his leg, and his kind mistress had tied it up with a piece of faded red calico and an end of ragged rope. He gave us a civil neigh, and looked at us curiously. Then an impertinent little yellow-and-white dog, with one ear standing up straight and the other drooping over, began to bark with all his might; but he retreated when he saw Kate's great dog, who was walking solemnly by her side and did not deign to notice him. Just now Mrs. Bonny appeared at the door of the house, shading her eyes with her hand, to see who was coming. "Landy!" said she, "if it ain't old Parson Lorimer! And who be these with ye?"

"This is Miss Kate Lancaster of Boston, Miss Katharine Brandon's niece, and her friend Miss Denis."

"Pleased to see ye," said the old woman; "walk in and lay off your things." And we followed her into the house. I wish you could have seen her: she wore a man's coat, cut off so that it made an odd short jacket, and a pair of men's boots much the worse for wear; also, some short skirts, beside two or three aprons, the inner one being a dress-apron, as she took off the outer ones and threw them into a corner; and on her head was a tight cap, with strings to tie under her chin. I thought it was a nightcap, and that she had forgotten to take it off, and dreaded her mortification if she should suddenly become conscious of it; but I need not have troubled myself, for while we were with her she pulled it on and tied it tighter, as if she considered it ornamental.

There were only two rooms in the house; we went into the kitchen, which was occupied by a flock of hens and one turkey. The latter was evidently undergoing a course of medical treatment behind the stove, and was allowed to stay with us, while the hens were remorselessly hustled out with a hemlock broom. They all congregated on the doorstep, apparently wishing to hear everything that was said.

"Ben up on the mountain?" asked our hostess. "Real sightly place. Goin' to be a master lot o' rosbries; get any down to the shore sence I quit comin'?"

"O yes," said Mr. Lorimer, "but we miss seeing you."

"I s'pose so," said Mrs. Bonny, smoothing her apron complacently; "but I'm getting old, and I tell 'em I'm goin' to take my comfort; sence 'he' died, I don't put myself out no great; I've got money enough to keep me long's I live. Beckett's folks goes down often, and I sends by them for what store stuff I want."

"How are you now?" asked the minister; "I think I heard you were ill in the spring."

"Stirrin', I'm obliged to ye. I wasn't laid up long, and I was so's I could get about most of the time. I've got the best bitters ye ever see, good for the spring of the year. S'pose yer sister, Miss Lorimer, wouldn't like some? she used to be weakly lookin'." But her brother refused the offer, saying that she had not been so well for many years.

"Do you often get out to church nowadays, Mrs. Bonny? I believe Mr. Reid preaches in the school-house sometimes, down by the great ledge; doesn't he?"

"Well, yes, he does; but I don't know as I get much of any good. Parson Reid, he's a worthy creatur', but he never seems to have nothin' to say about foreordination and them p'ints. Old Parson Padelford was the man! I used to set under his preachin' a good deal; I had an aunt living down to East Parish. He'd get worked up, and he'd shut up the Bible and preach the hair off your head, 'long at the end of the sermon. Couldn't understand more nor a quarter part what he said," said Mrs. Bonny, admiringly. "Well, we were a-speaking about the meeting over to the ledge; I don't know's I like them people any to speak of. They had a great revival over there in the fall, and one Sunday I thought's how I'd go; and when I got there, who should be a-prayin' but old Ben Patey,—he always lays out to get converted,—and he kep' it up diligent till I couldn't stand it no longer; and by and by says he, 'I've been a wanderer'; and I up and says, 'Yes, you have, I'll back ye up on that, Ben; ye've wandered around my wood-lot and spoilt half the likely young oaks and ashes I've got, a-stealing your basket-stuff.' And the folks laughed out loud, and up he got and cleared. He's an awful old thief, and he's no idea of being anything else. I wa'n't a-goin' to set there and hear him makin' b'lieve to the Lord. If anybody's heart is in it, I ain't a-goin' to hender 'em; I'm a professor, and I ain't ashamed of it, week-days nor Sundays neither. I can't bear to see folks so pious to meeting, and cheat yer eye-teeth out Monday morning. Well, there! we ain't none of us perfect; even old Parson Moody was round-shouldered, they say."

"You were speaking of the Becketts just now," said Mr. Lorimer (after we had stopped laughing, and Mrs. Bonny had settled her big steel-bowed spectacles, and sat looking at him with an expression of extreme wisdom. One might have ventured to call her "peart," I think). "How do they get on? I am seldom in this region nowadays, since Mr. Reid has taken it under his charge."

"They get along, somehow or 'nother," replied Mrs. Bonny; "they've got the best farm this side of the ledge, but they're dreadful lazy and shiftless, them young folks. Old Mis' Hate-evil Beckett was tellin' me the other day—she that was Samanthy Barnes, you know—that one of the boys got fighting, the other side of the mountain, and come home with his nose broke and a piece o' one ear bit off. I forget which ear it was. Their mother is a real clever, willin' woman, and she takes it to heart, but it's no use for her to say anything. Mis' Hate-evil Beckett, says she, 'It does make my man feel dreadful to see his brother's folks carry on so.' 'But there,' says I, 'Mis' Beckett, it's just such things as we read of; Scriptur' is fulfilled: In the larter days there shall be disobedient children.'"

This application of the text was too much for us, but Mrs. Bonny looked serious, and we did not like to laugh. Two or three of the exiled fowls had crept slyly in, dodging underneath our chairs, and had perched themselves behind the stove. They were long-legged, half-grown creatures, and just at this minute one rash young rooster made a manful attempt to crow. "Do tell!" said his mistress, who rose in great wrath, "you needn't be so forth-putting, as I knows on!" After this we were urged to stay and have some supper. Mrs. Bonny assured us she could pick a likely young hen in no time, fry her with a bit of pork, and get us up "a good meat tea"; but we had to disappoint her, as we had some distance to walk to the house where we had left our horses, and a long drive home.

Kate asked if she would be kind enough to lend us a tumbler (for ours was in the basket, which was given into Tommy's charge). We were thirsty, and would like to go back to the spring and get some water.

"Yes, dear," said Mrs. Bonny, "I've got a glass, if it's so's I can find it." And she pulled a chair under the little cupboard over the fireplace, mounted it, and opened the door. Several things fell out at her, and after taking a careful survey she went in, head and shoulders, until I thought that she would disappear altogether; but soon she came back, and reaching in took out one treasure after another, putting them on the mantel-piece or dropping them on the floor. There were some bunches of dried herbs, a tin horn, a lump of tallow in a broken plate, a newspaper, and an old boot, with a number of turkey-wings tied together, several bottles, and a steel trap, and finally, such a tumbler! which she produced with triumph, before stepping down. She poured out of it on the table a mixture of old buttons and squash-seeds, beside a lump of beeswax which she said she had lost, and now pocketed with satisfaction. She wiped the tumbler on her apron and handed it to Kate, but we were not so thirsty as we had been, though we thanked her and went down to the spring, coming back as soon as possible, for we could not lose a bit of the conversation.

There was a beautiful view from the doorstep, and we stopped a minute there. "Real sightly, ain't it?" said Mrs. Bonny. "But you ought to be here and look across the woods some morning just at sun-up. Why, the sky is all yaller and red, and them low lands topped with fog! Yes, it's nice weather, good growin' weather, this week. Corn and all the rest of the trade looks first-rate. I call it a forrard season. It's just such weather as we read of, ain't it?"

"I don't remember where, just at this moment," said Mr. Lorimer.

"Why, in the almanac, bless ye!" said she, with a tone of pity in her grum voice; could it be possible he didn't know,—the Deephaven minister!

We asked her to come and see us. She said she had always thought she'd get a chance some time to see Miss Katharine Brandon's house. She should be pleased to call, and she didn't know but she should be down to the shore before very long. She was 'shamed to look so shif'less that day, but she had some good clothes in a chist in the bedroom, and a boughten bonnet with a good cypress veil, which she had when "he" died. She calculated they would do, though they might be old-fashioned, some. She seemed greatly pleased at Mr. Lorimer's having taken the trouble to come to see her. All those people had a great reverence for "the minister." We were urged to come again in "rosbry" time, which was near at hand, and she gave us messages for some of her old customers and acquaintants. "I believe some of those old creatur's will never die," said she; "why, they're getting to be ter'ble old, ain't they, Mr. Lorimer? There! ye've done me a sight of good, and I wish I could ha' found the Bible, to hear ye read a Psalm." When Mr. Lorimer shook hands with her, at leaving, she made him a most reverential courtesy. He was the greatest man she knew; and once during the call, when he was speaking of serious things in his simple, earnest way, she had so devout a look, and seemed so interested, that Kate and I, and Mr. Lorimer himself, caught a new, fresh meaning in the familiar words he spoke.

Living there in the lonely clearing, deep in the woods and far from any neighbor, she knew all the herbs and trees and the harmless wild creatures who lived among them, by heart; and she had an amazing store of tradition and superstition, which made her so entertaining to us that we went to see her many times before we came away in the autumn. We went with her to find some pitcher-plants, one day, and it was wonderful how much she knew about the woods, what keen observation she had. There was something so wild and unconventional about Mrs. Bonny that it was like taking an afternoon walk with a good-natured Indian. We used to carry her offerings of tobacco, for she was a great smoker, and advised us to try it, if ever we should be troubled with nerves, or "narves," as she pronounced the name of that affliction.

XI

In Shadow

Soon after we went to Deephaven we took a long drive one day with Mr. Dockum, the kindest and silentest of men. He had the care of the Brandon property, and had some business at that time connected with a large tract of pasture-land perhaps ten miles from town. We had heard of the coast-road which led to it, how rocky and how rough and wild it was, and when Kate heard by chance that Mr. Dockum meant to go that way, she asked if we might go with him. He said he would much rather take us than "go sole alone," but he should be away until late and we must take our dinner, which we did not mind doing at all.

After we were three or four miles from Deephaven the country looked very different. The shore was so rocky that there were almost no places where a boat could put in, so there were no fishermen in the region, and the farms were scattered wide apart; the land was so poor that even the trees looked hungry. At the end of our drive we left the horse at a lonely little farm-house close by the sea. Mr. Dockum was to walk a long way inland through the woods with a man whom he had come to meet, and he told us if we followed the shore westward a mile or two we should find some very high rocks, for which he knew we had a great liking. It was a delightful day to spend out of doors; there was an occasional whiff of east-wind. Seeing us seemed to be a perfect godsend to the people whose nearest neighbors lived far out of sight. We had a long talk with them before we went for our walk. The house was close by the water by a narrow cove, around which the rocks were low, but farther down the shore the land rose more and more, and at last we stood at the edge of the highest rocks of all and looked far down at the sea, dashing its white spray high over the ledges that quiet day. What could it be in winter when there was a storm and the great waves came thundering in?

After we had explored the shore to our hearts' content and were tired, we rested for a while in the shadow of some gnarled pitch-pines which stood close together, as near the sea as they dared. They looked like a band of outlaws; they were such wild-looking trees. They seemed very old, and as if their savage fights with the winter winds had made them hard-hearted. And yet the little wild-flowers and the thin green grass-blades were growing fearlessly close around their feet; and there were some comfortable birds'-nests in safe corners of their rough branches.

When we went back to the house at the cove we had to wait some time for Mr. Dockum. We succeeded in making friends with the children, and gave them some candy and the rest of our lunch, which luckily had been even more abundant than usual. They looked thin and pitiful, but even in that lonely place, where they so seldom saw a stranger or even a neighbor, they showed that there was an evident effort to make them look like other children, and they were neatly dressed, though there could be no mistake about their being very poor. One forlorn little soul, with honest gray eyes and a sweet, shy smile, showed us a string of beads which she wore round her neck; there were perhaps two dozen of them, blue and white, on a bit of twine, and they were the dearest things in all her world. When we came away we were so glad that we could give the man more than he asked us for taking care of the horse, and his thanks touched us.

"I hope ye may never know what it is to earn every dollar as hard as I have. I never earned any money as easy as this before. I don't feel as if I ought to take it. I've done the best I could," said the man, with the tears coming into his eyes, and a huskiness in his voice. "I've done the best I could, and I'm willin' and my woman is, but everything seems to have been ag'in' us; we never seem to get forehanded. It looks sometimes as if the Lord had forgot us, but my woman she never wants me to say that; she says He ain't, and that we might be worse off,—but I don' know. I haven't had my health; that's hendered me most. I'm a boat-builder by trade, but the business's all run down; folks buys 'em second-hand nowadays, and you can't make nothing. I can't stand it to foller deep-sea fishing, and—well, you see what my land's wuth. But my oldest boy, he's getting ahead. He pushed off this spring, and he works in a box-shop to Boston; a cousin o' his mother's got him the chance. He sent me ten dollars a spell ago and his mother a shawl. I don't see how he done it, but he's smart!"

This seemed to be the only bright spot in their lives, and we admired the shawl and sat down in the house awhile with the mother, who seemed kind and patient and tired, and to have great delight in talking about what one should wear. Kate and I thought and spoke often of these people afterward, and when one day we met the man in Deephaven we sent some things to the children and his wife, and begged him to come to the house whenever he came to town; but we never saw him again, and though we made many plans for going again to the cove, we never did. At one time the road was reported impassable, and we put off our second excursion for this reason and others until just before we left Deephaven, late in October.

We knew the coast-road would be bad after the fall rains, and we found that Leander, the eldest of the Dockum boys, had some errand that way, so he went with us. We enjoyed the drive that morning in spite of the rough road. The air was warm, and sweet with the smell of bayberry-bushes and pitch-pines and the delicious saltness of the sea, which was not far from us all the way. It was a perfect autumn day. Sometimes we crossed pebble beaches, and then went farther inland, through woods and up and down steep little hills; over shaky bridges which crossed narrow salt creeks in the marsh-lands. There was a little excitement about the drive, and an exhilaration in the air, and we laughed at jokes forgotten the next minute, and sang, and were jolly enough. Leander, who had never happened to see us in exactly this hilarious state of mind before, seemed surprised and interested, and became unusually talkative, telling us a great many edifying particulars about the people whose houses we passed, and who owned every wood-lot along the road. "Do you see that house over on the pi'nt?" he asked. "An old fellow lives there that's part lost his mind. He had a son who was drowned off Cod Rock fishing, much as twenty-five years ago, and he's worn a deep path out to the end of the pi'nt where he goes out every hand's turn o' the day to see if he can't see the boat coming in." And Leander looked round to see if we were not amused, and seemed puzzled because we didn't laugh. Happily, his next story was funny.

We saw a sleepy little owl on the dead branch of a pine-tree; we saw a rabbit cross the road and disappear in a clump of juniper, and squirrels run up and down trees and along the stone-walls with acorns in their mouths. We passed straggling thickets of the upland sumach, leafless, and holding high their ungainly spikes of red berries; there were sturdy barberry-bushes along the lonely wayside, their unpicked fruit hanging in brilliant clusters. The blueberry-bushes made patches of dull red along the hillsides. The ferns were whitish-gray and brown at the edges of the woods, and the asters and golden-rods which had lately looked so gay in the open fields stood now in faded, frost-bitten companies. There were busy flocks of birds flitting from field to field, ready to start on their journey southward.

SARAH ORNE JEWETT

When we reached the house, to our surprise there was no one in sight and the place looked deserted. We left the wagon, and while Leander went toward the barn, which stood at a little distance, Kate and I went to the house and knocked. I opened the door a little way and said "Hallo!" but nobody answered. The people could not have moved away, for there were some chairs standing outside the door, and as I looked in I saw the bunches of herbs hanging up, and a trace of corn, and the furniture was all there. It was a great disappointment, for we had counted upon seeing the children again. Leander said there was nobody at the barn, and that they must have gone to a funeral; he couldn't think of anything else.

Just now we saw some people coming up the road, and we thought at first that they were the man and his wife coming back; but they proved to be strangers, and we eagerly asked what had become of the family.

"They're dead, both on 'em. His wife she died about nine weeks ago last Sunday, and he died day before yesterday. Funeral's going to be this afternoon. Thought ye were some of her folks from up country, when we were coming along," said the man.

"Guess they won't come nigh," said the woman, scornfully; "'fraid they'd have to help provide for the children. I was half-sister to him, and I've got to take the two least ones."

"Did you say he was going to be buried this afternoon?" asked Kate, slowly. We were both more startled than I can tell.

"Yes," said the man, who seemed much better-natured than his wife. She appeared like a person whose only aim in life was to have things over with. "Yes, we're going to bury at two o'clock. They had a master sight of trouble, first and last."

Leander had said nothing all this time. He had known the man, and had expected to spend the day with him and to get him to go on two miles farther to help bargain for a dory. He asked, in a disappointed way, what had carried him off so sudden.

"Drink," said the woman, relentlessly. "He ain't been good for nothing since his wife died: she was took with a fever along in the first of August. I'd ha' got up from it!"

"Now don't be hard on the dead, Marthy," said her husband. "I guess they done the best they could. They weren't shif'less, you know; they never had no health; 't was against wind and tide with 'em all the time." And Kate asked, "Did you say he was your brother?"

"Yes. I was half-sister to him," said the woman, promptly, with perfect unconsciousness of Kate's meaning.

"And what will become of those poor children?"

"I've got the two youngest over to my place to take care on, and the two next them has been put out to some folks over to the cove. I dare say like's not they'll be sent back."

"They're clever child'n, I guess," said the man, who spoke as if this were the first time he had dared take their part. "Don't be ha'sh, Marthy! Who knows but they may do for us when we get to be old?" And then she turned and looked at him with utter contempt. "I can't stand it to hear men-folks talking on what they don't know nothing about," said she. "The ways of Providence is dreadful myster'ous," she went on with a whine, instead of the sharp tone of voice which we had heard before. "We've had a hard row, and we've just got our own children off our hands and able to do for themselves, and now here are these to be fetched up."

"But perhaps they'll be a help to you; they seem to be good little things," said Kate. "I saw them in the summer, and they seemed to be pleasant children, and it is dreadfully hard for them to be left alone. It's not their fault, you know. We brought over something for them; will you be kind enough to take the basket when you go home?"

"Thank ye, I'm sure," said the aunt, relenting slightly. "You can speak to my man about it, and he'll give it to somebody that's going by. I've got to walk in the procession. They'll be obliged, I'm sure. I s'pose you're the young ladies that come here right after the Fourth o' July, ain't you? I should be pleased to have you call and see the child'n if you're over this way again. I heard 'em talk about you last time I was over. Won't ye step into the house and see him? He looks real natural," she added. But we said, "No, thank you."

Leander told us he believed he wouldn't bother about the dory that day, and he should be there at the house whenever we were ready. He evidently considered it a piece of good luck that he had happened to arrive in time for the funeral. We spoke to the man about the things we had brought for the children, which seemed to delight him, poor soul, and we felt sure he would be kind to them. His wife shouted to him from a window of the house that he'd better not loiter round, or they wouldn't be half ready when the folks began to come, and we said good by to him and went away.

It was a beautiful morning, and we walked slowly along the shore to the high rocks and the pitch-pine trees which we had seen before; the air was deliciously fresh, and one could take long deep breaths of it. The tide was coming in, and the spray dashed higher and higher. We climbed about the rocks and went down in some of the deep cold clefts into which the sun could seldom shine. We gathered some wild-flowers; bits of pimpernel and one or two sprigs of fringed gentian which had bloomed late in a sheltered place, and a pale little bouquet of asters. We sat for a long time looking off to sea, and we could talk or think of almost nothing beside what we had seen and heard at the farm-house. We said how much we should like to go to that funeral, and we even made up our minds to go back in season, but we gave up the idea: we had no right there, and it would seem as if we were merely curious, and we were afraid our presence would make the people ill at ease, the minister especially. It would be an intrusion.

We spoke of the children, and tried to think what could be done for them: we were afraid they would be told so many times that it was lucky they did not have to go to the poor-house, and yet we could not help pitying the hard-worked, discouraged woman whom we had seen, in spite of her bitterness. Poor soul! she looked like a person to whom nobody had ever been very kind, and for whom life had no pleasures: its sunshine had never been warm enough to thaw the ice at her heart.

We remembered how we knocked at the door and called loudly, but there had been no answer, and we wondered how we should have felt if we had gone farther into the room and had found the dead man in his coffin, all alone in the house. We thought of our first visit, and what he had said to us, and we wished we had come again sooner, for we might have helped them so much more if we had only known.

"What a pitiful ending it is," said Kate. "Do you realize that the family is broken up, and the children are to be half strangers to each other? Did you not notice that they seemed very fond of each other when we saw them in the summer? There was not half the roughness and apparent carelessness of one another which one so often sees in the country. Theirs was such a little world; one can understand how, when the man's wife died, he was bewildered and discouraged, utterly at a loss. The thoughts of winter, and of the little children, and of the struggles he had already come through against poverty and disappointment were terrible thoughts; and like a boat adrift at sea, the waves of his misery brought him in against the rocks, and his simple life was wrecked."

"I suppose his grandest hopes and wishes would have been realized in a good farm and a thousand or two dollars in safe keeping," said I. "Do you remember that merry little song in 'As You Like It'?

> *'Who doth ambition shun*
> *And loves to live i' the sun,*
> *Seeking the food he eats,*
> *And pleased with what he gets';*

and

> *'Here shall he see*
> *No enemy*
> *But winter and rough weather.'*

That is all he lived for, his literal daily bread. I suppose what would be prosperity to him would be miserably insufficient for some other people. I wonder how we can help being conscious, in the midst of our comforts and pleasures, of the lives which are being starved to death in more ways than one."

"I suppose one thinks more about these things as one grows older," said Kate, thoughtfully. "How seldom life in this world seems to be a success! Among rich or poor only here and there one touches satisfaction, though the one who seems to have made an utter failure may really be the greatest conqueror. And, Helen, I find that I understand better and better how unsatisfactory, how purposeless and disastrous, any life must be which is not a Christian life! It is like being always in the dark, and wandering one knows not where, if one is not learning more and more what it is to have a friendship with God."

By the middle of the afternoon the sky had grown cloudy, and a wind seemed to be coming in off the sea, and we unwillingly decided that we must go home. We supposed that the funeral would be all over with, but found we had been mistaken when we reached the cove. We seated ourselves on a rock near the water; just beside us was the old boat, with its killick and painter stretched ashore, where its owner had left it.

There were several men standing around the door of the house, looking solemn and important, and by and by one of them came over to us, and we found out a little more of the sad story. We liked this man, there was so much pity in his face and voice. "He was a real willin', honest man, Andrew was," said our new friend, "but he used to be sickly, and seemed to have no luck, though for a year or two he got along some better. When his wife died he was sore afflicted, and couldn't get over it, and he didn't know what to do or what was going to become of 'em with winter comin' on, and—well—I may's well tell ye; he took to drink and it killed him right off. I come over two or three times and made some gruel and fixed him up's well's I could, and the little gals done the best they could, but he faded right out, and didn't know anything the last time I see him, and he died Sunday mornin', when the tide begun to ebb. I always set a good deal by Andrew; we used to play together down to the great cove; that's where he was raised, and my folks lived there too. I've got one o' the little gals. I always knowed him and his wife."

Just now we heard the people in the house singing "China," the Deephaven funeral hymn, and the tune suited well that day, with its wailing rise and fall; it was strangely plaintive. Then the funeral exercises were over, and the man with whom we had just been speaking led to the door a horse and rickety wagon, from which the seat had been taken, and when the coffin had been put in he led the horse down the road a little way, and we watched the mourners come out of the house two by two. We heard some one scold in a whisper because the wagon was twice as far off as it need have been. They evidently had a rigid funeral etiquette, and felt it important that everything should be carried out according to rule. We saw a forlorn-looking kitten, with a bit of faded braid round its neck, run across the road in terror and presently appear again on the stone-wall, where she sat looking at the people. We saw the dead man's eldest son, of whom he had told us in the summer with such pride. He had shown his respect for his father as best he could, by a black band on his hat and a pair of black cotton gloves a world too large for him. He looked so sad, and cried bitterly as he stood alone at the head of the people. His aunt was next, with a handkerchief at her eyes, fully equal to the proprieties of the occasion, though I fear her grief was not so heartfelt as her husband's, who dried his eyes on his coat-sleeve again and again. There were perhaps twenty of the mourners, and there was much whispering among those who walked last. The minister and some others fell into line, and the procession went slowly down the slope; a strange shadow had fallen over everything. It was like a November day, for the air felt cold and bleak. There were some great sea-fowl high in the air, fighting their way toward the sea against the wind, and giving now and then a wild, far-off ringing cry. We could hear the dull sound of the sea, and at a little distance from the land the waves were leaping high, and breaking in white foam over the isolated ledges.

The rest of the people began to walk or drive away, but Kate and I stood watching the funeral as it crept along the narrow, crooked road. We had never seen what the people called "walking funerals" until we came to Deephaven, and there was something piteous about this; the mourners looked so few, and we could hear the rattle of the wagon-wheels. "He's gone, ain't he?" said some one near us. That was it,—*gone*.

Before the people had entered the house, there had been, I am sure, an indifferent, business-like look, but when they came out, all that was changed; their faces were awed by the presence of death, and the indifference had given place to uncertainty. Their neighbor was immeasurably their superior now. Living, he had been a failure by their own low standards; but now, if he could come back, he would know secrets, and be wise beyond anything they could imagine, and who could know the riches of which he might have come into possession?

To Kate and me there came a sudden consciousness of the mystery and inevitableness of death; it was not fear, thank God! but a thought of how certain it was that some day it would be a mystery to us no longer. And there was a thought, too, of the limitation of this present life; we were waiting there, in company with the people, the great sea, and the rocks and fields themselves, on this side the boundary. We knew just then how close to this familiar, every-day world might be the other, which at times before had seemed so far away, out of reach of even our thoughts, beyond the distant stars.

We stayed awhile longer, until the little black funeral had crawled out of sight; until we had seen the last funeral guest go away and the door had been shut and fastened with a queer old padlock and some links of rusty chain. The door fitted loosely, and the man gave it a vindictive shake, as if he thought that the poor house had somehow been to blame, and that after a long desperate struggle for life under its roof and among the stony fields the family must go away defeated. It is not likely that any one else will ever go to live there. The man to whom the farm was mortgaged will add the few forlorn acres to his pasture-land, and the thistles which the man who is dead had fought so many years will march in next summer and take unmolested possession.

I think to-day of that fireless, empty, forsaken house, where the winter sun shines in and creeps slowly along the floor; the bitter cold is in and around the house, and the snow has sifted in at every crack; outside it is untrodden by any living creature's footstep. The wind blows and rushes and shakes the loose window-sashes in their frames, while the padlock knocks—knocks against the door.

XII

Miss Chauncey

The Deephaven people used to say sometimes complacently, that certain things or certain people were "as dull as East Parish." Kate and I grew curious to see that part of the world which was considered duller than Deephaven itself; and as upon inquiry we found that it was not out of reach, one day we went there.

It was like Deephaven, only on a smaller scale. The village—though it is a question whether that is not an exaggerated term to apply—had evidently seen better days. It was on the bank of a river, and perhaps half a mile from the sea. There were a few old buildings there, some with mossy roofs and a great deal of yellow lichen on the sides of the walls next the sea; a few newer houses, belonging to fishermen; some dilapidated fish-houses; and a row of fish-flakes. Every house seemed to have a lane of its own, and all faced different ways except two fish-houses, which stood amiably side by side. There was a church, which we had been told was the oldest in the region. Through the windows we saw the high pulpit and sounding-board, and finally found the keys at a house near by; so we went in and looked around at our leisure. A rusty foot-stove stood in one of the old square pews, and in the gallery there was a majestic bass-viol with all its strings snapped but the largest, which gave out a doleful sound when we touched it.

After we left the church we walked along the road a little way, and came in sight of a fine old house which had apparently fallen into ruin years before. The front entrance was a fine specimen of old-fashioned workmanship, with its columns and carvings, and the fence had been a grand affair in its day, though now it could scarcely stand alone. The long range of out-buildings were falling piece by piece; one shed had been blown down entirely by a late high wind. The large windows had many panes of glass, and the great chimneys were built of the bright red bricks which used to be brought from over-seas in the days of the colonies. We noticed the gnarled lilacs in the yard, the wrinkled cinnamon-roses, and a flourishing company of French pinks, or "bouncing Bets," as Kate called them.

"Suppose we go in," said I; "the door is open a little way. There surely

SARAH ORNE JEWETT

must be some stories about its being haunted. We will ask Miss Honora." And we climbed over the boards which were put up like pasture-bars across the wide front gateway.

"We shall certainly meet a ghost," said Kate.

Just as we stood on the steps the door was pulled wide open; we started back, and, well-grown young women as we are, we have confessed since that our first impulse was to run away. On the threshold there stood a stately old woman who looked surprised at first sight of us, then quickly recovered herself and stood waiting for us to speak. She was dressed in a rusty black satin gown, with scant, short skirt and huge sleeves; on her head was a great black bonnet with a high crown and a close brim, which came far out over her face. "What is your pleasure?" said she; and we felt like two awkward children. Kate partially recovered her wits, and asked which was the nearer way to Deephaven.

"There is but one road, past the church and over the hill. It cannot be missed." And she bowed gravely, when we thanked her and begged her pardon, we hardly knew why, and came away.

We looked back to see her still standing in the doorway. "Who in the world can she be?" said Kate. And we wondered and puzzled and talked over "the ghost" until we saw Miss Honora Carew, who told us that it was Miss Sally Chauncey.

"Indeed, I know her, poor old soul!" said Miss Honora; "she has such a sad history. She is the last survivor of one of the most aristocratic old colonial families. The Chaunceys were of great renown until early in the present century, and then their fortunes changed. They had always been rich and well-educated, and I suppose nobody ever had a gayer, happier time than Miss Sally did in her girlhood, for they entertained a great deal of company and lived in fine style; but her father was unfortunate in business, and at last was utterly ruined at the time of the embargo; then he became partially insane, and died after many years of poverty. I have often heard a tradition that a sailor to whom he had broken a promise had cursed him, and that none of the family had died in their beds or had any good luck since. The East Parish people seem to believe in it, and it is certainly strange what terrible sorrow has come to the Chaunceys. One of Miss Sally's brothers, a fine young officer in the navy who was at home on leave, asked her one day if she could get on without him, and she said yes, thinking he meant to go back to sea; but in a few minutes she heard the noise of a pistol in his room, and hurried in to find him lying dead on the floor. Then there was another brother who was insane, and who became so violent that he was chained for years in one of the upper chambers, a dangerous prisoner. I have heard his horrid cries myself, when I was a young girl," said Miss Honora, with a shiver.

"Miss Sally is insane, and has been for many years, and this seems to me the saddest part of the story. When she first lost her reason she was sent to a hospital, for there was no one who could take care of her. The mania was so acute that no one had the slightest thought that she would recover or even live long. Her guardian sold the furniture and pictures and china, almost everything but clothing, to pay the bills at the hospital, until the house was fairly empty; and then one spring day, I remember it well, she came home in her right mind, and, without a thought of what was awaiting her, ran eagerly into her home. It was a terrible shock, and she never has recovered from it, though after a long illness her insanity took a mild form, and she has always been perfectly harmless. She has been alone many years, and no one can persuade her to leave the old house, where she seems to be contented, and does not realize her troubles; though she lives mostly in the past, and has little idea of the present, except in her house affairs, which seem pitiful to me, for I remember the housekeeping of the Chaunceys when I was a child. I have always been to see her, and she usually knows me, though I have been but seldom of late years. She is several years older than I. The town makes her an allowance every year, and she has some friends who take care that she does not suffer, though her wants are few. She is an elegant woman still, and some day, if you like, I will give you something to carry to her, and a message, if I can think of one, and you must go to make her a call. I hope she will happen to be talkative, for I am sure you would enjoy her. For many years she did not like to see strangers, but some one has told me lately that she seems to be pleased if people go to see her."

You may be sure it was not many days before Kate and I claimed the basket and the message, and went again to East Parish. We boldly lifted the great brass knocker, and were dismayed because nobody answered. While we waited, a girl came up the walk and said that Miss Sally lived up stairs, and she would speak to her if we liked. "Sometimes she don't have sense enough to know what the knocker means," we were told. There was evidently no romance about Miss Sally to our new acquaintance.

"Do you think," said I, "that we might go in and look around the lower rooms? Perhaps she will refuse to see us."

"Yes, indeed," said the girl; "only run the minute I speak; you'll have time enough, for she walks slow and is a little deaf."

So we went into the great hall with its wide staircase and handsome cornices and panelling, and then into the large parlor on the right, and through it to a smaller room looking out on the garden, which sloped down to the river. Both rooms had fine carved mantels, with Dutch-tiled fireplaces, and in the cornices we saw the fastenings where pictures had hung,—old portraits, perhaps. And what had become of them? The girl did not know: the house had been the same ever since she could remember, only it would all fall through into the cellar soon. But the old lady was proud as Lucifer, and wouldn't hear of moving out.

The floor in the room toward the river was so broken that it was not safe, and we came back through the hall and opened the door at the foot of the stairs. "Guess you won't want to stop long there," said the girl. Three old hens and a rooster marched toward us with great solemnity when we looked in. The cobwebs hung in the room, as they often do in old barns, in long, gray festoons; the lilacs outside grew close against the two windows where the shutters were not drawn, and the light in the room was greenish and dim.

Then we took our places on the threshold, and the girl went up stairs and announced us to Miss Sally, and in a few minutes we heard her come along the hall.

"Sophia," said she, "where are the gentry waiting?" And just then she came in sight round the turn of the staircase. She wore the same great black bonnet and satin gown, and looked more old-fashioned and ghostly than before. She was not tall, but very erect, in spite of her great age, and her eyes seemed to "look through you" in an uncanny way. She slowly descended the stairs and came toward us with a courteous greeting, and when we had introduced ourselves as Miss Carew's friends she gave us each her hand in a most cordial way and said she was pleased to see us. She bowed us into the parlor and brought us two rickety, straight-backed chairs, which, with an old table, were all the furniture there was in the room. "Sit ye down," said she, herself taking a place in the window-seat. I have seen few more elegant women than Miss Chauncey. Thoroughly at her ease, she had the manner of a lady of the olden times, using the quaint fashion of speech which she had been taught in her girlhood. The long words and ceremonious phrases suited her extremely well. Her hands were delicately shaped, and she folded them in her lap, as no doubt she had learned to do at boarding-school so many years before. She asked Kate and me if we knew any young ladies at that school in Boston, saying that most of her intimate friends had left when she did, but some of the younger ones were there still.

She asked for the Carews and Mr. Lorimer, and when Kate told her that she was Miss Brandon's niece, and asked if she had not known her, she said, "Certainly, my dear; we were intimate friends at one time, but I have seen her little of late."

"Do you not know that she is dead?" asked Kate.

"Ah, they say every one is 'dead,' nowadays. I do not comprehend the silly idea!" said the old lady, impatiently. "It is an excuse, I suppose. She could come to see me if she chose, but she was always a ceremonious body, and I go abroad but seldom now; so perhaps she waits my visit. I will not speak uncourteously, and you must remember me to her kindly."

Then she asked us about other old people in Deephaven, and about families in Boston whom she had known in her early days. I think every one of whom she spoke was dead, but we assured her that they were all well and prosperous, and we hoped we told the truth. She asked about the love-affairs of men and women who had died old and gray-headed within our remembrance; and finally she said we must pardon her for these tiresome questions, but it was so rarely she saw any one direct from Boston, of whom she could inquire concerning these old friends and relatives of her family.

Something happened after this which touched us both inexpressibly: she sat for some time watching Kate with a bewildered look, which at last faded away, a smile coming in its place. "I think you are like my mother," she said; "did any one ever say to you that you are like my mother? Will you let me see your forehead? Yes; and your hair is only a little darker." Kate had risen when Miss Chauncey did, and they stood side by side. There was a tone in the old lady's voice which brought the tears to my eyes. She stood there some minutes looking at Kate. I wonder what her thoughts were. There was a kinship, it seemed to me, not of blood, only that they both were of the same stamp and rank: Miss Chauncey of the old generation and Kate Lancaster of the new. Miss Chauncey turned to me, saying, "Look up at the portrait and you will see the likeness too, I think." But when she turned and saw the bare wainscoting of the room, she looked puzzled, and the bright flash which had lighted up her face was gone in an instant, and she sat down again in the window-seat; but we were glad that she had forgotten. Presently she said, "Pardon me, but I forget your question."

Miss Carew had told us to ask her about her school-days, as she nearly always spoke of that time to her; and, to our delight, Miss Sally told us a long story about her friends and about her "coming-out party," when boat-loads of gay young guests came down from Riverport, and all the gentry from Deephaven. The band from the fort played for the dancing, the garden was lighted, the card-tables were in this room, and a grand supper was served. She also remembered what some of her friends wore, and her own dress was a silver-gray brocade with rosebuds of three colors. She told us how she watched the boats go off up river in the middle of the summer night; how sweet the music sounded; how bright the moonlight was; how she wished we had been there at her party.

"I can't believe I am an old woman. It seems only yesterday," said she, thoughtfully. And then she lost the idea, and talked about Kate's great-grandmother, whom she had known, and asked us how she had been this summer.

She asked us if we would like to go up stairs where she had a fire, and we eagerly accepted, though we were not in the least cold. Ah, what a sorry place it was! She had gathered together some few pieces of her old furniture, which half filled one fine room, and here she lived. There was a tall, handsome chest of drawers, which I should have liked much to ransack. Miss Carew had told us that Miss Chauncey had large claims against the government, dating back sixty or seventy years, but nobody could ever find the papers; and I felt sure that they must be hidden away in some secret drawer. The brass handles and trimmings were blackened, and the wood looked like ebony. I wanted to climb up and look into the upper part of this antique piece of furniture, and it seemed to me I could at once put my hand on a package of "papers relating to the embargo."

On a stand near the window was an old Bible, fairly worn out with constant use. Miss Chauncey was religious; in fact, it was the only subject about which she was perfectly sane. We saw almost nothing of her insanity that day, though afterward she was different. There were days when her mind seemed clear; but sometimes she was silent, and often she would confuse Kate with Miss Brandon, and talk to her of long-forgotten plans and people. She would rarely speak of anything more than a minute or two, and then would drift into an entirely foreign subject.

She urged us that afternoon to stay to luncheon with her; she said she could not offer us dinner, but she would give us tea and biscuit, and no doubt we should find something in Miss Carew's basket, as she was always kind in remembering her fancies. Miss Honora had told us to decline, if she asked us to stay; but I should have liked to see her sit at the head of her table, and to be a guest at such a lunch-party.

Poor creature! it was a blessed thing that her shattered reason made her unconscious of the change in her fortunes, and incapable of comparing the end of her life with its beginning. To herself she was still Miss Chauncey, a gentlewoman of high family, possessed of unusual worldly advantages. The remembrance of her cruel trials and sorrows had faded from her mind. She had no idea of the poverty of her surroundings when she paced back and forth, with stately steps, on the ruined terraces of her garden; the ranks of lilies and the conserve-roses were still in bloom for her, and the box-borders were as trimly kept as ever; and when she pointed out to us the distant steeples of Riverport, it was plain to see that it was still the Riverport of her girlhood. If the boat-landing at the foot of the garden had long ago dropped into the river and gone out with the tide; if the maids and men who used to do her bidding were all out of hearing; if there had been no dinner company that day and no guests were expected for the evening,—what did it matter? The twilight had closed around her gradually, and she was alone in her house, but she did not heed the ruin of it or the absence of her friends. On the morrow, life would again go on.

We always used to ask her to read the Bible to us, after Mr. Lorimer had told us how grand and beautiful it was to listen to her. I shall never hear some of the Psalms or some chapters of Isaiah again without being reminded of her; and I remember just now, as I write, one summer afternoon when Kate and I had lingered later than usual, and we sat in the upper room looking out on the river and the shore beyond, where the light had begun to grow golden as the day drew near sunset. Miss Sally had opened the great book at random and read slowly, "In my Father's house are many mansions"; and then, looking off for a moment at a leaf which had drifted into the window-recess, she repeated it: "In my Father's house are many mansions; if it were not so, I would have told you." Then she went on slowly to the end of the chapter, and with her hands clasped together on the Bible she fell into a reverie, and the tears came into our eyes as we watched her look of perfect content. Through all her clouded years the promises of God had been her only certainty.

Miss Chauncey died early in the winter after we left Deephaven, and one day when I was visiting Kate in Boston Mr. Lorimer came to see us, and told us about her.

It seems that after much persuasion she was induced to go to spend the winter with a neighbor, her house having become uninhabitable, and she was, beside, too feeble to live alone. But her fondness for her old home was too strong, and one day she stole away from the people who took care of her, and crept in through the cellar, where she had to wade through half-frozen water, and then went up stairs, where she seated herself at a front window and called joyfully to the people who went by, asking them to come in to see her, as she had got home again. After this she was very ill, and one day, when she was half delirious, they missed her, and found her at last sitting on her hall stairway, which she was too feeble to climb. She lived but a short time afterwards, and in her last days her mind seemed perfectly clear. She said over and over again how good God had always been to her, and she was gentle, and unwilling to be a trouble to those who had the care of her.

Mr. Lorimer spoke of her simple goodness, and told us that though she had no other sense of time, and hardly knew if it were summer or winter, she was always sure when Sunday came, and always came to church when he preached at East Parish, her greatest pleasure seeming to be to give money, if there was a contribution. "She may be a lesson to us," added the old minister, reverently; "for, though bewildered in mind, bereft of riches and friends and all that makes this world dear to many of us, she was still steadfast in her simple faith, and was never heard to complain of any of the burdens which God had given her."

XIII

LAST DAYS IN DEEPHAVEN

When the summer was ended it was no sorrow to us, for we were even more fond of Deephaven in the glorious autumn weather than we had ever been before. Mr. Lancaster was abroad longer than he had intended to be at first, and it was late in the season before we left. We were both ready to postpone going back to town as late as possible; but at last it was time for my friend to re-establish the Boston housekeeping, and to take up the city life again. I must admit we half dreaded it: we were surprised to find how little we cared for it, and how well one can get on without many things which are thought indispensable.

For the last fortnight we were in the house a good deal, because the weather was wet and dreary. At one time there was a magnificent storm, and we went every day along the shore in the wind and rain for a mile or two to see the furious great breakers come plunging in against the rocks. I never had seen such a wild, stormy sea as that; the rage of it was awful, and the whole harbor was white with foam. The wind had blown northeast steadily for days, and it seemed to me that the sea never could be quiet and smooth and blue again, with soft white clouds sailing over it in the sky. It was a treacherous sea; it was wicked; it had all the trembling land in its power, if it only dared to send its great waves far ashore. All night long the breakers roared, and the wind howled in the chimneys, and in the morning we always looked fearfully across the surf and the tossing gray water to see if the lighthouse were standing firm on its rock. It was so slender a thing to hold its own in such a wide and monstrous sea. But the sun came out at last, and not many days afterward we went out with Danny and Skipper Scudder to say good by to Mrs. Kew. I have been some voyages at sea, but I never was so danced about in a little boat as I was that day. There was nothing to fear with so careful a crew, and we only enjoyed the roughness as we went out and in, though it took much manoeuvring to land us at the island.

It was very sad work to us—saying good by to our friends, and we tried to make believe that we should spend the next summer in Deephaven, and we meant at any rate to go down for a visit. We were glad when the people said they should miss us, and that they hoped we should not forget them and the old place. It touched us to find that they cared so much for us, and we said over and over again how happy we had been, and that it was such a satisfactory summer. Kate laughingly proposed one evening, as we sat talking by the fire and were particularly contented, that we should copy the Ladies of Llangollen, and remove ourselves from society and its distractions.

"I have thought often, lately," said my friend, "what a good time they must have had, and I feel a sympathy and friendliness for them which I never felt before. We could have guests when we chose, as we have had this summer, and we could study and grow very wise, and what could be pleasanter? But I wonder if we should grow very lazy if we stayed here all the year round; village life is not stimulating, and there would not be much to do in winter,—though I do not believe that need be true; one may be busy and useful in any place."

"I suppose if we really belonged in Deephaven we should think it a hard fate, and not enjoy it half so much as we have this summer," said I. "Our idea of happiness would be making long visits in Boston; and we should be heart-broken when we had to come away and leave our lunch-parties, and symphony concerts, and calls, and fairs, the reading-club and the childrens' hospital. We should think the people uncongenial and behind the times, and that the Ridge road was stupid and the long sands desolate; while we remembered what delightful walks we had taken out Beacon Street to the three roads, and over the Cambridge Bridge. Perhaps we should even be ashamed of the dear old church for being so out of fashion. We should have the blues dreadfully, and think there was no society here, and wonder why we had to live in such a town."

"What a gloomy picture!" said Kate, laughing. "Do you know that I have understood something lately better than I ever did before,—it is that success and happiness are not things of chance with us, but of choice. I can see how we might so easily have had a dull summer here. Of course it is our own fault if the events of our lives are hindrances; it is we who make them bad or good. Sometimes it is a conscious choice, but oftener unconscious. I suppose we educate ourselves for taking the best of life or the worst, do not you?"

"Dear old Deephaven!" said Kate, gently, after we had been silent a little while. "It makes me think of one of its own old ladies, with its clinging to the old fashions and its respect for what used to be respectable when it was young. I cannot make fun of what was once dear to somebody, and which realized somebody's ideas of beauty or fitness. I don't dispute the usefulness of a new, bustling, manufacturing town with its progressive ideas; but there is a simple dignity in a town like Deephaven, as if it tried to be loyal to the traditions of its ancestors. It quietly accepts its altered circumstances, if it has seen better days, and has no harsh feelings toward the places which have drawn away its business, but it lives on, making its old houses and boats and clothes last as long as possible."

"I think one cannot help," said I, "having a different affection for an old place like Deephaven from that which one may have for a newer town. Here—though there are no exciting historical associations and none of the veneration which one has for the very old cities and towns abroad—it is impossible not to remember how many people have walked the streets and lived in the houses. I was thinking to-day how many girls might have grown up in this house, and that their places have been ours; we have inherited their pleasures, and perhaps have carried on work which they began. We sit in somebody's favorite chair and look out of the windows at the sea, and have our wishes and our hopes and plans just as they did before us. Something of them still lingers where their lives were spent. We are often reminded of our friends who have died; why are we not reminded as surely of strangers in such a house as this,—finding some trace of the lives which were lived among the sights we see and the things we handle, as the incense of many masses lingers in some old cathedral, and one catches the spirit of longing and prayer where so many heavy hearts have brought their burdens and have gone away comforted?"

"When I first came here," said Kate, "it used to seem very sad to me to find Aunt Katharine's little trinkets lying about the house. I have often thought of what you have just said. I heard Mrs. Patton say the other day that there is no pocket in a shroud, and of course it is better that we should carry nothing out of this world. Yet I can't help wishing that it were possible to keep some of my worldly goods always. There are one or two books of mine and some little things which I have had a long time, and of which I have grown very fond. It makes me so sorry to think of their being neglected and lost. I cannot believe I shall forget these earthly treasures when I am in heaven, and I wonder if I shall not miss them. Isn't it strange to think of not reading one's Bible any more? I suppose this is a very low view of heaven, don't you?" And we both smiled.

"I think the next dwellers in this house ought to find a decided atmosphere of contentment," said I. "Have you ever thought that it took us some time to make it your house instead of Miss Brandon's? It used to seem to me that it was still under her management, that she was its mistress; but now it belongs to you, and if I were ever to come back without you I should find you here."

IT IS BEWILDERING TO KNOW that this is the last chapter, and that it must not be long. I remember so many of our pleasures of which I have hardly said a word. There were our guests, of whom I have told you nothing, and of whom there was so much to say. Of course we asked my Aunt Mary to visit us, and Miss Margaret Tennant, and many of our girlfriends. All the people we know who have yachts made the port of Deephaven if they were cruising in the neighboring waters. Once a most cheerful party of Kate's cousins and some other young people whom we knew very well came to visit us in this way, and the yacht was kept in the harbor a week or more, while we were all as gay as bobolinks and went frisking about the country, and kept late hours in the sober old Brandon house. My Aunt Mary, who was with us, and Kate's aunt, Mrs. Thorniford, who knew the Carews, and was commander of the yacht-party, tried to keep us in order, and to make us ornaments to Deephaven society instead of reproaches and stumbling-blocks. Kate's younger brothers were with us, waiting until it was time for them to go back to college, and I think there never had been such picnics in Deephaven before, and I fear there never will be again.

We are fond of reading, and we meant to do a great deal of it, as every one does who goes away for the summer; but I must confess that our grand plans were not well carried out. Our German dictionaries were on the table in the west parlor until the sight of them mortified us, and finally, to avoid their silent reproach, I put them in the closet, with the excuse that it would be as easy to get them there, and they would be out of the way. We used to have the magazines sent us from town; you would have smiled at the box of books which we carried to Deephaven, and indeed we sent two or three times for others; but I do not remember that we ever carried out that course of study which we had planned with so much interest. We were out of doors so much that there was often little time for anything else.

Kate said one day that she did not care, in reading, to be always making new acquaintances, but to be seeing more of old ones; and I think it is a very wise idea. We each have our pet books; Kate carries with her a much-worn copy of "Mr. Rutherford's Children," which has been her delight ever since she can remember. Sibyl and Chryssa are dear old friends, though I suppose now it is not merely what Kate reads, but what she associates with the story. I am not often separated from Jean Ingelow's "Stories told to a Child," that charmingly wise and pleasant little book. It is always new, like Kate's favorite. It is very hard to make a list of the books one likes best, but I remember that we had "The Village on the Cliff," and "Henry Esmond," and "Tom Brown at Rugby," with his more serious ancestor, "Sir Thomas Browne." I am sure we had "Fenelon," for we always have that; and there was "Pet Marjorie," and "Rab," and "Annals of a Parish," and "The Life of the Reverend Sydney Smith"; beside Miss Tytler's "Days of Yore," and "The Holy and Profane State," by Thomas Fuller, from which Kate gets so much entertainment and profit. We read Mr. Emerson's essays together, out of doors, and some stories which had been our dear friends at school, like "Leslie Goldthwaite." There was a very good library in the house, and we both like old books, so we enjoyed that. And we used to read the Spectator, and many old-fashioned stories and essays and sermons, with much more pleasure because they had such quaint old brown leather bindings. You will not doubt that we had some cherished volumes of poetry, or that we used to read them aloud to each other when we sat in our favorite corner of the rocks at the shore, or were in the pine woods of an afternoon.

We used to go out to tea, and do a great deal of social visiting, which was very pleasant. Dinner-parties were not in fashion, though it was a great attention to be asked to spend the day, which courtesy we used to delight in extending to our friends; and we entertained company in that way often. When we first went out we were somewhat interesting on account of our clothes, which were of later pattern than had been adopted generally in Deephaven. We used to take great pleasure in arraying ourselves on high days and holidays, since when we went wandering on shore, or out sailing or rowing, we did not always dress as befitted our position in the town. Fish-scales and blackberry-briers so soon disfigure one's clothes.

We became in the course of time learned in all manner of 'longshore lore, and even profitably employed ourselves one morning in going clam-digging with old Ben Horn, a most fascinating ancient mariner. We both grew so well and brown and strong, and Kate and I did not get tired of each other at all, which I think was wonderful, for few friendships would bear such a test. We were together always, and alone together a great deal; and we became wonderfully well acquainted. We are such good friends that we often were silent for a long time, when mere acquaintances would have felt compelled to talk and try to entertain each other.

Before we left the leaves had fallen off all the trees except the oaks, which make in cold weather one of the dreariest sounds one ever hears: a shivering rustle, which makes one pity the tree and imagine it shelterless and forlorn. The sea had looked rough and cold for many days, and the old house itself had grown chilly,—all the world seemed waiting for the snow to come. There was nobody loitering on the wharves, and when we went down the street we walked fast, arm in arm, to keep warm. The houses were shut up as close as possible, and the old sailors did not seem cheery any longer; they looked forlorn, and it was not a pleasant prospect to be so long weather-bound in port. If they ventured out, they put on ancient great-coats, with huge flaps to the pockets and large horn buttons, and they looked contemptuously at the vane, which always pointed to the north or east. It felt like winter, and the captains rolled more than ever as they walked, as if they were on deck in a heavy sea. The rheumatism claimed many victims, and there was one day, it must be confessed, when a biting, icy fog was blown in-shore, that Kate and I were willing to admit that we could be as comfortable in town, and it was almost time for sealskin jackets.

In the front yards we saw the flower-beds black with frost, except a few brave pansies which had kept green and had bloomed under the tall china-aster stalks, and one day we picked some of these little flowers to put between the leaves of a book and take away with us. I think we loved Deephaven all the more in those last days, with a bit of compassion in our tenderness for the dear old town which had so little to amuse it. So long a winter was coming, but we thought with a sigh how pleasant it would be in the spring.

You would have smiled at the treasures we brought away with us. We had become so fond of even our fishing-lines; and this very day you may see in Kate's room two great bunches of Deephaven cat-o'-nine-tails. They were much in our way on the journey home, but we clung affectionately to these last sheaves of our harvest.

The morning we came away our friends were all looking out from door or window to see us go by, and after we had passed the last house and there was no need to smile any longer, we were very dismal. The sun was shining again bright and warm as if the Indian summer were beginning, and we wished that it had been a rainy day.

The thought of Deephaven will always bring to us our long quiet summer days, and reading aloud on the rocks by the sea, the fresh salt air, and the glory of the sunsets; the wail of the Sunday psalm-singing at church, the yellow lichen that grew over the trees, the houses, and the stone-walls; our boating and wanderings ashore; our importance as members of society, and how kind every one was to us both. By and by the Deephaven warehouses will fall and be used for firewood by the fisher-people, and the wharves will be worn away by the tides. The few old gentlefolks who still linger will be dead then; and I wonder if some day Kate Lancaster and I will go down to Deephaven for the sake of old times, and read the epitaphs in the burying-ground, look out to sea, and talk quietly about the girls who were so happy there one summer long before. I should like to walk along the beach at sunset, and watch the color of the marshes and the sea change as the light of the sky goes out. It would make the old days come back vividly. We should see the roofs and chimneys of the village, and the great Chantrey elms look black against the sky. A little later the marsh fog would show faintly white, and we should feel it deliciously cold and wet against our hands and faces; when we looked up there would be a star; the crickets would chirp loudly; perhaps some late sea-birds would fly inland. Turning, we should see the lighthouse lamp shine out over the water, and the great sea would move and speak to us lazily in its idle, high-tide sleep.

SARAH ORNE JEWETT

SELECTED STORIES AND SKETCHES

An Autumn Holiday

I had started early in the afternoon for a long walk; it was just the weather for walking, and I went across the fields with a delighted heart. The wind came straight in from the sea, and the sky was bright blue; there was a little tinge of red still lingering on the maples, and my dress brushed over the late golden-rods, while my old dog, who seemed to have taken a new lease of youth, jumped about wildly and raced after the little birds that flew up out of the long brown grass—the constant little chickadees, that would soon sing before the coming of snow. But this day brought no thought of winter; it was one of the October days when to breathe the air is like drinking wine, and every touch of the wind against one's face is a caress: like a quick, sweet kiss, that wind is. You have a sense of companionship; it is a day that loves you.

I went strolling along, with this dear idle day for company; it was a pleasure to be alive, and to go through the dry grass, and to spring over the stone walls and the shaky pasture fences. I stopped by each of the stray apple-trees that came in my way, to make friends with it, or to ask after its health, if it were an old friend. These old apple-trees make very charming bits of the world in October; the leaves cling to them later than to the other trees, and the turf keeps short and green underneath; and in this grass, which was frosty in the morning, and has not quite dried yet, you can find some cold little cider apples, with one side knurly, and one shiny bright red or yellow cheek. They are wet with dew, these little apples, and a black ant runs anxiously over them when you turn them round and round to see where the best place is to bite. There will almost always be a bird's nest in the tree, and it is most likely to be a robin's nest. The prehistoric robins must have been cave dwellers, for they still make their nests as much like cellars as they can, though they follow the new fashion and build them aloft. One always has a thought of spring at the sight of a robin's nest. It is so little while ago that it was spring, and we were so glad to have the birds come back, and the life of the new year was just showing itself; we were looking forward to so much growth and to the realization and perfection of so many things. I think the sadness of autumn, or the pathos of it, is like that of elderly people. We have seen how the flowers looked when they bloomed and have eaten the fruit when it was ripe; the questions have had their answer, the days we waited for have come and gone.

Everything has stopped growing. And so the children have grown to be men and women, their lives have been lived, the autumn has come. We have seen what our lives would be like when we were older; success or disappointment, it is all over at any rate. Yet it only makes one sad to think it is autumn with the flowers or with one's own life, when one forgets that always and always there will be the spring again.

I am very fond of walking between the roads. One grows so familiar with the highways themselves. But once leap the fence and there are a hundred roads that you can take, each with its own scenery and entertainment. Every walk of this kind proves itself a tour of exploration and discovery, and the fields of my own town, which I think I know so well, are always new fields. I find new ways to go, new sights to see, new friends among the things that grow, and new treasures and pleasures every summer; and later, when the frosts have come and the swamps have frozen, I can go everywhere I like all over my world.

That afternoon I found something I had never seen before—a little grave alone in a wide pasture which had once been a field. The nearest house was at least two miles away, but by hunting for it I found a very old cellar, where the child's home used to be, not very far off, along the slope. It must have been a great many years ago that the house had stood there; and the small slate head-stone was worn away by the rain and wind, so there was nothing to be read, if indeed there had ever been any letters on it. It had looked many a storm in the face, and many a red sunset. I suppose the woods near by had grown and been cut, and grown again, since it was put there. There was an old sweet-brier bush growing on the short little grave, and in the grass underneath I found a ground-sparrow's nest. It was like a little neighborhood, and I have felt ever since as if I belonged to it; and I wondered then if one of the young ground-sparrows was not always sent to take the nest when the old ones were done with it, so they came back in the spring year after year to live there, and there were always the stone and the sweet-brier bush and the birds to remember the child. It was such a lonely place in that wide field under the great sky, and yet it was so comfortable too; but the sight of the little grave at first touched me strangely, and I tried to picture to myself the procession that came out from the house the day of the funeral, and I thought of the mother in the evening after all the people had gone home, and how she missed the baby, and kept seeing the new grave out here in the twilight as she went about her work. I suppose the family moved away, and so all the rest were buried elsewhere.

I often think of this place, and I link it in my thoughts with something I saw once in the water when I was out at sea: a little boat that some child had lost, that had drifted down the river and out to sea; too long a voyage, for it was a sad little wreck, with even its white sail of a hand-breadth half under water, and its twine rigging trailing astern. It was a silly little boat, and no loss, except to its owner, to whom it had seemed as brave and proud a thing as any ship of the line to you and me. It was a shipwreck of his small hopes, I suppose, and I can see it now, the toy of the great winds and waves, as it floated on its way, while I sailed on mine, out of sight of land.

The little grave is forgotten by everybody but me, I think: the mother must have found the child again in heaven a very long time ago: but in the winter I shall wonder if the snow has covered it well, and next year I shall go to see the sweet-brier bush when it is in bloom. God knows what use that life was, the grave is such a short one, and nobody knows whose little child it was; but perhaps a thousand people in the world to-day are better because it brought a little love into the world that was not there before.

I sat so long here in the sun that the dog, after running after all the birds, and even chasing crickets, and going through a great piece of affectation in barking before an empty woodchuck's hole to kill time, came to sit patiently in front of me, as if he wished to ask when I would go on. I had never been in this part of the pasture before. It was at one side of the way I usually took, so presently I went on to find a favorite track of mine, half a mile to the right, along the bank of a brook. There had been heavy rains the week before, and I found more water than usual running, and the brook was apparently in a great hurry. It was very quiet along the shore of it; the frogs had long ago gone into winter-quarters, and there was not one to splash into the water when he saw me coming. I did not see a musk-rat either, though I knew where their holes were by the piles of fresh-water mussel shells that they had untidily thrown out at their front door. I thought it might be well to hunt for mussels myself, and crack them in search of pearls, but it was too serene and beautiful a day. I was not willing to disturb the comfort of even a shell-fish. It was one of the days when one does not think of being tired: the scent of the dry everlasting flowers, and the freshness of the wind, and the cawing of the crows, all come to me as I think of it, and I remember that I went a long way before I began to think of going home again. I knew I could not be far from a cross-road, and when I climbed a low hill I saw a house which I was glad to make the end of my walk—for a time, at any rate. It was some time since I had seen the old woman who lived there, and I liked her dearly, and was sure of a welcome. I went down through the pasture lane, and just then I saw my father drive away up the road, just too far for me to make him hear when I called. That seemed too bad at first, until I remembered that he would come back again over the same road after a while, and in the mean time I could make my call. The house was low and long and unpainted, with a great many frost-bitten flowers about it. Some hollyhocks were bowed down despairingly, and the morning-glory vines were more miserable still. Some of the smaller plants had been covered to keep them from freezing, and were braving out a few more days, but no shelter would avail them much longer. And already nobody minded whether the gate was shut or not, and part of the great flock of hens were marching proudly about among the wilted posies, which they had stretched their necks wistfully through the fence for all summer. I heard the noise of spinning in the house, and my dog scurried off after the cat as I went in the door. I saw Miss Polly Marsh and her sister, Mrs. Snow, stepping back and forward together spinning yarn at a pair of big wheels. The wheels made such a noise with their whir and creak, and my friends were talking so fast as they twisted and turned the yarn, that they did not hear my footstep, and I stood in the doorway watching them, it was such a quaint and pretty sight. They went together like a pair of horses, and kept step with each other to and fro. They were about the same size, and were cheerful old bodies, looking a good deal alike, with their checked handkerchiefs over their smooth gray hair, their dark gowns made short in the skirts, and their broad little feet in gray stockings and low leather shoes without heels. They stood straight, and though they were quick at their work they moved stiffly; they were talking busily about some one.

"I could tell by the way the doctor looked that he didn't think there was much of anything the matter with her," said Miss Polly Marsh. "'You needn't tell me,' says I, the other day, when I see him at Miss Martin's. 'She'd be up and about this minute if she only had a mite o' resolution;' and says he, 'Aunt Polly, you're as near right as usual;'" and the old lady stopped to laugh a little. "I told him that wa'n't saying much," said she, with an evident consciousness of the underlying compliment and the doctor's good opinion. "I never knew one of that tribe that hadn't a queer streak and wasn't shif'less; but they're tougher than ellum roots;"

and she gave the wheel an emphatic turn, while Mrs. Snow reached for more rolls of wool, and happened to see me.

"Wherever did you come from?" said they, in great surprise. "Why, you wasn't anywhere in sight when I was out speaking to the doctor," said Mrs. Snow. "Oh, come over horseback, I suppose. Well, now, we're pleased to see ye."

"No," said I, "I walked across the fields. It was too pleasant to stay in the house, and I haven't had a long walk for some time before." I begged them not to stop spinning, but they insisted that they should not have turned the wheels a half-dozen times more, even if I had not come, and they pushed them back to the wall before they came to sit down to talk with me over their knitting—for neither of them were ever known to be idle. Mrs. Snow was only there for a visit; she was a widow, and lived during most of the year with her son; and Aunt Polly was at home but seldom herself, as she was a famous nurse, and was often in demand all through that part of the country. I had known her all my days. Everybody was fond of the good soul, and she had been one of the most useful women in the world. One of my pleasantest memories is of a long but not very painful illness one winter, when she came to take care of me. There was no end either to her stories or her kindness. I was delighted to find her at home that afternoon, and Mrs. Snow also.

Aunt Polly brought me some of her gingerbread, which she knew I liked, and a stout little pitcher of milk, and we sat there together for a while, gossiping and enjoying ourselves. I told all the village news that I could think of, and I was just tired enough to know it, and to be contented to sit still for a while in the comfortable three-cornered chair by the little front window. The October sunshine lay along the clean kitchen floor, and Aunt Polly darted from her chair occasionally to catch stray little wisps of wool which the breeze through the door blew along from the wheels. There was a gay string of red peppers hanging over the very high mantel-shelf, and the wood-work in the room had never been painted, and had grown dark brown with age and smoke and scouring. The clock ticked solemnly, as if it were a judge giving the laws of time, and felt itself to be the only thing that did not waste it. There was a bouquet of asparagus and some late sprigs of larkspur and white petunias on the table underneath, and a Leavitt's Almanac lay on the county paper, which was itself lying on the big Bible, of which Aunt Polly made a point of reading two chapters every day in course. I remember her saying, despairingly, one night, half to herself, "I don' know but I may skip the Chronicles next time," but I have never to this day believed that she did. They asked me at once to come into the best room, but I liked the old kitchen best. "Who was it that you were talking about as I came in?" said I. "You said you didn't believe there was much the matter with her." And Aunt Polly clicked her knitting-needles faster, and told me that it was Mary Susan Ash, over by Little Creek.

"They're dreadful nervous, all them Ashes," said Mrs. Snow. "You know young Joe Adams's wife, over our way, is a sister to her, and she's forever a-doctorin'. Poor fellow! *he's* got a drag. I'm real sorry for Joe; but, land sakes alive! he might 'a known better. They said she had an old green bandbox with a gingham cover, that was stowed full o' vials, that she moved with the rest of her things when she was married, besides some she car'd in her hands. I guess she ain't in no more hurry to go than any of the rest of us. I've lost every mite of patience with her. I was over there last week one day, and she'd had a call from the new supply—you know Adams's folks is Methodists—and he was took in by her. She made out she'd got the consumption, and she told how many complaints she had, and what a sight o' medicine she took, and she groaned and sighed, and her voice was so weak you couldn't more than just hear it. I stepped right into the bedroom after he'd been prayin' with her, and was taking leave. You'd thought, by what he said, she was going right off then. She was coughing dreadful hard, and I knew she hadn't no more cough than I had. So says I, 'What's the matter, Adaline? I'll get ye a drink of water. Something in your throat, I s'pose. I hope you won't go and get cold, and have a cough.' She looked as if she could 'a bit me, but I was just as pleasant 's could be. Land! to see her laying there, I suppose the poor young fellow thought she was all gone. He meant well. I wish he had seen her eating apple-dumplings for dinner. She felt better 'long in the first o' the afternoon before he come. I says to her, right before him, that I guessed them dumplings did her good, but she never made no answer. She will have these dyin' spells. I don't know's she can help it, but she needn't act as if it was a credit to anybody to be sick and laid up. Poor Joe, he come over for me last week another day, and said she'd been havin' spasms, and asked me if there wa'n't something I could think of. 'Yes,' says I; 'you just take a pail o' stone-cold water, and throw it square into her face; that'll bring her out of it;' and he looked at me a minute, and then he burst out a-laughing—he couldn't help it. He's too good to her; that's the trouble."

SARAH ORNE JEWETT

"You never said that to her about the dumplings?" said Aunt Polly, admiringly. "Well, *I* shouldn't ha' dared;" and she rocked and knitted away faster than ever, while we all laughed. "Now with Mary Susan it's different. I suppose she does have the neurology, and she's a poor broken-down creature. I do feel for her more than I do for Adaline. She was always a willing girl, and she worked herself to death, and she can't help these notions, nor being an Ash neither."

"I'm the last one to be hard on anybody that's sick, and in trouble," said Mrs. Snow.

"Bless you, she set up with Ad'line herself three nights in one week, to my knowledge. It's more'n I would do," said Aunt Polly, as if there were danger that I should think Mrs. Snow's kind heart to be made of flint.

"It ain't what I call watching," said she, apologetically. "We both doze off, and then when the folks come in in the morning she'll tell what a sufferin' night she's had. She likes to have it said she has to have watchers."

"It's strange what a queer streak there is running through the whole of 'em," said Aunt Polly, presently. "It always was so, far back's you can follow 'em. Did you ever hear about that great-uncle of theirs that lived over to the other side o' Denby, over to what they call the Denby Meadows? We had a cousin o' my father's that kept house for him (he was a single man), and I spent most of a summer and fall with her once when I was growing up. She seemed to want company: it was a lonesome sort of a place."

"There! I don't know when I have thought to' that," said Mrs. Snow, looking much amused. "What stories you did use to tell, after you come home, about the way he used to act! Dear sakes! she used to keep us laughing till we was tired. Do tell her about him, Polly; she'll like to hear."

"Well, I've forgot a good deal about it: you see it was much as fifty years ago. I wasn't more than seventeen or eighteen years old. He was a very respectable man, old Mr. Dan'el Gunn was, and a cap'n in the militia in his day. Cap'n Gunn, they always called him. He was well off, but he got sun-struck, and never was just right in his mind afterward. When he was getting over his sickness after the stroke he was very wandering, and at last he seemed to get it into his head that he was his own sister Patience that died some five or six years before: she was single too, and she always lived with him. They said when he got so's to sit up in his arm-chair of an afternoon, when he was getting better, he fought 'em dreadfully because they fetched him his own clothes to put on; he said they was brother Dan'el's clothes. So, sure enough, they got out an old double gown, and let him put it on, and he was as peaceable as could be. The doctor told 'em to humor him, but they thought it was a fancy he took, and he would forget it; but the next day he made 'em get the double gown again, and a cap too, and there he used to set up alongside of his bed as prim as a dish. When he got round again so he could set up all day, they thought he wanted the dress; but no; he seemed to be himself, and had on his own clothes just as usual in the morning; but when he took his nap after dinner and waked up again, he was in a dreadful frame o' mind, and had the trousers and coat off in no time, and said he was Patience. He used to fuss with some knitting-work he got hold of somehow; he was good-natured as could be, and sometimes he would make 'em fetch him the cat, because Patience used to have a cat that set in her lap while she knit. I wasn't there then, you know, but they used to tell me about it. Folks used to call him Miss Dan'el Gunn.

"He'd been that way some time when I went over. I'd heard about his notions, and I was scared of him at first, but I found out there wasn't no need. Don't you know I was sort o' 'fraid to go, 'Lizabeth, when Cousin Statiry sent for me after she went home from that visit she made here? She'd told us about him, but sometimes, 'long at the first of it, he used to be cross. He never was after I went there. He was a clever, kind-hearted man, if ever there was one," said Aunt Polly, with decision. "He used to go down to the corner to the store sometimes in the morning, and he would see to business. And before he got feeble sometimes he would work out on the farm all the morning, stiddy as any of the men; but after he come in to dinner he would take off his coat, if he had it on, and fall asleep in his arm-chair, or on a l'unge there was in his bedroom, and when he waked up he would be sort of bewildered for a while, and then he'd step round quick's he could, and get his dress out o' the clothes-press, and the cap, and put 'em on right over the rest of his clothes. He was always small-featured and smooth-shaved, and I don' know as, to come in sudden, you would have thought he was a man, except his hair stood up short and straight all on the top of his head, as men-folks had a fashion o' combing their hair then, and I must say he did make a dreadful ordinary-looking woman. The neighbors got used to his ways, and, land! I never thought nothing of it after the first week or two.

SARAH ORNE JEWETT

"His sister's clothes that he wore first was too small for him, and so my cousin Statiry, that kep' his house, she made him a linsey-woolsey dress with a considerable short skirt, and he was dreadful pleased with it, she said, because the other one never would button over good, and showed his wais'coat, and she and I used to make him caps; he used to wear the kind all the old women did then, with a big crown, and close round the face. I've got some laid away up-stairs now that was my mother's—she wore caps very young, mother did. His nephew that lived with him carried on the farm, and managed the business, but he always treated the cap'n as if he was head of everything there. Everybody pitied the cap'n; folks respected him; but you couldn't help laughing, to save ye. We used to try to keep him in, afternoons, but we couldn't always."

"Tell her about that day he went to meeting," said Mrs. Snow.

"Why, one of us always used to stay to home with him; we took turns; and somehow or 'nother he never offered to go, though by spells he would be constant to meeting in the morning. Why, bless you, you never'd think anything ailed him a good deal of the time, if you saw him before noon, though sometimes he would be freaky, and hide himself in the barn, or go over in the woods, but we always kept an eye on him. But this Sunday there was going to be a great occasion. Old Parson Croden was going to preach; he was thought more of than anybody in this region: you've heard tell of him a good many times, I s'pose. He was getting to be old, and didn't preach much. He had a colleague, they set so much by him in his parish, and I didn't know's I'd ever get another chance to hear him, so I didn't want to stay to home, and neither did Cousin Statiry; and Jacob Gunn, old Mr. Gunn's nephew, he said it might be the last time ever he'd hear Parson Croden, and he set in the seats anyway; so we talked it all over, and we got a young boy to come and set 'long of the cap'n till we got back. He hadn't offered to go anywhere of an afternoon for a long time. I s'pose he thought women ought to be stayers at home according to Scripture.

"Parson Ridley—his wife was a niece to old Dr. Croden—and the old doctor they was up in the pulpit, and the choir was singing the first hymn—it was a fuguing tune, and they was doing their best: seems to me it was 'Canterbury New.' Yes, it was; I remember I thought how splendid it sounded, and Jacob Gunn he was a-leading off; and I happened to look down the aisle, and who should I see but the poor old cap'n in his cap and gown parading right into meeting before all the folks! There! I wanted to go through the floor. Everybody 'most had seen him at home, but, my goodness! to have him come into meeting!"

"What did you do?" said I.

"Why, nothing," said Miss Polly; "there was nothing *to* do. I thought I should faint away; but I called Cousin Statiry's 'tention, and she looked dreadful put to it for a minute; and then says she, 'Open the door for him; I guess he won't make no trouble,' and, poor soul, he didn't. But to see him come up the aisle! He'd fixed himself nice as he could, poor creatur; he'd raked out Miss Patience's old Navarino bonnet with green ribbons and a willow feather, and set it on right over his cap, and he had her bead bag on his arm, and her turkey-tail fan that he'd got out of the best room; and he come with little short steps up to the pew: and I s'posed he'd set by the door; but no, he made to go by us, up into the corner where she used to set, and took her place, and spread his dress out nice, and got his handkerchief out o' his bag, just's he'd seen her do. He took off his bonnet all of a sudden, as if he'd forgot it, and put it under the seat, like he did his hat—that was the only thing he did that any woman wouldn't have done—and the crown of his cap was bent some. I thought die I should. The pew was one of them up aside the pulpit, a square one, you know, right at the end of the right-hand aisle, so I could see the length of it and out of the door, and there stood that poor boy we'd left to keep the cap'n company, looking as pale as ashes. We found he'd tried every way to keep the old gentleman at home, but he said he got f'erce as could be, so he didn't dare to say no more, and Cap'n Gunn drove him back twice to the house, and that's why he got in so late. I didn't know but it was the boy that had set him on to go to meeting when I see him walk in, and I could 'a wrung his neck; but I guess I misjudged him; he was called a stiddy boy. He married a daughter of Ichabod Pinkham's over to Oak Plains, and I saw a son of his when I was taking care of Miss West last spring through that lung fever—looked like his father. I wish I'd thought to tell him about that Sunday. I heard he was waiting on that pretty Becket girl, the orphan one that lives with Nathan Becket. Her father and mother was both lost at sea, but she's got property."

"What did they say in church when the captain came in, Aunt Polly?" said I.

"Well, a good many of them laughed—they couldn't help it, to save them; but the cap'n he was some hard o' hearin', so he never noticed it, and he set there in the corner and fanned him, as pleased and satisfied as could be. The singers they had the worst time, but they had just come to the end of a verse, and they played on the instruments a good while in between, but I could see 'em shake, and I s'pose the tune did stray a little, though they went through it well. And after the first fun of it was over, most of the folks felt bad. You see, the cap'n had been very much looked up to, and it was his misfortune, and he set there quiet, listening to the preaching. I see some tears in some o' the old folks' eyes: they hated to see him so broke in his mind, you know. There was more than usual of 'em out that day; they knew how bad he'd feel if he realized it. A good Christian man he was, and dreadful precise, I've heard 'em say."

"Did he ever go again?" said I.

"I seem to forget," said Aunt Polly. "I dare say. I wasn't there but from the last of June into November, and when I went over again it wasn't for three years, and the cap'n had been dead some time. His mind failed him more and more along at the last. But I'll tell you what he did do, and it was the week after that very Sunday, too. He heard it given out from the pulpit that the Female Missionary Society would meet with Mis' William Sands the Thursday night o' that week—the sewing society, you know; and he looked round to us real knowing; and Cousin Statiry, says she to me, under her bonnet, 'You don't s'pose he'll want to go?' and I like to have laughed right out. But sure enough he did, and what do you suppose but he made us fix over a handsome black watered silk for him to wear, that had been his sister's best dress. He said he'd outgrown it dreadful quick. Cousin Statiry she wished to heaven she'd thought to put it away, for Jacob had given it to her, and she was meaning to make it over for herself; but it didn't do to cross the cap'n and Jacob Gunn gave Statiry another one—the best he could get, but it wasn't near so good a piece, she thought. He set everything by Statiry, and so did the cap'n, and well they might.

"We hoped he'd forget all about it the next day; but he didn't; and I always thought well of those ladies, they treated him so handsome, and tried to make him enjoy himself. He did eat a great supper; they kep' a-piling up his plate with everything. I couldn't help wondering if some of 'em would have put themselves out much if it had been some poor flighty old woman. The cap'n he was as polite as could be, and when Jacob come to walk home with him he kissed 'em all round and asked 'em to meet at his house. But the greatest was—land! I don't know when I've thought so much about those times—one afternoon he was setting at home in the keeping-room, and Statiry was there, and Deacon Abel

Pinkham stopped in to see Jacob Gunn about building some fence, and he found he'd gone to mill, so he waited a while, talking friendly, as they expected Jacob might be home; and the cap'n was as pleased as could be, and he urged the deacon to stop to tea. And when he went away, says he to Statiry, in a dreadful knowing way, 'Which of us do you consider the deacon come to see?' You see, the deacon was a widower. Bless you! when I first come home I used to set everybody laughing, but I forget most of the things now. There was one day, though"—

"Here comes your father," said Mrs. Snow. "Now we mustn't let him go by or you'll have to walk 'way home." And Aunt Polly hurried out to speak to him, while I took my great bunch of golden-rod, which already drooped a little, and followed her, with Mrs. Snow, who confided to me that the captain's nephew Jacob had offered to Polly that summer she was over there, and she never could see why she didn't have him: only love goes where it is sent, and Polly wasn't one to marry for what she could get if she didn't like the man. There was plenty that would have said yes, and thank you too, sir, to Jacob Gunn.

That was a pleasant afternoon. I reached home when it was growing dark and chilly, and the early autumn sunset had almost faded in the west. It was a much longer way home around by the road than by the way I had come across the fields.

From a Mournful Villager

Lately I have been thinking, with much sorrow, of the approaching extinction of front yards, and of the type of New England village character and civilization with which they are associated. Formerly, because I lived in an old-fashioned New England village, it would have been hard for me to imagine that there were parts of the country where the Front yard, as I knew it, was not in fashion, and that Grounds (however small) had taken its place. No matter how large a piece of land lay in front of a house in old times, it was still a front yard, in spite of noble dimension and the skill of practiced gardeners.

There are still a good many examples of the old manner of out-of-door life and customs, as well as a good deal of the old-fashioned provincial society, left in the eastern parts of the New England States; but put side by side with the society that is American rather than provincial, one discovers it to be in a small minority. The representative United States citizen will be, or already is, a Westerner, and his instincts and ways of looking at things have certain characteristics of their own which are steadily growing more noticeable.

For many years New England was simply a bit of Old England transplanted. We all can remember elderly people whose ideas were wholly under the influence of their English ancestry. It is hardly more than a hundred years since we were English colonies, and not independent United States, and the customs and ideas of the mother country were followed from force of habit. Now one begins to see a difference; the old traditions have had time to almost die out even in the most conservative and least changed towns, and a new element has come in. The true characteristics of American society, as I have said, are showing themselves more and more distinctly to the westward of New England, and come back to it in a tide that steadily sweeps away the old traditions. It rises over the heads of the prim and stately idols before which our grandfathers and grandmothers bowed down and worshiped, and which we ourselves were at least taught to walk softly by as they toppled on their thrones.

One cannot help wondering what a lady of the old school will be like a hundred years from now! But at any rate she will not be in heart and thought and fashion of good breeding as truly an Englishwoman as if she had never stepped out of Great Britain. If one of our own elderly ladies were suddenly dropped into the midst of provincial English society, she would be quite at home; but west of her own Hudson River she is lucky if she does not find herself behind the times, and almost a stranger and a foreigner.

And yet from the first there was a little difference, and the colonies were New England and not Old. In some ways more radical, yet in some ways more conservative, than the people across the water, they showed a new sort of flower when they came into bloom in this new climate and soil. In the old days there had not been time for the family ties to be broken and forgotten. Instead of the unknown English men and women who are our sixth and seventh cousins now, they had first and second cousins then; but there was little communication between one country and the other, and the mutual interest in every-day affairs had to fade out quickly. A traveler was a curiosity, and here, even between the villages themselves, there was far less intercourse than we can believe possible. People stayed on their own ground; their horizons were of small circumference, and their whole interest and thought were spent upon their own land, their own neighbors, their own affairs, while they not only were contented with this state of things but encouraged it. One has only to look at the high-walled pews of the old churches, at the high fences of the town gardens, and at even the strong fortifications around some family lots in the burying-grounds, to be sure of this. The interviewer was not besought and encouraged in those days,—he was defied. In that quarter, at least, they had the advantage of us. Their interest was as real and heartfelt in each other's affairs as ours, let us hope; but they never allowed idle curiosity to show itself in the world's market-place, shameless and unblushing.

There is so much to be said in favor of our own day, and the men and women of our own time, that a plea for a recognition of the quaintness and pleasantness of village life in the old days cannot seem unwelcome, or without deference to all that has come with the later years of ease and comfort, or of discovery in the realms of mind or matter. We are beginning to cling to the elderly people who are so different from ourselves, and for this reason: we are paying them instinctively the honor that is due from us to our elders and betters; they have that grand prestige and dignity that only comes with age; they are like old wines, perhaps no better than many others when they were young, but now after many years they have come to be worth nobody knows how many dollars a dozen, and the connoisseurs make treasures of the few bottles of that vintage which are left.

SARAH ORNE JEWETT

It was a restricted and narrowly limited life in the old days. Religion, or rather sectarianism, was apt to be simply a matter of inheritance, and there was far more bigotry in every cause and question,—a fiercer partisanship; and because there were fewer channels of activity, and those undivided into specialties, there was a whole-souled concentration of energy that was as efficient as it was sometimes narrow and short-sighted. People were more contented in the sphere of life to which it had pleased God to call them, and they do not seem to have been so often sorely tempted by the devil with a sight of the kingdoms of the world and the glory of them. We are more likely to busy ourselves with finding things to do than in doing with our might the work that is in our hands already. The disappearance of many of the village front yards may come to be typical of the altered position of woman, and mark a stronghold on her way from the much talked-of slavery and subjection to a coveted equality. She used to be shut off from the wide acres of the farm, and had no voice in the world's politics; she must stay in the house, or only hold sway out of doors in this prim corner of land where she was queen. No wonder that women clung to their rights in their flower-gardens then, and no wonder that they have grown a little careless of them now, and that lawn mowers find so ready a sale. The whole world is their front yard nowadays!

THERE MIGHT BE WRITTEN A history of front yards in New England which would be very interesting to read. It would end in a treatise upon landscape gardening and its possibilities, and wild flights of imagination about the culture of plants under glass, the application of artificial heat in forcing, and the curious mingling and development of plant life, but it would begin in the simple time of the early colonists. It must have been hard when, after being familiar with the gardens and parks of England and Holland, they found themselves restricted to front yards by way of pleasure grounds. Perhaps they thought such things were wrong, and that having a pleasant place to walk about in out of doors would encourage idle and lawless ways in the young; at any rate, for several years it was more necessary to raise corn and potatoes to keep themselves from starving than to lay out alleys and plant flowers and box borders among the rocks and stumps. There is a great pathos in the fact that in so stern and hard a life there was time or place for any gardens at all. I can picture to myself the little slips and cuttings that had been brought over in the ship, and more carefully guarded than any of the household goods; I can see the women look at them tearfully when they came into bloom, because nothing else could be a better reminder of their old home. What fears there must have been lest the first winter's cold might kill them, and with what love and care they must have been tended! I know a rose-bush, and a little while ago I knew an apple-tree, that were brought over by the first settlers; the rose still blooms, and until it was cut down the old tree bore apples. It is strange to think that civilized New England is no older than the little red roses that bloom in June on that slope above the river in Kittery. Those earliest gardens were very pathetic in the contrast of their extent and their power of suggestion and association. Every seed that came up was thanked for its kindness, and every flower that bloomed was the child of a beloved ancestry.

It would be interesting to watch the growth of the gardens as life became easier and more comfortable in the colonies. As the settlements grew into villages and towns, and the Indians were less dreadful, and the houses were better and more home-like, the busy people began to find a little time now and then when they could enjoy themselves soberly. Beside the fruits of the earth they could have some flowers and a sprig of sage and southernwood and tansy, or lavender that had come from Surrey and could be dried to be put among the linen as it used to be strewn through the chests and cupboards in the old country.

I like to think of the changes as they came slowly; that after a while tender plants could be kept through the winter, because the houses were better built and warmer, and were no longer rough shelters which were only meant to serve until there could be something better. Perhaps the parlor, or best room, and a special separate garden for the flowers were two luxuries of the same date, and they made a noticeable change in the manner of living,—the best room being a formal recognition of the claims of society, and the front yard an appeal for the existence of something that gave pleasure,—beside the merely useful and wholly necessary things of life. When it was thought worth while to put a fence around the flower-garden the respectability of art itself was established and made secure. Whether the house was a fine one, and its inclosure spacious, or whether it was a small house with only a narrow bit of ground in front, this yard was kept with care, and it was different from the rest of the land altogether. The children were not often allowed to play there, and the family did not use the front door except upon occasions of more or less ceremony. I think that many of the old front yards could tell stories of the lovers who found it hard to part under the stars, and lingered over the gate; and who does not remember the solemn group of men who gather there at funerals, and stand with their heads uncovered as the mourners go out and come in, two by two. I have always felt rich in the possession of an ancient York tradition of an old fellow who demanded, as he lay dying, that the grass in his front yard should be cut at once; it was no use to have it trodden down and spoilt by the folks at the funeral. I always hoped it was good hay weather; but he must have been certain of that when he spoke. Let us hope he did not confuse this world with the next, being so close upon the borders of it! It was not man-like to think of the front yard, since it was the special domain of the women,—the men of the family respected but ignored it,—they had to be teased in the spring to dig the flower beds, but it was the busiest time of the year; one should remember that.

I think many people are sorry, without knowing why, to see the fences pulled down; and the disappearance of plain white palings causes almost as deep regret as that of the handsome ornamental fences and their high posts with urns or great white balls on top. A stone coping does not make up for the loss of them; it always looks a good deal like a lot in a cemetery, for one thing; and then in a small town the grass is not smooth, and looks uneven where the flower-beds were not properly smoothed down. The stray cows trample about where they never went before; the bushes and little trees that were once protected grow ragged and scraggly and out at elbows, and a few forlorn flowers come up of themselves, and try hard to grow and to bloom. The ungainly red tubs that are perched on little posts have plants in them, but the poor posies look as if they would rather be in the ground, and as if they are held too near the fire of the sun. If everything must be neglected and forlorn so much the more reason there should be a fence, if but to hide it. Americans are too fond of being stared at; they apparently feel as if it were one's duty to one's neighbor. Even if there is nothing really worth looking at about a house, it is still exposed to the gaze of the passers-by. Foreigners are far more sensible than we, and the out-of-door home life among them is something we might well try to copy. They often have their meals served out of doors, and one can enjoy an afternoon nap in a hammock, or can take one's work out into the shady garden with great satisfaction, unwatched; and even a little piece of ground can be made, if shut in and kept for the use and pleasure of the family alone, a most charming unroofed and trellised summer ante-room to the house. In a large, crowded town it would be selfish to conceal the rare bits of garden, where the sight of anything green is a godsend; but where there is the whole wide country of fields and woods within easy reach I think there should be high walls around our gardens, and that we lose a great deal in not making them entirely separate from the highway; as much as we should lose in making the walls of our parlors and dining-rooms of glass, and building the house as close to the street as possible.

But to go back to the little front yards: we are sorry to miss them and their tangle or orderliness of roses and larkspur and honeysuckle, Canterbury bells and London pride, lilacs and peonies. These may all bloom better than ever in the new beds that are cut in the turf; but with the side fences that used to come from the corners of the house to the front fence, other barriers, as I have said here over and over, have been taken away, and the old-fashioned village life is becoming extinct. People do not know what they lose when they make way with the reserve, the separateness, the sanctity of the front yard of their grandmothers. It is like writing down the family secrets for any one to read; it is like having everybody call you by your first name and sitting in any pew in church, and like having your house in the middle of a road, to take away the fence which, slight as it may be, is a fortification round your home. More things than one may come in without being asked. We Americans had better build more fences than take any away from our lives. There should be gates for charity to go out and in, and kindness and sympathy too, but his life and his house are together each man's stronghold and castle, to be kept and defended.

I was much amused once at thinking that the fine old solid paneled doors were being unhinged faster than ever nowadays, since so many front gates have disappeared, and the click of the latch can no longer give notice of the approach of a guest. Now the knocker sounds or the bell rings without note or warning, and the village housekeeper cannot see who is coming in until they have already reached the door. Once the guests could be seen on their way up the walk. It must be a satisfaction to look through the clear spots of the figured ground-glass in the new doors, and I believe if there is a covering inside few doors will be found unprovided with a peephole. It was better to hear the gate open and shut, and if it caught and dragged as front gates are very apt to do you could have time always for a good look out of the window at the approaching friend.

There are few of us who cannot remember a front-yard garden which seemed to us a very paradise in childhood. It was like a miracle when the yellow and white daffies came into bloom in the spring, and there was a time when tiger-lilies and the taller rose-bushes were taller than we were, and we could not look over their heads as we do now. There were always a good many lady's-delights that grew under the bushes, and came up anywhere in the chinks of the walk of the door-step, and there was a little green sprig called ambrosia that was a famous stray-away. Outside the fence one was not unlikely to see a company of French pinks, which were forbidden standing-room inside as if they were tiresome poor relations of the other flowers. I always felt a sympathy for French pinks,—they have a fresh, sweet look, as if they resigned themselves to their lot in life and made the best of it, and remembered that they had the sunshine and rain, and could see what was going on in the world, if they were outlaws.

I like to remember being sent on errands, and being asked to wait while the mistress of the house picked some flowers to send back to my mother. They were almost always prim, flat bouquets in those days; the larger flowers were picked first and stood at the back and looked over the heads of those that were shorter of stem and stature, and the givers always sent a message that they had not stopped to arrange them. I remember that I had even then a great dislike to lemon verbena, and that I would have waited patiently outside a gate all the afternoon if I knew that some one would kindly give me a sprig of lavender in the evening. And lilies did not seem to me overdressed, but it was easy for me to believe that Solomon in all his glory was not arrayed like a great yellow marigold, or even the dear little single ones that were yellow and brown, and bloomed until the snow came.

I wish that I had lived for a little while in those days when lilacs were a new fashion, and it was a great distinction to have some growing in a front yard. It always seems as if lilacs and poplars belonged to the same generation with a certain kind of New English gentlemen and ladies, who were ascetic and severe in some of their fashions, while in others they were more given to pleasuring and mild revelry than either their ancestors or the people who have lived in their houses since. Fifty years ago there seems to have been a last tidal wave of Puritanism which swept over the country, and drowned for a time the sober feasting and dancing which before had been considered no impropriety in the larger villages. Whist-playing was clung to only by the most worldly citizens, and, as for dancing, it was made a sin in itself and a reproach, as if every step was taken willfully in seven-leagued boots toward a place which is to be the final destination of all the wicked.

A single poplar may have a severe and uncharitable look, but a row of them suggests the antique and pleasing pomp and ceremony of their early days, before the sideboard cupboards were only used to keep the boxes of strings and nails and the duster; and the best decanters were put on a high shelf, while the plain ones were used for vinegar in the kitchen closet. There is far less social visiting from house to house than there used to be. People in the smaller towns have more acquaintances who live at a distance than was the case before the days of railroads, and there are more guests who come from a distance, which has something to do with making tea-parties and the entertainment of one's neighbors less frequent than in former times. But most of the New England towns have changed their characters in the last twenty years, since the manufactories have come in and brought together large numbers either of foreigners or of a different class of people from those who used to make the most of the population. A certain class of families is rapidly becoming extinct. There will be found in the older villages very few persons left who belong to this class, which was once far more important and powerful; the oldest churches are apt to be most thinly attended simply because a different sort of ideas, even of heavenly things, attract the newer residents. I suppose that elderly people have said, ever since the time of Shem, Ham, and Japhet's wives in the ark, that society is nothing to what it used to be, and we may expect to be always told what unworthy successors we are of our grandmothers. But the fact remains that a certain element of American society is fast dying out, giving place to the new; and with all our glory and pride in modern progress and success we cling to the old associations regretfully. There is nothing to take the place of the pleasure we have in going to see our old friends in the parlors which have changed little since our childhood. No matter how advanced in years we seem to ourselves we are children still to the gracious hostess. Thank Heaven for the friends who have always known us! They may think us unreliable and young still; they may not understand that we have become busy and more or less important people to ourselves and to the world,—we are pretty sure to be without honor in our own country, but they will never forget us, and we belong to each other and always shall.

I have received many kindnesses at my friends' hands, but I do not know that I have ever felt myself to be a more fortunate or honored guest than I used years ago, when I sometimes went to call upon an elderly friend of my mother who lived in most pleasant and stately fashion. I used to put on my very best manner, and I have no doubt that my thoughts were well ordered, and my conversation as proper as I knew how to make it. I can remember that I used to sit on a tall ottoman, with nothing to lean against, and my feet were off soundings, I was so high above the floor. We used to discuss the weather, and I said that I went to school (sometimes), or that it was then vacation, as the case might be, and we tried to make ourselves agreeable to each other. Presently my lady would take her keys out of her pocket, and sometimes a maid would come to serve me, or else she herself would bring me a silver tray with some pound-cakes baked in hearts and rounds, and a small glass of wine, and I proudly felt that I was a guest, though I was such a little thing an attention was being paid me, and a thrill of satisfaction used to go over me for my consequence and importance. A handful of sugar-plums would have seemed nothing beside this entertainment. I used to be careful not to crumble the cake, and I used to eat it with my gloves on, and a pleasant fragrance would cling for some time afterward to the ends of the short Lisle-thread fingers. I have no doubt that my manners as I took leave were almost as distinguished as those of my hostess, though I might have been wild and shy all the rest of the week. It was not many years ago that I went to my old friend's funeral—and saw them carry her down the long, wide walk, between the tall box borders which were her pride; and all the air was heavy and sweet with the perfume of the early summer blossoms; the white lilacs and the flowering currants were still in bloom, and the rows of her dear Dutch tulips stood dismayed in their flaunting colors and watched her go away.

My sketch of the already out-of-date or fast vanishing village fashions perhaps should be ended here, but I cannot resist a wish to add another bit of autobiography of which I have been again and again reminded in writing these pages. The front yard I knew best belonged to my grandfather's house. My grandmother was a proud and solemn woman, and she hated my mischief, and rightly thought my elder sister a much better child than I. I used to be afraid of her when I was in the house, but I shook off even her authority and forgot I was under anybody's rule when I was out of doors. I was first cousin to a caterpillar if they called me to come in, and I was own sister to a giddy-minded bobolink when I ran away across the fields, as I used to do very often.

But when I was a very little child indeed my world was bounded by the fences that were around my home; there were wide green yards and tall elm-trees to shade them; there was a long line of barns and sheds, and one of these had a large room in its upper story, with an old ship's foresail spread over the floor, and made a capital play-room in wet weather. Here fruit was spread in the fall, and there were some old chests and pieces of furniture that had been discarded; it was like the garret, only much pleasanter. The children in the village now cannot possibly be so happy as I was then. I used to mount the fence next the street and watch the people go in and out of the quaint-roofed village shops that stood in a row on the other side, and looked as if they belonged to a Dutch or old English town. They were burnt down long ago, but they were charmingly picturesque; the upper stories sometimes projected over the lower, and the chimneys were sometimes clustered together and built of bright red bricks.

And I was too happy when I could smuggle myself into the front yard, with its four lilac bushes and its white fences to shut it in from the rest of the world, beside other railings that went from the porch down each side of the brick walk, which was laid in a pattern, and had H.C., 1818, cut deeply into one of the bricks near the door-step. The H.C. was for Henry Currier, the mason, who had signed this choice bit of work as if it were a picture, and he had been dead so many years that I used to think of his initials as if the corner brick were a little grave-stone for him. The knocker used to be so bright that it shone at you, and caught your eye bewilderingly, as you came in from the street on a sunshiny day. There were very few flowers, for my grandmother was old and feeble when I knew her, and could not take care of them; but I remember that there were blush roses, and white roses, and cinnamon roses all in a tangle in one corner, and I used to pick the crumpled petals of those to make myself a delicious coddle with ground cinnamon and damp brown sugar. In the spring I used to find the first green grass there, for it was warm and sunny, and I used to pick the little French pinks when they dared show their heads in the cracks of the flag-stones that were laid around the house. There were small shoots of lilac, too, and their leaves were brown and had a faint, sweet fragrance, and a little later the dandelions came into bloom; the largest ones I knew grew there, and they have always been to this day my favorite flowers.

I had my trials and sorrows in this paradise, however; I lost a cent there one day which I never have found yet! And one morning, there suddenly appeared in one corner a beautiful, dark-blue *fleur-de-lis*, and I joyfully broke its neck and carried it into the house, but everybody had seen it, and wondered that I could not have left it alone. Besides this, it befell me later to sin more gravely still; my grandmother had kept some plants through the winter on a three-cornered stand built like a flight of steps, and when the warm spring weather came this was put out of doors. She had a cherished tea-rose bush, and what should I find but a bud on it; it was opened just enough to give a hint of its color. I was very pleased; I snapped it off at once, for I had heard so many times that it was hard to make roses bloom; and I ran in through the hall and up the stairs, where I met my grandmother on the square landing. She sat down in the window-seat, and I showed her proudly what was crumpled in my warm little fist. I can see it now!—it had no stem at all, and for many days afterward I was bowed down with a sense of my guilt and shame, for I was made to understand it was an awful thing to have blighted and broken a treasured flower like that.

It must have been the very next winter that my grandmother died. She had a long illness which I do not remember much about; but the night she died might have been yesterday night, it is all so fresh and clear in my mind. I did not live with her in the old house then, but in a new house close by, across the yard. All the family were at the great house, and I could see that lights were carried hurriedly from one room to another. A servant came to fetch me, but I would not go with her; my grandmother was dying, whatever that might be, and she was taking leave of every one—she was ceremonious even then. I did not dare to go with the rest; I had an intense curiosity to see what dying might be like, but I was afraid to be there with her, and I was also afraid to stay at home alone. I was only five years old. It was in December, and the sky seemed to grow darker and darker, and I went out at last to sit on a door-step and cry softly to myself, and while I was there some one came to another door next the street, and rang the bell loudly again and again. I suppose I was afraid to answer the summons—indeed, I do not know that I thought of it; all the world had been still before, and the bell sounded loud and awful through the empty house. It seemed as if the messenger from an unknown world had come to the wrong house to call my poor grandmother away; and that loud ringing is curiously linked in my mind with the knocking at the gate in "Macbeth." I never can think of one without the other, though there was no fierce Lady Macbeth to bid me not be lost so poorly in my thoughts; for when they

An October Ride

I t was a fine afternoon, just warm enough and just cool enough, and I started off alone on horseback, though I do not know why I should say alone when I find my horse such good company. She is called Sheila, and she not only gratifies one's sense of beauty, but is very interesting in her character, while her usefulness in this world is beyond question. I grow more fond of her every week; we have had so many capital good times together, and I am certain that she is as much pleased as I when we start out for a run.

I do not say to every one that I always pronounce her name in German fashion because she occasionally shies, but that is the truth. I do not mind her shying, or a certain mysterious and apparently unprovoked jump, with which she sometimes indulges herself, and no one else rides her, so I think she does no harm, but I do not like the principle of allowing her to be wicked, unrebuked and unhindered, and some day I shall give my mind to admonishing this four-footed Princess of Thule, who seems at present to consider herself at the top of royalty in this kingdom or any other. I believe I should not like her half so well if she were tamer and entirely and stupidly reliable; I glory in her good spirits and I think she has a right to be proud and willful if she chooses. I am proud myself of her quick eye and ear, her sure foot, and her slender, handsome chestnut head. I look at her points of high breeding with admiration, and I thank her heartily for all the pleasure she has given me, and for what I am sure is a steadfast friendship between us,—and a mutual understanding that rarely knows a disappointment or a mistake. She is careful when I come home late through the shadowy, twilighted woods, and I can hardly see my way; she forgets then all her little tricks and capers, and is as steady as a clock with her tramp, tramp, over the rough, dark country roads. I feel as if I had suddenly grown a pair of wings when she fairly flies over the ground and the wind whistles in my ears. There never was a time when she could not go a little faster, but she is willing to go step by step through the close woods, pushing her way through the branches, and stopping considerately when a bough that will not bend tries to pull me off the saddle. And she never goes away and leaves me when I dismount to get some flowers or a drink of spring water, though sometimes she thinks what fun it would be. I cannot speak of all her virtues for I have not learned them yet. We are still new friends, for I have only ridden her two years and I feel all the fascination of the first meeting every time I go out with her, she is so unexpected in her ways; so amusing, so sensible, so brave, and in every way so delightful a horse.

It was in October, and it was a fine day to look at, though some of the great clouds that sailed through the sky were a little too heavy-looking to promise good weather on the morrow, and over in the west (where the wind was coming from) they were packed close together and looked gray and wet. It might be cold and cloudy later, but that would not hinder my ride; it is a capital way to keep warm, to come along a smooth bit of road on the run, and I should have time at any rate to go the way I wished, so Sheila trotted quickly through the gate and out of the village. There was a flicker of color left on the oaks and maples, and though it was not Indian-summer weather it was first cousin to it. I took off my cap to let the wind blow through my hair; I had half a mind to go down to the sea, but it was too late for that; there was no moon to light me home. Sheila took the strip of smooth turf just at the side of the road for her own highway, she tossed her head again and again until I had my hand full of her thin, silky mane, and she gave quick pulls at her bit and hurried little jumps ahead as if she expected me already to pull the reins tight and steady her for a hard gallop. I patted her and whistled at her, I was so glad to see her again and to be out riding, and I gave her part of her reward to begin with, because I knew she would earn it, and then we were on better terms than ever. She has such a pretty way of turning her head to take the square lump of sugar, and she never bit my fingers or dropped the sugar in her life.

Down in the lower part of the town on the edge of York, there is a long tract of woodland, covering what is called the Rocky Hills; rough, high land, that stretches along from beyond Agamenticus, near the sea, to the upper part of Eliot, near the Piscataqua River. Standing on Agamenticus, the woods seem to cover nearly the whole of the country as far as one can see, and there is hardly a clearing to break this long reach of forest of which I speak; there must be twenty miles of it in an almost unbroken line. The roads cross it here and there, and one can sometimes see small and lonely farms hiding away in the heart of it. The trees are for the most part young growth of oak or pine, though I could show you yet many a noble company of great pines that once would have been marked with the king's arrow, and many a royal old oak which has been overlooked in the search for ships' knees and plank for the navy yard, and piles for the always shaky, up-hill and down, pleasant old Portsmouth bridge. The part of these woods which I know best lies on either side the already old new road to York on the Rocky Hills, and here I often ride, or even take perilous rough drives through the cart-paths, the wood roads which are busy thoroughfares in the winter, and are silent and shady, narrowed by green branches and carpeted with slender brakes, and seldom traveled over, except by me, all summer long.

It was a great surprise, or a succession of surprises, one summer, when I found that every one of the old uneven tracks led to or at least led by what had once been a clearing, and in old days must have been the secluded home of some of the earliest adventurous farmers of this region. It must have taken great courage, I think, to strike the first blow of one's axe here in the woods, and it must have been a brave certainty of one's perseverance that looked forward to the smooth field which was to succeed the unfruitful wilderness. The farms were far enough apart to be very lonely, and I suppose at first the cry of fierce wild creatures in the forest was an every-day sound, and the Indians stole like snakes through the bushes and crept from tree to tree about the houses watching, begging, and plundering, over and over again. There are some of these farms still occupied, where the land seems to have become thoroughly civilized, but most of them were deserted long ago; the people gave up the fight with such a persistent willfulness and wildness of nature and went away to the village, or to find more tractable soil and kindlier neighborhoods.

I do not know why it is these silent, forgotten places are so delightful to me; there is one which I always call my farm, and it was a long time after I knew it well before I could find out to whom it had once belonged. In some strange way the place has become a part of my world and to belong to my thoughts and my life.

I suppose every one can say, "I have a little kingdom where I give laws." Each of us has truly a kingdom in thought, and a certain spiritual possession. There are some gardens of mine where somebody plants the seeds and pulls the weeds for me every year without my ever taking a bit of trouble. I have trees and fields and woods and seas and houses, I own a great deal of the world to think and plan and dream about. The picture belongs most to the man who loves it best and sees entirely its meaning. We can always have just as much as we can take of things, and we can lay up as much treasure as we please in the higher world of thought that can never be spoiled or hindered by moth or rust, as lower and meaner wealth can be.

As for this farm of mine, I found it one day when I was coming through the woods on horseback trying to strike a shorter way out into the main road. I was pushing through some thick underbrush, and looking ahead I noticed a good deal of clear sky as if there were an open place just beyond, and presently I found myself on the edge of a clearing. There was a straggling orchard of old apple-trees, the grass about them was close and short like the wide door-yard of an old farmhouse and into this cleared space the little pines were growing on every side. The old pines stood a little way back watching their children march in upon their inheritance, as if they were ready to interfere and protect and defend, if any trouble came. I could see that it would not be many years, if they were left alone, before the green grass would be covered, and the old apple-trees would grow mossy and die for lack of room and sunlight in the midst of the young woods. It was a perfect acre of turf, only here and there I could already see a cushion of juniper, or a tuft of sweet fern or bayberry. I walked the horse about slowly, picking a hard little yellow apple here and there from the boughs over my head, and at last I found a cellar all grown over with grass, with not even a bit of a crumbling brick to be seen in the hollow of it. No doubt there were some underground. It was a very large cellar, twice as large as any I had ever found before in any of these deserted places, in the woods or out. And that told me at once that there had been a large house above it, an unusual house for those old days; the family was either a large one, or it had made for itself more than a merely sufficient covering and shelter, with no inch of unnecessary room. I knew I was on very high land, but the trees were so tall and close that I could not see beyond them. The wind blew over pleasantly and it was a curiously protected and hidden place, sheltered and quiet, with its one small crop of cider apples dropping ungathered to the ground, and unharvested there, except by hurrying black ants and sticky, witless little snails.

I suppose my feeling toward this place was like that about a ruin, only this seemed older than a ruin. I could not hear my horse's foot-falls, and an apple startled me when it fell with a soft thud, and I watched it roll a foot or two and then stop, as if it knew it never would have anything more to do in the world. I remembered the Enchanted Palace and the Sleeping Beauty in the Wood, and it seemed as if I were on the way to it, and this was a corner of that palace garden. The horse listened and stood still, without a bit of restlessness, and when we heard the far cry of a bird she looked round at me, as if she wished me to notice that we were not alone in the world, after all. It was strange, to be sure, that people had lived there, and had had a home where they were busy, and where the fortunes of life had found them; that they had followed out the law of existence in its succession of growth and flourishing and failure and decay, within that steadily narrowing circle of trees.

The relationship of untamed nature to what is tamed and cultivated is a very curious and subtle thing to me; I do not know if every one feels it so intensely. In the darkness of an early autumn evening I sometimes find myself whistling a queer tune that chimes in with the crickets' piping and the cries of the little creatures around me in the garden. I have no thought of the rest of the world. I wonder what I am; there is a strange self-consciousness, but I am only a part of one great existence which is called nature. The life in me is a bit of all life, and where I am happiest is where I find that which is next of kin to me, in friends, or trees, or hills, or seas, or beside a flower, when I turn back more than once to look into its face.

The world goes on year after year. We can use its forces, and shape and mould them, and perfect this thing or that, but we cannot make new forces; we only use the tools we find to carve the wood we find. There is nothing new; we discover and combine and use. Here is the wild fruit,—the same fruit at heart as that with which the gardener wins his prize. The world is the same world. You find a diamond, but the diamond was there a thousand years ago; you did not make it by finding it. We grow spiritually, until we grasp some new great truth of God; but it was always true, and waited for us until we came. What is there new and strange in the world except ourselves! Our thoughts are our own; God gives our life to us moment by moment, but He gives it to be our own.

> "Ye on your harps must lean to hear
> A secret chord that mine will bear."

As I looked about me that day I saw the difference that men had made slowly fading out of sight. It was like a dam in a river; when it is once swept away the river goes on the same as before. The old patient, sublime forces were there at work in their appointed way, but perhaps by and by, when the apple-trees are gone and the cellar is only a rough hollow in the woods, some one will again set aside these forces that have worked unhindered, and will bring this corner of the world into a new use and shape. What if we could stop or change forever the working of these powers! But Nature repossesses herself surely of what we boldly claim. The pyramids stand yet, it happens, but where are all those cities that used also to stand in old Egypt, proud and strong, and dating back beyond men's memories or traditions,—turned into sand again and dust that is like all the rest of the desert, and blows about in the wind? Yet there cannot be such a thing as life that is lost. The tree falls and decays, in the dampness of the woods, and is part of the earth under foot, but another tree is growing out of it; perhaps it is part of its own life that is springing again from the part of it that died. God must always be putting again to some use the life that is withdrawn; it must live, because it is Life. There can be no confusion to God in this wonderful world, the new birth of the immortal, the new forms of the life that is from everlasting to everlasting, or the new way in which it comes. But it is only God who can plan and order it all,—who is a father to his children, and cares for the least of us. I thought of his unbroken promises; the people who lived and died in that lonely place knew Him, and the chain of events was fitted to their thoughts and lives, for their development and education. The world was made for them, and God keeps them yet; somewhere in his kingdom they are in their places,—they are not lost; while the trees they left grow older, and the young trees spring up, and the fields they cleared are being covered over and turned into wild land again.

I HAD VISITED THIS FARM of mine many times since that first day, but since the last time I had been there I had found out, luckily, something about its last tenant. An old lady whom I knew in the village had told me that when she was a child she remembered another very old woman, who used to live here all alone, far from any neighbors, and that one afternoon she had come with her mother to see her. She remembered the house very well; it was larger and better than most houses in the region. Its owner was the last of her family; but why she lived alone, or what became of her at last, or of her money or her goods, or who were her relatives in the town, my friend did not know. She was a thrifty, well-to-do old soul, a famous weaver and spinner, and she used to come to the meeting-house at the Old Fields every Sunday, and sit by herself in a square pew. Since I knew this, the last owner of my farm has become very real to me, and I thought of her that day a great deal, and could almost see her as she sat alone on her door-step in the twilight of a summer evening, when the thrushes were calling in the woods; or going down the hills to church, dressed in quaint fashion, with a little sadness in her face as she thought of her lost companions and how she did not use to go to church alone. And I pictured her funeral to myself, and watched her carried away at last by the narrow road that wound among the trees; and there was nobody left in the house after the neighbors from the nearest farms had put it to rights, and had looked over her treasures to their hearts' content. She must have been a fearless woman, and one could not stay in such a place as this, year in and year out, through the long days of summer and the long nights of winter, unless she found herself good company.

I do not think I could find a worse avenue than that which leads to my farm, I think sometimes there must have been an easier way out which I have yet failed to discover, but it has its advantages, for the trees are beautiful and stand close together, and I do not know such green brakes anywhere as those which grow in the shadiest places. I came into a well-trodden track after a while, which led into a small granite quarry, and then I could go faster, and at last I reached a pasture wall which was quickly left behind and I was only a little way from the main road. There were a few young cattle scattered about in the pasture, and some of them which were lying down got up in a hurry and stared at me suspiciously as I rode along. It was very uneven ground, and I passed some stiff, straight mullein stalks which stood apart together in a hollow as if they wished to be alone. They always remind me of the rigid old Scotch Covenanters, who used to gather themselves together in companies, against the law, to worship God in some secret hollow of the bleak hill-side. Even the smallest and youngest of the mulleins was a Covenanter at heart; they had all put by their yellow flowers, and they will stand there, gray and unbending, through the fall rains and winter snows, to keep their places and praise God in their own fashion, and they take great credit to themselves for doing it, I have no doubt, and think it is far better to be a stern and respectable mullein than a straying, idle clematis, that clings and wanders, and cannot bear wet weather. I saw members of the congregation scattered through the pasture and felt like telling them to hurry, for the long sermon had already begun! But one ancient worthy, very late on his way to the meeting, happened to stand in our way, and Sheila bit his dry head off, which was a great pity.

After I was once on the high road it was not long before I found myself in another part of the town altogether. It is great fun to ride about the country; one rouses a great deal of interest; there seems to be something exciting in the sight of a girl on horseback, and people who pass you in wagons turn to look after you, though they never would take the trouble if you were only walking. The country horses shy if you go by them fast, and sometimes you stop to apologize. The boys will leave anything to come and throw a stone at your horse. I think Sheila would like to bite a boy, though sometimes she goes through her best paces when she hears them hooting, as if she thought they were admiring her, which I never allow myself to doubt. It is considered a much greater compliment if you make a call on horseback than if you came afoot, but carriage people are nothing in the country to what they are in the city.

I was on a good road and Sheila was trotting steadily, and I did not look at the western sky behind me until I suddenly noticed that the air had grown colder and the sun had been for a long time behind a cloud; then I found there was going to be a shower, in a very little while, too. I was in a thinly settled part of the town, and at first I could not think of any shelter, until I remembered that not very far distant there was an old house, with a long, sloping roof, which had formerly been the parsonage of the north parish; there had once been a church near by, to which most of the people came who lived in this upper part of the town. It had been for many years the house of an old minister, of widespread fame in his day; I had always heard of him from the elderly people, and I had often thought I should like to go into his house, and had looked at it with great interest, but until within a year or two there had been people living there. I had even listened with pleasure to a story of its being haunted, and this was a capital chance to take a look at the old place, so I hurried toward it.

As I went in at the broken gate it seemed to me as if the house might have been shut up and left to itself fifty years before, when the minister died, so soon the grass grows up after men's footsteps have worn it down, and the traces are lost of the daily touch and care of their hands. The home lot was evidently part of a pasture, and the sheep had nibbled close to the door-step, while tags of their long, spring wool, washed clean by summer rains, were caught in the rose-bushes near by.

It had been a very good house in its day, and had a dignity of its own, holding its gray head high, as if it knew itself to be not merely a farm-house, but a Parsonage. The roof looked as if the next winter's weight of snow might break it in, and the window panes had been loosened so much in their shaking frames that many of them had fallen out on the north side of the house, and were lying on the long grass underneath, blurred and thin but still unbroken. That was the last letter of the house's death warrant, for now the rain could get in, and the crumbling timbers must loose their hold of each other quickly. I had found a dry corner of the old shed for the horse and left her there, looking most ruefully over her shoulder after me as I hurried away, for the rain had already begun to spatter down in earnest. I was not sorry when I found that somebody had broken a pane of glass in the sidelight of the front door, near the latch, and I was very pleased when I found that by reaching through I could unfasten a great bolt and let myself in, as perhaps some tramp in search of shelter had done before me. However, I gave the blackened brass knocker a ceremonious rap or two, and I could have told by the sound of it, if in no other way, that there was nobody at home. I looked up to see a robin's nest on the cornice overhead, and I had to push away the lilacs and a withered hop vine which were both trying to cover up the door.

It gives one a strange feeling, I think, to go into an empty house so old as this. It was so still there that the noise my footsteps made startled me, and the floor creaked and cracked as if some one followed me about. There was hardly a straw left or a bit of string or paper, but the rooms were much worn, the bricks in the fire-places were burnt out, rough and crumbling, and the doors were all worn smooth and round at the edges. The best rooms were wainscoted, but up-stairs there was a long, unfinished room with a little square window at each end, under the sloping roof, and as I listened there to the rain I remembered that I had once heard an old man say wistfully, that he had slept in just such a "linter" chamber as this when he was a boy, and that he never could sleep anywhere now so well as he used there while the rain fell on the roof just over his bed.

Down-stairs I found a room which I knew must have been the study. It was handsomely wainscoted, and the finish of it was even better than that of the parlor. It must have been a most comfortable place, and I fear the old parson was luxurious in his tastes and less ascetic, perhaps, than the more puritanical members of his congregation approved.

There was a great fire-place with a broad hearth-stone, where I think he may have made a mug of flip sometimes, and there were several curious, narrow, little cupboards built into the wall at either side, and over the fire-place itself two doors opened and there were shelves inside, broader at the top as the chimney sloped back. I saw some writing on one of these doors and went nearer to read it. There was a date at the top, some time in 1802, and his reverence had had a good quill pen and ink which bravely stood the test of time; he must have been a tall man to have written so high. I thought it might be some record of a great storm or other notable event in his house or parish, but I was amused to find that he had written there on the unpainted wood some valuable recipes for the medical treatment of horses. "It is Useful for a Sprain—and For a Cough, Take of Elecampane"—and so on. I hope he was not a hunting parson, but one could hardly expect to find any reference to the early fathers or federal head-ship in Adam on the cupboard door. I thought of the stories I had heard of the old minister and felt very well acquainted with him, though his books had been taken down and his fire was out, and he himself had gone away. I was glad to think what a good, faithful man he was, who spoke comfortable words to his people and lived pleasantly with them in this quiet country place so many years. There are old people living who have told me that nobody preaches nowadays as he used to preach, and that he used to lift his hat to everybody; that he liked a good dinner, and always was kind to the poor.

I thought as I stood in the study, how many times he must have looked out of the small-paned western windows across the fields, and how in his later days he must have had a treasure of memories of the people who had gone out of that room the better for his advice and consolation, the people whom he had helped and taught and ruled. I could not imagine that he ever angrily took his parishioners to task for their errors of doctrine; indeed, it was not of his active youth and middle age that I thought at all, but of the last of his life, when he sat here in the sunshine of a winter afternoon, and the fire flickered and snapped on the hearth, and he sat before it in his arm-chair with a brown old book which he laid on his knee while he thought and dozed, and roused himself presently to greet somebody who came in, a little awed at first, to talk with him. It was a great thing to be a country minister in those old days, and to be such a minister as he was; truly the priest and ruler of his people. The times have changed, and the temporal power certainly is taken away. The divine right of ministers is almost as little believed in as that of kings, by many people; it is not possible for the influence to be so great, the office and the man are both looked at with less reverence. It is a pity that it should be so, but the conservative people who like old-fashioned ways cannot tell where to place all the blame. And it is very odd to think that these iconoclastic and unpleasant new times of ours will, a little later, be called old times, and that the children, when they are elderly people, will sigh to have them back again.

I was very glad to see the old house, and I told myself a great many stories there, as one cannot help doing in such a place. There must have been so many things happen in so many long lives which were lived there; people have come into the world and gone out of it again from those square rooms with their little windows, and I believe if there are ghosts who walk about in daylight I was only half deaf to their voices, and heard much of what they tried to tell me that day. The rooms which had looked empty at first were filled again with the old clergymen, who met together with important looks and complacent dignity, and eager talk about some minor point in theology that is yet unsettled; the awkward, smiling couples, who came to be married; the mistress of the house, who must have been a stately person in her day; the little children who, under all their shyness, remembered the sugar-plums in the old parson's pockets,—all these, and even the tall cane that must have stood in the entry, were visible to my mind's eye. And I even heard a sermon from the old preacher who died so long ago, on the beauty of a life well spent.

The rain fell steadily and there was no prospect of its stopping, though I could see that the clouds were thinner and that it was only a shower. In the kitchen I found an old chair which I pulled into the study, which seemed more cheerful than the rest of the house, and then I remembered that there were some bits of board in the kitchen also, and the thought struck me that it would be good fun to make a fire in the old fire-place. Everything seemed right about the chimney. I even went up into the garret to look at it there, for I had no wish to set the parsonage on fire, and I brought down a pile of old corn husks for kindlings which I found on the garret floor. I built my fire carefully, with two bricks for andirons, and when I lit it it blazed up gayly, I poked it and it crackled, and though I was very well contented there alone I wished for some friend to keep me company, it was selfish to have so much pleasure with no one to share it. The rain came faster than ever against the windows, and the room would have been dark if it had not been for my fire, which threw out a magnificent yellow light over the old brown wood-work. I leaned back and watched the dry sticks fall apart in red coals and thought I might have to spend the night there, for if it were a storm and not a shower I was several miles from home, and a late October rain is not like a warm one in June to fall upon one's shoulders. I could hear the house leaking when it rained less heavily, and the soot dropped down the chimney and great drops of water came down, too, and spluttered in the fire. I thought what a merry thing it would be if a party of young people ever had to take refuge there, and I could almost see their faces and hear them laugh, though until that minute they had been strangers to me.

But the shower was over at last, and my fire was out, and the last pale shining of the sun came into the windows, and I looked out to see the distant fields and woods all clear again in the late afternoon light. I must hurry to get home before dark, so I raked up the ashes and left my chair beside the fire-place, and shut and fastened the front door after me, and went out to see what had become of my horse, shaking the dust and cobwebs off my dress as I crossed the wet grass to the shed. The rain had come through the broken roof and poor Sheila looked anxious and hungry as if she thought I might have meant to leave her there till morning in that dismal place. I offered her my apologies, but she made even a shorter turn than usual when I had mounted, and we scurried off down the road, spattering ourselves as we went. I hope the ghosts who live in the parsonage watched me with friendly eyes, and I looked back myself, to see a thin blue whiff of smoke still coming up from the great chimney. I wondered who it was that had made the first fire there,—but I think I shall have made the last.

Tom's Husband

I shall not dwell long upon the circumstances that led to the marriage of my hero and heroine; though their courtship was, to them, the only one that has ever noticeably approached the ideal, it had many aspects in which it was entirely commonplace in other people's eyes. While the world in general smiles at lovers with kindly approval and sympathy, it refuses to be aware of the unprecedented delight which is amazing to the lovers themselves.

But, as has been true in many other cases, when they were at last married, the most ideal of situations was found to have been changed to the most practical. Instead of having shared their original duties, and, as school-boys would say, going halves, they discovered that the cares of life had been doubled. This led to some distressing moments for both our friends; they understood suddenly that instead of dwelling in heaven they were still upon earth, and had made themselves slaves to new laws and limitations. Instead of being freer and happier than ever before, they had assumed new responsibilities; they had established a new household, and must fulfill in some way or another the obligations of it. They looked back with affection to their engagement; they had been longing to have each other to themselves, apart from the world, but it seemed that they never felt so keenly that they were still units in modern society. Since Adam and Eve were in Paradise, before the devil joined them, nobody has had a chance to imitate that unlucky couple. In some respects they told the truth when, twenty times a day, they said that life had never been so pleasant before; but there were mental reservations on either side which might have subjected them to the accusation of lying. Somehow, there was a little feeling of disappointment, and they caught themselves wondering—though they would have died sooner than confess it—whether they were quite so happy as they had expected. The truth was, they were much happier than people usually are, for they had an uncommon capacity for enjoyment. For a little while they were like a sail-boat that is beating and has to drift a few minutes before it can catch the wind and start off on the other tack. And they had the same feeling, too, that any one is likely to have who has been long pursuing some object of his ambition or desire. Whether it is a coin, or a picture, or a stray volume of some old edition of Shakespeare, or whether it is an office under government or a lover, when fairly in one's grasp there is a loss of the eagerness that was felt in pursuit. Satisfaction, even after one has dined well, is not so interesting and eager a feeling as hunger.

My hero and heroine were reasonably well established to begin with: they each had some money, though Mr. Wilson had most. His father had at one time been a rich man, but with the decline, a few years before, of manufacturing interests, he had become, mostly through the fault of others, somewhat involved; and at the time of his death his affairs were in such a condition that it was still a question whether a very large sum or a moderately large one would represent his estate. Mrs. Wilson, Tom's step-mother, was somewhat of an invalid; she suffered severely at times with asthma, but she was almost entirely relieved by living in another part of the country. While her husband lived, she had accepted her illness as inevitable, and rarely left home; but during the last few years she had lived in Philadelphia with her own people, making short and wheezing visits only from time to time, and had not undergone a voluntary period of suffering since the occasion of Tom's marriage, which she had entirely approved. She had a sufficient property of her own, and she and Tom were independent of each other in that way. Her only other stepchild was a daughter, who had married a navy officer, and had at this time gone out to spend three years (or less) with her husband, who had been ordered to Japan.

It is not unfrequently noticed that in many marriages one of the persons who choose each other as partners for life is said to have thrown himself or herself away, and the relatives and friends look on with dismal forebodings and ill-concealed submission. In this case it was the wife who might have done so much better, according to public opinion. She did not think so herself, luckily, either before marriage or afterward, and I do not think it occurred to her to picture to herself the sort of career which would have been her alternative. She had been an only child, and had usually taken her own way. Some one once said that it was a great pity that she had not been obliged to work for her living, for she had inherited a most uncommon business talent, and, without being disreputably keen at a bargain, her insight into the practical working of affairs was very clear and far-reaching. Her father, who had also been a manufacturer, like Tom's, had often said it had been a mistake that she was a girl instead of a boy. Such executive ability as hers is often wasted in the more contracted sphere of women, and is apt to be more a disadvantage than a help. She was too independent and self-reliant for a wife; it would seem at first thought that she needed a wife herself more than she did a husband. Most men like best the women whose natures cling and appeal to theirs for protection. But Tom Wilson, while he did not wish to be protected himself, liked these very qualities in his wife which would have displeased some other men; to tell the truth, he was very much in love with his wife just as she was. He was a successful collector of almost everything but money, and during a great part of his life he had been an invalid, and he had grown, as he laughingly confessed, very old-womanish. He had been badly lamed, when a boy, by being caught in some machinery in his father's mill, near which he was idling one afternoon, and though he had almost entirely outgrown the effect of his injury, it had not been until after many years. He had been in college, but his eyes had given out there, and he had been obliged to leave in the middle of his junior year, though he had kept up a pleasant intercourse with the members of his class, with whom he had been a great favorite. He was a good deal of an idler in the world. I do not think his ambition, except in the case of securing Mary Dunn for his wife, had ever been distinct; he seemed to make the most he could of each day as it came, without making all his days' works tend toward some grand result, and go toward the upbuilding of some grand plan and purpose. He consequently gave no promise of being either distinguished or great. When his eyes would allow, he was an indefatigable reader; and although he would have said that he read only for amusement, yet he amused himself with books that were well worth the time he spent over them.

The house where he lived nominally belonged to his step-mother, but she had taken for granted that Tom would bring his wife home to it, and assured him that it should be to all intents and purposes his. Tom was deeply attached to the old place, which was altogether the pleasantest in town. He had kept bachelor's hall there most of the time since his father's death, and he had taken great pleasure, before his marriage, in refitting it to some extent, though it was already comfortable and furnished in remarkably good taste. People said of him that if it had not been for his illnesses, and if he had been a poor boy, he probably would have made something of himself. As it was, he was not very well known by the towns-people, being somewhat reserved, and not taking much interest in their every-day subjects of conversation. Nobody liked him so well as they liked his wife, yet there was no reason why he should be disliked enough to have much said about him.

After our friends had been married for some time, and had outlived the first strangeness of the new order of things, and had done their duty to their neighbors with so much apparent willingness and generosity that even Tom himself was liked a great deal better than he ever had been before, they were sitting together one stormy evening in the library, before the fire. Mrs. Wilson had been reading Tom the letters which had come to him by the night's mail. There was a long one from his sister in Nagasaki, which had been written with a good deal of ill-disguised reproach. She complained of the smallness of the income of her share in her father's estate, and said that she had been assured by American friends that the smaller mills were starting up everywhere, and beginning to do well again. Since so much of their money was invested in the factory, she had been surprised and sorry to find by Tom's last letters that he had seemed to have no idea of putting in a proper person as superintendent, and going to work again. Four per cent. on her other property, which she had been told she must soon expect instead of eight, would make a great difference to her. A navy captain in a foreign port was obliged to entertain a great deal, and Tom must know that it cost them much more to live than it did him, and ought to think of their interests. She hoped he would talk over what was best to be done with their mother (who had been made executor, with Tom, of his father's will).

Tom laughed a little, but looked disturbed. His wife had said something to the same effect, and his mother had spoken once or twice in her letters of the prospect of starting the mill again. He was not a bit of a business man, and he did not feel certain, with the theories which he had arrived at of the state of the country, that it was safe yet to spend the money which would have to be spent in putting the mill in order. "They think that the minute it is going again we shall be making money hand over hand, just as father did when we were children," he said. "It is going to cost us no end of money before we can make anything. Before father died he meant to put in a good deal of new machinery, I remember. I don't know anything about the business myself, and I would have sold out long ago if I had had an offer that came anywhere near the value. The larger mills are the only ones that are good for anything now, and we should have to bring a crowd of French Canadians here; the day is past for the people who live in this part of the country to go into the factory again. Even the Irish all go West when they come into the country, and don't come to places like this any more."

"But there are a good many of the old work-people down in the village," said Mrs. Wilson. "Jack Towne asked me the other day if you weren't going to start up in the spring."

Tom moved uneasily in his chair. "I'll put you in for superintendent, if you like," he said, half angrily, whereupon Mary threw the newspaper at him; but by the time he had thrown it back he was in good humor again.

"Do you know, Tom," she said, with amazing seriousness, "that I believe I should like nothing in the world so much as to be the head of a large business? I hate keeping house,—I always did; and I never did so much of it in all my life put together as I have since I have been married. I suppose it isn't womanly to say so, but if I could escape from the whole thing I believe I should be perfectly happy. If you get rich when the mill is going again, I shall beg for a housekeeper, and shirk everything. I give you fair warning. I don't believe I keep this house half so well as you did before I came here."

Tom's eyes twinkled. "I am going to have that glory,—I don't think you do, Polly; but you can't say that I have not been forbearing. I certainly have not told you more than twice how we used to have things cooked. I'm not going to be your kitchen-colonel."

"Of course it seemed the proper thing to do," said his wife, meditatively; "but I think we should have been even happier than we have if I had been spared it. I have had some days of wretchedness that I shudder to think of. I never know what to have for breakfast; and I ought not to say it, but I don't mind the sight of dust. I look upon housekeeping as my life's great discipline;" and at this pathetic confession they both laughed heartily.

"I've a great mind to take it off your hands," said Tom. "I always rather liked it, to tell the truth, and I ought to be a better housekeeper,—I have been at it for five years; though housekeeping for one is different from what it is for two, and one of them a woman. You see you have brought a different element into my family. Luckily, the servants are pretty well drilled. I do think you upset them a good deal at first!"

Mary Wilson smiled as if she only half heard what he was saying. She drummed with her foot on the floor and looked intently at the fire, and presently gave it a vigorous poking. "Well?" said Tom, after he had waited patiently as long as he could.

"Tom! I'm going to propose something to you. I wish you would really do as you said, and take all the home affairs under your care, and let me start the mill. I am certain I could manage it. Of course I should get people who understood the thing to teach me. I believe I was made for it; I should like it above all things. And this is what I will do: I will bear the cost of starting it, myself,—I think I have money enough, or can get it; and if I have not put affairs in the right trim at the end of a year I will stop, and you may make some other arrangement. If I have, you and your mother and sister can pay me back."

"So I am going to be the wife, and you the husband," said Tom, a little indignantly; "at least, that is what people will say. It's a regular Darby and Joan affair, and you think you can do more work in a day than I can do in three. Do you know that you must go to town to buy cotton? And do you know there are a thousand things about it that you don't know?"

"And never will?" said Mary, with perfect good humor. "Why, Tom, I can learn as well as you, and a good deal better, for I like business, and you don't. You forget that I was always father's right-hand man after I was a dozen years old, and that you have let me invest my money and some of your own, and I haven't made a blunder yet."

Tom thought that his wife had never looked so handsome or so happy. "I don't care, I should rather like the fun of knowing what people will say. It is a new departure, at any rate. Women think they can do everything better than men in these days, but I'm the first man, apparently, who has wished he were a woman."

"Of course people will laugh," said Mary, "but they will say that it's just like me, and think I am fortunate to have married a man who will let me do as I choose. I don't see why it isn't sensible: you will be living exactly as you were before you married, as to home affairs; and since it was a good thing for you to know something about housekeeping then, I can't imagine why you shouldn't go on with it now, since it makes me miserable, and I am wasting a fine business talent while I do it. What do we care for people's talking about it?"

"It seems to me that it is something like women's smoking: it isn't wicked, but it isn't the custom of the country. And I don't like the idea of your going among business men. Of course I should be above going with you, and having people think I must be an idiot; they would say that you married a manufacturing interest, and I was thrown in. I can foresee that my pride is going to be humbled to the dust in every way," Tom declared in mournful tones, and began to shake with laughter. "It is one of your lovely castles in the air, dear Polly, but an old brick mill needs a better foundation than the clouds. No, I'll look around, and get an honest, experienced man for agent. I suppose it's the best thing we can do, for the machinery ought not to lie still any longer; but I mean to sell the factory as soon as I can. I devoutly wish it would take fire, for the insurance would be the best price we are likely to get. That is a famous letter from Alice! I am afraid the captain has been growling over his pay, or they have been giving too many little dinners on board ship. If we were rid of the mill, you and I might go out there this winter. It would be capital fun."

Mary smiled again in an absent-minded way. Tom had an uneasy feeling that he had not heard the end of it yet, but nothing more was said for a day or two. When Mrs. Tom Wilson announced, with no apparent thought of being contradicted, that she had entirely made up her mind, and she meant to see those men who had been overseers of the different departments, who still lived in the village, and have the mill put in order at once, Tom looked disturbed, but made no opposition; and soon after breakfast his wife formally presented him with a handful of keys, and told him there was some lamb in the house for dinner; and presently he heard the wheels of her little phaeton rattling off down the road. I should be untruthful if I tried to persuade any one that he was not provoked; he thought she would at least have waited for his formal permission, and at first he meant to take another horse, and chase her, and bring her back in disgrace, and put a stop to the whole thing. But something assured him that she knew what she was about, and he determined to let her have her own way. If she failed, it might do no harm, and this was the only ungallant thought he gave her. He was sure that she would do nothing unladylike, or be unmindful of his dignity; and he believed it would be looked upon as one of her odd, independent freaks, which always had won respect in the end, however much they had been laughed at in the beginning. "Susan," said he, as that estimable person went by the door with the dust-pan, "you may tell Catherine to come to me for orders about the house, and you may do so yourself. I am going to take charge again, as I did before I was married. It is no trouble to me, and Mrs. Wilson dislikes it. Besides, she is going into business, and will have a great deal else to think of."

"Yes, sir; very well, sir," said Susan, who was suddenly moved to ask so many questions that she was utterly silent. But her master looked very happy; there was evidently no disapproval of his wife; and she went on up the stairs, and began to sweep them down, knocking the dust-brush about excitedly, as if she were trying to kill a descending colony of insects.

Tom went out to the stable and mounted his horse, which had been waiting for him to take his customary after-breakfast ride to the post-office, and he galloped down the road in quest of the phaeton. He saw Mary talking with Jack Towne, who had been an overseer and a valued workman of his father's. He was looking much surprised and pleased.

"I wasn't caring so much about getting work, myself," he explained; "I've got what will carry me and my wife through; but it'll be better for the young folks about here to work near home. My nephews are wanting something to do; they were going to Lynn next week. I don't say but I should like to be to work in the old place again. I've sort of missed it, since we shut down."

"I'm sorry I was so long in overtaking you," said Tom, politely, to his wife. "Well, Jack, did Mrs. Wilson tell you she's going to start the mill? You must give her all the help you can."

"'Deed I will," said Mr. Towne, gallantly, without a bit of astonishment.

"I don't know much about the business yet," said Mrs. Wilson, who had been a little overcome at Jack Towne's lingo of the different rooms and machinery, and who felt an overpowering sense of having a great deal before her in the next few weeks. "By the time the mill is ready, I will be ready, too," she said, taking heart a little; and Tom, who was quick to understand her moods, could not help laughing, as he rode alongside. "We want a new barrel of flour, Tom, dear," she said, by way of punishment for his untimely mirth.

If she lost courage in the long delay, or was disheartened at the steady call for funds, she made no sign; and after a while the mill started up, and her cares were lightened, so that she told Tom that before next pay day she would like to go to Boston for a few days, and go to the theatre, and have a frolic and a rest. She really looked pale and thin, and she said she never worked so hard in all her life; but nobody knew how happy she was, and she was so glad she had married Tom, for some men would have laughed at it.

"I laughed at it," said Tom, meekly. "All is, if I don't cry by and by, because I am a beggar, I shall be lucky." But Mary looked fearlessly serene, and said that there was no danger at present.

It would have been ridiculous to expect a dividend the first year, though the Nagasaki people were pacified with difficulty. All the business letters came to Tom's address, and everybody who was not directly concerned thought that he was the motive power of the reawakened enterprise. Sometimes business people came to the mill, and were amazed at having to confer with Mrs. Wilson, but they soon had to respect her talents and her success. She was helped by the old clerk, who had been promptly recalled and reinstated, and she certainly did capitally well. She was laughed at, as she had expected to be, and people said they should think Tom would be ashamed of himself; but it soon appeared that he was not to blame, and what reproach was offered was on the score of his wife's oddity. There was nothing about the mill that she did not understand before very long, and at the end of the second year she declared a small dividend with great pride and triumph. And she was congratulated on her success, and every one thought of her project in a different way from the way they had thought of it in the beginning. She had singularly good fortune: at the end of the third year she was making money for herself and her friends faster than most people were, and approving letters began to come from Nagasaki. The Ashtons had been ordered to stay in that region, and it was evident that they were continually being obliged to entertain more instead of less. Their children were growing fast, too, and constantly becoming more expensive. The captain and his wife had already begun to congratulate themselves secretly that their two sons would in all probability come into possession, one day, of their uncle Tom's handsome property.

For a good while Tom enjoyed life, and went on his quiet way serenely. He was anxious at first, for he thought that Mary was going to make ducks and drakes of his money and her own. And then he did not exactly like the looks of the thing, either; he feared that his wife was growing successful as a business person at the risk of losing her womanliness. But as time went on, and he found there was no fear of that, he accepted the situation philosophically. He gave up his collection of engravings, having become more interested in one of coins and medals, which took up most of his leisure time. He often went to the city in pursuit of such treasures, and gained much renown in certain quarters as a numismatologist of great skill and experience. But at last his house (which had almost kept itself, and had given him little to do beside ordering the dinners, while faithful old Catherine and her niece Susan were his aids) suddenly became a great care to him. Catherine, who had been the main-stay of the family for many years, died after a short illness, and Susan must needs choose that time, of all others, for being married to one of the second hands in the mill. There followed a long and dismal season of experimenting, and for a time there was a procession of incapable creatures going in at one kitchen door and out of the other. His wife would not have liked to say so, but it seemed to her that Tom was growing fussy about the house affairs, and took more notice of those minor details than he used. She wished more than once, when she was tired, that he would not talk so much about the housekeeping; he seemed sometimes to have no other thought.

In the early days of Mrs. Wilson's business life, she had made it a rule to consult her husband on every subject of importance; but it had speedily proved to be a formality. Tom tried manfully to show a deep interest which he did not feel, and his wife gave up, little by little, telling him much about her affairs. She said that she liked to drop business when she came home in the evening; and at last she fell into the habit of taking a nap on the library sofa, while Tom, who could not use his eyes much by lamp-light, sat smoking or in utter idleness before the fire. When they were first married his wife had made it a rule that she should always read him the evening papers, and afterward they had always gone on with some book of history or philosophy, in which they were both interested. These evenings of their early married life had been charming to both of them, and from time to time one would say to the other that they ought to take up again the habit of reading together. Mary was so unaffectedly tired in the evening that Tom never liked to propose a walk; for, though he was not a man of peculiarly social nature, he had always been accustomed to pay an occasional evening visit to his neighbors in the village. And though he had little interest in the business world, and still less knowledge of it, after a while he wished that his wife would have more to say about what she was planning and doing, or how things were getting on. He thought that her chief aid, old Mr. Jackson, was far more in her thoughts than he. She was forever quoting Jackson's opinions. He did not like to find that she took it for granted that he was not interested in the welfare of his own property; it made him feel like a sort of pensioner and dependent, though, when they had guests at the house, which was by no means seldom, there was nothing in her manner that would imply that she thought herself in any way the head of the family. It was hard work to find fault with his wife in any way, though, to give him his due, he rarely tried.

But, this being a wholly unnatural state of things, the reader must expect to hear of its change at last, and the first blow from the enemy was dealt by an old woman, who lived near by, and who called to Tom one morning, as he was driving down to the village in a great hurry (to post a letter, which ordered his agent to secure a long-wished-for ancient copper coin, at any price), to ask him if they had made yeast that week, and if she could borrow a cupful, as her own had met with some misfortune. Tom was instantly in a rage, and he mentally condemned her to some undeserved fate, but told her aloud to go and see the cook. This slight delay, besides being killing to his dignity, caused him to lose the mail, and in the end his much-desired copper coin. It was a hard day for him, altogether; it was Wednesday, and the first days of the week having been stormy the washing was very late. And Mary came home to dinner provokingly good-natured. She had met an old school-mate and her husband driving home from the mountains, and had first taken them over her factory, to their great amusement and delight, and then had brought them home to dinner. Tom greeted them cordially, and manifested his usual graceful hospitality; but the minute he saw his wife alone he said in a plaintive tone of rebuke, "I should think you might have remembered that the servants are unusually busy to-day. I do wish you would take a little interest in things at home. The women have been washing, and I'm sure I don't know what sort of a dinner we can give your friends. I wish you had thought to bring home some steak. I have been busy myself, and couldn't go down to the village. I thought we would only have a lunch."

Mary was hungry, but she said nothing, except that it would be all right,—she didn't mind; and perhaps they could have some canned soup.

She often went to town to buy or look at cotton, or to see some improvement in machinery, and she brought home beautiful bits of furniture and new pictures for the house, and showed a touching thoughtfulness in remembering Tom's fancies; but somehow he had an uneasy suspicion that she could get along pretty well without him when it came to the deeper wishes and hopes of her life, and that her most important concerns were all matters in which he had no share. He seemed to himself to have merged his life in his wife's; he lost his interest in things outside the house and grounds; he felt himself fast growing rusty and behind the times, and to have somehow missed a good deal in life; he had a suspicion that he was a failure. One day the thought rushed over him that his had been almost exactly the experience of most women, and he wondered if it really was any more disappointing and ignominious to him than it was to women themselves. "Some of them may be contented with it," he said to himself, soberly. "People think women are designed for such careers by nature, but I don't know why I ever made such a fool of myself."

Having once seen his situation in life from such a standpoint, he felt it day by day to be more degrading, and he wondered what he should do about it; and once, drawn by a new, strange sympathy, he went to the little family burying ground. It was one of the mild, dim days that come sometimes in early November, when the pale sunlight is like the pathetic smile of a sad face, and he sat for a long time on the limp, frost-bitten grass beside his mother's grave.

But when he went home in the twilight his step-mother, who just then was making them a little visit, mentioned that she had been looking through some boxes of hers that had been packed long before and stowed away in the garret. "Everything looks very nice up there," she said, in her wheezing voice (which, worse than usual that day, always made him nervous); and added, without any intentional slight to his feelings, "I do think you have always been a most excellent housekeeper."

"I'm tired of such nonsense!" he exclaimed, with surprising indignation. "Mary, I wish you to arrange your affairs so that you can leave them for six months at least. I am going to spend this winter in Europe."

"Why, Tom, dear!" said his wife, appealingly. "I couldn't leave my business any way in the"—

But she caught sight of a look on his usually placid countenance that was something more than decision, and refrained from saying anything more.

And three weeks from that day they sailed.

SARAH ORNE JEWETT

Miss Debby's Neighbors

There is a class of elderly New England women which is fast dying out:—those good souls who have sprung from a soil full of the true New England instincts; who were used to the old-fashioned ways, and whose minds were stored with quaint country lore and tradition. The fashions of the newer generations do not reach them; they are quite unconscious of the western spirit and enterprise, and belong to the old days, and to a fast-disappearing order of things.

But a shrewder person does not exist than the spokeswoman of the following reminiscences, whose simple history can be quickly told, since she spent her early life on a lonely farm, leaving it only once for any length of time,—one winter when she learned her trade of tailoress. She afterward sewed for her neighbors, and enjoyed a famous reputation for her skill; but year by year, as she grew older, there was less to do, and at last, to use her own expression, "Everybody got into the way of buying cheap, ready-made-up clothes, just to save 'em a little trouble," and she found herself out of business, or nearly so. After her mother's death, and that of her favorite younger brother Jonas, she left the farm and came to a little house in the village, where she lived most comfortably the rest of her life, having a small property which she used most sensibly. She was always ready to render any special service with her needle, and was a most welcome guest in any household, and a most efficient helper. To be in the same room with her for a while was sure to be profitable, and as she grew older she was delighted to recall the people and events of her earlier life, always filling her descriptions with wise reflections and much quaint humor. She always insisted, not without truth, that the railroads were making everybody look and act of a piece, and that the young folks were more alike than people of her own day. It is impossible to give the delightfulness of her talk in any written words, as well as many of its peculiarities, for her way of going round Robin Hood's barn between the beginning of her story and its end can hardly be followed at all, and certainly not in her own dear loitering footsteps.

On an idle day her most devoted listener thought there was nothing better worth doing than to watch this good soul at work. A book was held open for the looks of the thing, but presently it was allowed to flutter its leaves and close, for Miss Debby began without any apparent provocation:—

"They may say whatever they have a mind to, but they can't persuade me that there's no such thing as special providences," and she twitched her strong linen thread so angrily through the carpet she was sewing, that it snapped and the big needle flew into the air. It had to be found before any further remarks could be made, and the listener also knelt down to search for it. After a while it was discovered clinging to Miss Debby's own dress, and after reharnessing it she went to work again at her long seam. It was always significant of a succession of Miss Debby's opinions when she quoted and berated certain imaginary persons whom she designated as "They," who stood for the opposite side of the question, and who merited usually her deepest scorn and fullest antagonism. Her remarks to these offending parties were always prefaced with "I tell 'em," and to the listener's mind "they" always stood rebuked, but not convinced, in spiritual form it may be, but most intense reality; a little group as solemn as Miss Debby herself. Once the listener ventured to ask who "they" were, in her early childhood, but she was only answered by a frown. Miss Debby knew as well as any one the difference between figurative language and a lie. Sometimes they said what was right and proper, and were treated accordingly; but very seldom, and on this occasion it seemed that they had ventured to trifle with sacred things.

"I suppose you're too young to remember John Ashby's grandmother? A good woman she was, and she had a dreadful time with her family. They never could keep the peace, and there was always as many as two of them who didn't speak with each other. It seems to come down from generation to generation like a—*curse!*" And Miss Debby spoke the last word as if she had meant it partly for her thread, which had again knotted and caught, and she snatched the offered scissors without a word, but said peaceably, after a minute or two, that the thread wasn't what it used to be. The next needleful proved more successful, and the listener asked if the Ashbys were getting on comfortably at present.

"They always behave as if they thought they needed nothing," was the response. "Not that I mean that they are any ways contented, but they never will give in that other folks holds a candle to 'em. There's one kind of pride that I do hate,—when folks is satisfied with their selves and don't see no need of improvement. I believe in self-respect, but I believe in respecting other folks's rights as much as your own; but it takes an Ashby to ride right over you. I tell 'em it's the spirit of the tyrants of old, and it's the kind of pride that goes before a fall. John Ashby's grandmother was a clever little woman as ever stepped. She came from over Hardwick way, and I think she kep' 'em kind of decent-behaved as long as she was round; but she got wore out a doin' of it, an' went down to her grave in a quick consumption. My mother set up with her the night she died. It was in May, towards the latter part, and an awful rainy night. It was the storm that always comes in apple-blossom time. I remember well that mother come crying home in the morning and told us Mis' Ashby was dead. She brought Marilly with her, that was about my own age, and was taken away within six months afterwards. She pined herself to death for her mother, and when she caught the scarlet fever she went as quick as cherry-bloom when it's just ready to fall and a wind strikes it. She wa'n't like the rest of 'em. She took after her mother's folks altogether.

"You know our farm was right next to theirs,—the one Asa Hopper owns now, but he's let it all run out,—and so, as we lived some ways from the stores, we had to be neighborly, for we depended on each other for a good many things. Families in lonesome places get out of one supply and another, and have to borrow until they get a chance to send to the village; or sometimes in a busy season some of the folks would have to leave work and be gone half a day. Land, you don't know nothing about old times, and the life that used to go on about here. You can't step into a house anywheres now that there ain't the county map and they don't fetch out the photograph book; and in every district you'll find all the folks has got the same chromo picture hung up, and all sorts of luxuries and makeshifts o' splendor that would have made the folks I was fetched up by stare their eyes out o' their heads. It was all we could do to keep along then; and if anybody was called rich, it was only because he had a great sight of land,—and then it was drudge, drudge the harder to pay the taxes. There was hardly any ready money; and I recollect well that old Tommy Simms was reputed wealthy, and it was told over fifty times a year that he'd got a solid four thousand dollars in the bank. He strutted round like a turkey-cock, and thought he ought to have his first say about everything that was going.

"I was talking about the Ashbys, wasn't I? I do' know's I ever told you about the fight they had after their father died about the old house. Joseph was married to a girl he met in camp-meeting time, who had a little property—two or three hundred dollars—from an old great uncle that she'd been keeping house for; and I don't know what other plans she may have had for spending of her means, but she laid most of it out in a husband; for Joseph never cared any great about her that I could see, though he always treated her well enough. She was a poor ignorant sort of thing, seven years older than he was; but she had a pleasant kind of a face, and seemed like an overgrown girl of six or eight years old. I remember just after they was married Joseph was taken down with a quinsy sore throat,—being always subject to them,—and mother was over in the forenoon, and she was one that was always giving right hand and left, and she told Susan Ellen—that was his wife—to step over in the afternoon and she would give her some blackberry preserve for him; she had some that was nice and it was very healing. So along about half-past one o'clock, just as we had got the kitchen cleared, and mother and I had got out the big wheels to spin a few rolls,—we always liked to spin together, and mother was always good company;—my brother Jonas—that was the youngest of us—looked out of the window, and says he: 'Here comes Joe Ashby's wife with a six-quart pail.'

"Mother she began to shake all over with a laugh she tried to swallow down, but I didn't know what it was all about, and in come poor Susan Ellen and lit on the edge of the first chair and set the pail down beside of her. We tried to make her feel welcome, and spoke about everything we could contrive, seein' as it was the first time she'd been over; and she seemed grateful and did the best she could, and lost her strangeness with mother right away, for mother was the best hand to make folks feel to home with her that I ever come across. There ain't many like her now, nor never was, I tell 'em. But there wa'n't nothing said about the six-quart pail, and there it set on the floor, until Susan Ellen said she must be going and mentioned that there was something said about a remedy for Joseph's throat. 'Oh, yes,' says mother, and she brought out the little stone jar she kept the preserve in, and there wa'n't more than the half of it full. Susan Ellen took up the cover off the pail, and I walked off into the bedroom, for I thought I should laugh, certain. Mother put in a big spoonful, and another, and I heard 'em drop, and she went on with one or two more, and then she give up. 'I'd give you the jar and welcome,' she says, 'but I ain't very well off for preserves, and I was kind of counting on this for tea in case my brother's folks are over.' Susan Ellen thanked her, and said Joseph would be obliged, and back she went acrost the pasture. I can see that big tin pail now a-shining in the sun.

"The old man was alive then, and he took a great spite against poor Susan Ellen, though he never would if he hadn't been set on by John; and whether he was mad because Joseph had stepped in to so much good money or what, I don't know,—but he twitted him about her, and

SARAH ORNE JEWETT

at last he and the old man between 'em was too much to bear, and Joe fitted up a couple o' rooms for himself in a building he'd put up for a kind of work-shop. He used to carpenter by spells, and he clapboarded it and made it as comfortable as he could, and he ordered John out of it for good and all; but he and Susan Ellen both treated the old sir the best they knew how, and Joseph kept right on with his farm work same as ever, and meant to lay up a little more money to join with his wife's, and push off as soon as he could for the sake of peace, though if there was anybody set by the farm it was Joseph. He was to blame for some things,—I never saw an Ashby that wasn't,—and I dare say he was aggravating. They were clearing a piece of woodland that winter, and the old man was laid up in the house with the rheumatism, off and on, and that made him fractious, and he and John connived together, till one day Joseph and Susan Ellen had taken the sleigh and gone to Freeport Four Corners to get some flour and one thing and another, and to have the horse shod beside, so they was likely to be gone two or three hours. John Jacobs was going by with his oxen, and John Ashby and the old man hailed him, and said they'd give him a dollar if he'd help 'em, and they hitched the two yoke, his and their'n, to Joseph's house. There wa'n't any foundation to speak of, the sills set right on the ground, and he'd banked it up with a few old boards and some pine spills and sand and stuff, just to keep the cold out. There wa'n't but a little snow, and the roads was smooth and icy, and they slipped it along as if it had been a hand-sled, and got it down the road a half a mile or so to the fork of the roads, and left it settin' there right on the heater-piece. Jacobs told afterward that he kind of disliked to do it, but he thought as long as their minds were set, he might as well have the dollar as anybody. He said when the house give a slew on a sideling piece in the road, he heard some of the crockery-ware smash down, and a branch of an oak they passed by caught hold of the stove-pipe that come out through one of the walls, and give that a wrench, but he guessed there wa'n't no great damage. Joseph may have given 'em some provocation before he went away in the morning,—I don't know *but* he did, and I don't know *as* he did,—but at any rate when he was coming home late in the afternoon he caught sight of his house (some of our folks was right behind, and they saw him), and he stood right up in the sleigh and shook his fist, he was so mad; but afterwards he bu'st out laughin'. It did look kind of curi's; it wa'n't bigger than a front entry, and it set up so pert right there on the heater-piece, as if he was calc'latin' to farm it. The folks said Susan Ellen covered up her face in her shawl and began to cry. I s'pose the pore thing was discouraged. Joseph was awful mad,—he was kind of laughing and cryin' together. Our folks stopped and asked him if there was anything they could do, and he said no; but Susan Ellen went in to view how things were, and they made up a fire, and then Joe took the horse home, and I guess they had it hot and heavy. Nobody supposed they'd ever make up 'less there was a funeral in the family to bring 'em together, the fight had gone so far,—but 'long in the winter old Mr. Ashby, the boys' father, was taken down with a spell o' sickness, and there wa'n't anybody they could get to come and look after the house. The doctor hunted, and they all hunted, but there didn't seem to be anybody—'twa'n't so thick settled as now, and there was no spare help—so John had to eat humble pie, and go and ask Susan Ellen if she wouldn't come back and let by-gones be by-gones. She was as good-natured a creatur' as ever stepped, and did the best she knew, and she spoke up as pleasant as could be, and said she'd go right off that afternoon and help 'em through.

"The old Ashby had been a hard drinker in his day and he was all broke down. Nobody ever saw him that he couldn't walk straight, but he got a crooked disposition out of it, if nothing else. I s'pose there never was a man loved sperit better. They said one year he was over to Cyrus Barker's to help with the haying, and there was a jug o' New England rum over by the spring with some gingerbread and cheese and stuff; and he went over about every half an hour to take something, and along about half-past ten he got the jug middling low, so he went to fill it up with a little water, and lost holt of it and it sunk, and they said he drunk the spring dry three times!

"Joe and Susan Ellen stayed there at the old place well into the summer, and then after planting they moved down to the Four Corners where they had bought a nice little place. Joe did well there,—he carried on the carpenter trade, and got smoothed down considerable, being amongst folks. John he married a Pecker girl, and got his match too; she was the only living soul he ever was afraid of. They lived on there a spell and—why, they must have lived there all of fifteen or twenty years, now I come to think of it, for the time they moved was after the railroad was built. 'Twas along in the winter and his wife she got a notion to buy a place down to the Falls below the Corners after the mills got started and have John work in the spinning-room while she took boarders. She said 'twa'n't no use staying on the farm, they couldn't make a living off from it now they'd cut the growth. Joe's folks and she never could get along, and they said she was dreadfully riled up hearing how much Joe was getting in the machine shop.

"They needn't tell me about special providences being all moonshine," said Miss Debby for the second time, "if here wa'n't a plain one, I'll never say one word more about it. You see, that very time Joe Ashby got a splinter in his eye and they were afraid he was going to lose his sight, and he got a notion that he wanted to go back to farming. He always set everything by the old place, and he had a boy growing up that neither took to his book nor to mill work, and he wanted to farm it too. So Joe got hold of John one day when he come in with some wood, and asked him why he wouldn't take his place for a year or two, if he wanted to get to the village, and let him go out to the old place. My brother Jonas was standin' right by and heard 'em and said he never heard nobody speak civiller. But John swore and said he wa'n't going to be caught in no such a trap as that. His father left him the place and he was going to do as he'd a mind to. There'd be'n trouble about the property, for old Mr. Ashby had given Joe some money he had in the bank. Joe had got to be well off, he could have bought most any farm about here, but he wanted the old place 'count of his attachment. He set everything by his mother, spite of her being dead so long. John hadn't done very well spite of his being so sharp, but he let out the best of the farm on shares, and bought a mis'able sham-built little house down close by the mills,—and then some idea or other got into his head to fit that up to let and move it to one side of the lot, and haul down the old house from the farm to live in themselves. There wa'n't no time to lose, else the snow would be gone; so he got a gang o' men up there and put shoes underneath the sills, and then they assembled all the oxen they could call in, and started. Mother was living then, though she'd got to be very feeble, and when they come for our yoke she wouldn't have Jonas let 'em go. She said the old house ought to stay in its place. Everybody had been telling John Ashby that the road was too hilly, and besides the house was too old to move, they'd rack it all to pieces dragging it so fur; but he wouldn't listen to no reason.

"I never saw mother so stirred up as she was that day, and when she see the old thing a moving she burst right out crying. We could see one end of it looking over the slope of the hill in the pasture between it and our house. There was two windows that looked our way, and I know Mis' Ashby used to hang a piece o' something white out o' one of 'em when she wanted mother to step over for anything. They set a good deal by each other, and Mis' Ashby was a lame woman. I shouldn't ha' thought John would had 'em haul the house right over the little gardin she thought so much of, and broke down the laylocks and flowering currant she set everything by. I remember when she died I wasn't more'n seven or eight year old, it was all in full bloom and mother she broke off a branch and laid into the coffin. I do' know as I've ever seen any since or set in a room and had the sweetness of it blow in at the windows without remembering that day,—'twas the first funeral I ever went to, and that may be some reason. Well, the old house started off and mother watched it as long as she could see it. She was sort o' feeble herself then, as I said, and we went on with the work,—'twas a Saturday, and we was baking and churning and getting things to rights generally. Jonas had been over in the swamp getting out some wood he'd cut earlier in the winter—and along in the afternoon he come in and said he s'posed I wouldn't want to ride down to the Corners so late, and I said I did feel just like it, so we started off. We went the Birch Ridge road, because he wanted to see somebody over that way,—and when we was going home by the straight road, Jonas laughed and said we hadn't seen anything of John Ashby's moving, and he guessed he'd got stuck somewhere. He was glad he hadn't nothing to do with it. We drove along pretty quick, for we were some belated, and we didn't like to leave mother all alone after it come dark. All of a sudden Jonas stood up in the sleigh, and says he, 'I don't believe but the cars is off the track;' and I looked and there did seem to be something the matter with 'em. They hadn't been running more than a couple o' years then, and we was prepared for anything.

"Jonas he whipped up the horse and we got there pretty quick, and I'll be bound if the Ashby house hadn't got stuck fast right on the track, and stir it one way or another they couldn't. They'd been there since quarter-past one, pulling and hauling,—and the men was all hoarse with yelling, and the cars had come from both ways and met there,—one each side of the crossing,—and the passengers was walking about, scolding and swearing,—and somebody'd gone and lit up a gre't bonfire. You never see such a sight in all your life! I happened to look up at the old house, and there were them two top windows that used to look over to our place, and they had caught the shine of the firelight, and made the poor old thing look as if it was scared to death. The men was banging at it with axes and crowbars, and it was dreadful distressing. You pitied it as if it was a live creatur'. It come from such a quiet place, and always looked kind of comfortable, though so much war had gone on amongst the Ashbys. I tell you it was a judgment on John, for they got it shoved back after a while, and then wouldn't touch it again,—not one of the men,—nor let their oxen. The plastering was all stove, and the outside walls all wrenched apart,—and John never did anything more about it; but let it set there all summer, till it burnt down, and there was an end, one night in September. They supposed some traveling folks slept in it and set it afire, or else some boys did it for fun. I was glad it was out of the way. One day, I know, I was coming by with mother, and she said it made her feel bad to see the little strips of leather by the fore door, where Mis' Ashby had nailed up a rosebush once. There! there ain't an Ashby alive now of the old stock, except young John. Joe's son went off to sea, and I believe he was lost somewhere in the China seas, or else he died of a fever; I seem to forget. He was called a smart boy, but he never could seem to settle down to anything. Sometimes I wonder folks is as good as they be, when I consider what comes to 'em from their folks before 'em, and how they're misshaped by nature. Them Ashbys never was like other folks, and yet some good streak or other there was in every one of 'em. You can't expect much from such hindered creator's,—it's just like beratin' a black and white cat for being a poor mouser. It ain't her fault that the mice see her quicker than they can a gray one. If you get one of them masterful dispositions put with a good strong will towards the right, that's what makes the best of men; but all them Ashbys cared about was to grasp and get, and be cap'ns. They liked to see other folks put down, just as if it was going to set them up. And they didn't know nothing. They make me think of some o' them old marauders that used to hive up into their castles, in old times, and then go out a-over-setting and plundering. And I tell you that same sperit was in 'em. They was born a couple o' hundred years too late. Kind of left-over folks, as it were." And Miss Debby indulged in a quiet chuckle as she bent over her work. "John he got captured by his wife,—she carried too many guns for him. I believe he died very poor and her own son wouldn't support her, so she died over in Freeport poor-house. And Joe got along better; his wife was clever but rather slack, and it took her a good while to see through things. She married again pretty quick after he died. She had as much as seven or eight thousand dollars, and she was taken just as she stood by a roving preacher that was holding meetings here in the winter time. He sold out her place here, and they went up country

A Note About the Author

Sarah Orne Jewett (1849–1909) was an American novelist and poet whose work was often set in the northeast region. She studied at Berwick Academy where she become an avid reader and writer. Jewett published her first story, "Jenny Garrow's Lovers" in 1868 followed by the novels *A Country Doctor* (1884), *A Marsh Island* (1885) and *The Tory Lover* (1901). Jewett was best-known for her detailed accounts of New England life in the late nineteenth and early twentieth centuries.

A Note from the Publisher

Spanning many genres, from non-fiction essays to literature classics to children's books and lyric poetry, Mint Edition books showcase the master works of our time in a modern new package. The text is freshly typeset, is clean and easy to read, and features a new note about the author in each volume. Many books also include exclusive new introductory material. Every book boasts a striking new cover, which makes it as appropriate for collecting as it is for gift giving. Mint Edition books are only printed when a reader orders them, so natural resources are not wasted. We're proud that our books are never manufactured in excess and exist only in the exact quantity they need to be read and enjoyed.

Discover more of your favorite classics with Bookfinity™.

- Track your reading with custom book lists.
- Get great book recommendations for your personalized Reader Type.
- Add reviews for your favorite books.
- AND MUCH MORE!

Visit **bookfinity.com** and take the fun Reader Type quiz to get started.

Enjoy our classic and modern companion pairings!

Printed in the USA
CPSIA information can be obtained
at www.ICGtesting.com
JSHW021943130324
59154JS00004B/216